After her mother had fallen asleep, Kate left the room

She walked to where the soda machine hummed and moths dashed themselves to death against the bare light bulb burning above. She fed coins into the machine and pushed the button for iced tea. There was a crashing thump as the can landed in the dispenser, but she left it there because iced tea wasn't what she'd really come out here for.

She'd come to think about what her mother had said about Hayden deserving a father and Mitch deserving to know he had a son. Why did mothers always have to be right?

Mitchell McCray. For years she'd tried not to think about him, but as her son grew, that became increasingly impossible. Hayden looked way too much like his father. She tried to forget how she'd behaved that night, because a part of her just couldn't believe Mitch had so easily, so effortlessly swept her off her feet.

Dear Reader,

Stories are sometimes like stray cats. You don't go looking for them; they find you. This past December I went online to shop for a new dog sled. Sled Dog Central links to all related sites, and their main page announced the shocking news that Susan Butcher, four-time winner of the 1100-mile Iditarod Sled Dog Race, had recently been diagnosed with acute myelogenous leukemia.

Susan's influence on the lives of others has been profound. At twenty-nine, I watched her being interviewed during the Iditarod by an ABC news correspondent and was awed. She was inspirational, forging her way boldly through the middle of the magnificent Alaskan wilderness, driving her beloved team of sled dogs and handily beating the male-dominated field. Women all over the world rode the runners with her and thrilled to her victory, not just once but four times. Her courage and determination changed our world. How could such a strong-spirited woman with two beautiful daughters and a devoted husband be diagnosed with such a life-threatening disease?

While researching her illness I learned about the critical need for bone marrow donors and joined the donor registry. Then I wrote this story, hopefully to open the eyes of others who might want to help save a life. The characters in this story are fictional, but there's nothing fictional about leukemia. Progress is being made in the treatments, and the long-term survival rate is climbing, especially for children, but we still have a long way to go. To find out more about how to become a donor, go to www.marrow.org.

Whoever said "If you have your health, you have everything?" was right. Count your blessings and cherish each day. Love your little ones and sing them to sleep. Life is short.

Nadia Nichols
www.nadianichols.com

FROM OUT
OF THE BLUE
Nadia Nichols

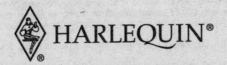

TORONTO • NEW YORK • LONDON
AMSTERDAM • PARIS • SYDNEY • HAMBURG
STOCKHOLM • ATHENS • TOKYO • MILAN • MADRID
PRAGUE • WARSAW • BUDAPEST • AUCKLAND

ISBN-13: 978-0-373-71394-3
ISBN-10:   0-373-71394-0

FROM OUT OF THE BLUE

www.eHarlequin.com

Printed in U.S.A.

ABOUT THE AUTHOR

Nadia went to the dogs at the age of twenty-nine and currently operates a kennel of thirty Alaskan huskies. She has raced for fifteen years in northern New England and Canada, works at the family-owned Harraseeket Inn in Freeport, Maine, and is also a registered Maine guide.

She began her writing career at the age of five, when she made her first sale, a short story called "The Bear," to her mother for 25 cents. This story was such a blockbuster that her mother bought every other story Nadia wrote and kept her in ice cream money throughout much of her childhood.

Now all her royalties go toward buying dog food. She can be reached at nadianichols@aol.com.

Books by Nadia Nichols

HARLEQUIN SUPERROMANCE

For Susan

CHAPTER ONE

FUNNY, HOW SMALL the house looked from the curb. It was the exact same size as all the other cookie-cutter houses on the base with the exact same size lawn in front, but now that it was no longer her home, it looked sad and abandoned and small. The lawn was dry and brown and the bushes against the foundation drooped in the Southern California heat. The street was quiet. No curious onlookers were on hand for her departure. Her CO had kept his promise that there would be no farewell fuss or fanfare. Her furniture and belongings were packed away into the moving van and the crew was ready to roll. One of the men was closing the van's rear door while the other approached with a clipboard.

"If I could just get your signature on the bottom, ma'am, we'll be on our way."

She took the pen and clipboard and signed her full name on the line: Katherine Carolyn Jones. She left off the part she was leaving behind—"Captain." As of three days ago, when ten years of Navy life had come to a premature end, she was officially a civilian. She handed the clipboard back. "Thank you. See you in a few days."

"Montana's not that far. We might even beat you there."

"You will. We're taking the scenic route," she said.

He climbed into the cab of the moving van with his partner, started up the truck and pulled away from the curb.

She wasn't aware that her mother was standing beside her until she spoke. "Honey? You all right?"

"Sure. Just a little hot, that's all." Kate slipped her arm around her mother's waist. Ruth Jones had been like a rock the past few days, throughout the long, arduous process of packing up. Dressed in blue jeans and a T-shirt, Ruth radiated that ageless Montana cowgirl vitality and had the lean, fit build to match. Her graying hair was neatly bound into a braid that hung between her shoulders.

"Montana'll seem chilly to you after all these years away." She glanced toward the car. "Maybe we should get going. Hayden's getting antsy. He keeps asking where Rosa's gone."

Kate followed her mother's gaze to where her young son fidgeted in the backseat along with Wiggins, the family cat. Neither of them enjoyed riding in vehicles, and the journey was just beginning. This was the first time Hayden would be separated from the woman who'd cared for him during Kate's frequent absences from his life. Rosa's tearful goodbye the day before had been heartrending, but she'd refused to come to Montana. It was too far from her family in Mexico. Too cold and snowy. She would stay in California and find another nanny job. Kate knew that wouldn't be difficult. The fifty-eight-year-old woman was marvelous with children, and an excellent cook and housekeeper to boot. Kate would miss her calm, cheerful competence very much, along with her chicken relleno, green chili stew and guacamole salads.

Hayden was already missing her. He was fussy and ir-ritable and nothing his mother or grandmother did or said seemed to comfort him. It would take them at least three days to drive to Montana because Kate was determined to make it an enjoyable road trip and not a marathon. Her mother's company would be a good distraction. It would keep her from thinking about why she was giving up the life she'd loved and the career she'd worked so hard for.

She took one final look at her house and was walking toward the car when the base's postal truck turned the corner and made the requisite stop at the bank of mailboxes that served all the houses on the street. She groaned as her own mailbox was opened and a handful of what were no doubt huge medical bills were stuffed inside. "Hang on a sec, Mom. I'll be right back." She trotted up to the postal truck and leaned in the window. "Hey, Charlie, do me a favor?"

"Sure, Captain. What's up?" A fixture on the base, Charlie had a broad, friendly face and a ready smile.

"I put in a change of address form a couple of days ago. Can you check to make sure it's gone through? I shouldn't be getting any more mail delivered here."

Charlie frowned. "You being transferred?"

"Something like that. Will you do that for me?"

"You know I will, but I wish I didn't have to. Good luck, Captain. Won't be the same around here without you stirring the pot and keeping the flyboys on their toes, but I figured something was up when I passed that moving van."

As he drove off, Kate reached into her mailbox for the last time, drawing out a sheaf of envelopes. Some junk mail, a phone bill and two medical bills. She stuffed the junk mail back in the box for Charlie to deal with and tucked the bills into the visor pocket when she slipped into the car. The hot seat stung her legs, so when she started the engine, she maxed the air conditioner. Cool air poured forth from the vents as she put the car into gear. "Okay, gang, let's rock and roll."

Hayden was complaining loudly that Wiggins had clawed him—he'd let the cat out of the pet carrier against her orders—and her mother was talking about the wildflowers blooming on the flanks of the mountains back home, naming each and every one, but the voices faded into silence as they approached the guardhouse.

"Wow," Ruth said. "I've never seen anything like that before."

Kate had slowed the car but forced herself to continue driving toward the gate. Ranks of officers in dress uniform flanked both sides of the road and stood at attention, saluting her as she exited the base for the final time. She recognized them all, of course. She'd flown with some of them, commanded others and lived among many for the past four years. She focused her eyes forward, tightened her hands on the wheel and willed herself to remain visibly impassive while inside she fell completely apart. Her CO had promised her this wouldn't happen. He'd sworn to keep her resignation and departure, and the reasons for both, in the strictest of confidences. Yet here they were, the men and women she'd served with, saying a final goodbye the only way they knew how, even though she was no longer a naval officer—just a thirty-two-year-old civilian mother returning home to fight the toughest battle of her life.

At the very end of the row of uniformed officers, Kate saw her CO, and next to him, in the flesh, stood the legendary Fleet Admiral Ransom Gates, the highest ranking officer in the United States Navy. Feeling overwhelmed as Admiral Gates approached the car, Kate put the vehicle into Park and struggled to unbuckle her seat belt. He waved a hand, stilling her.

"At ease," he said, leaning toward her open window. "Your commanding officer informed me of your resignation. But since you're one of the finest officers in my fleet, I'm not accepting it. As of now you're on an extended emergency medical leave, with full benefits and pay."

"But, sir…"

"I've done a little research. I know what you're up against and I'm aware it could be two years before you're out of the woods, but there isn't a doubt in my mind that you'll make it all the way back." He passed her a letter-sized sheet of paper and riveted her with eyes as blue and cold as the oceans he ruled. "You're a fighter, Captain. Beat this thing. That's an order."

"Yes, sir." Kate took the paper from him, recognizing her own signature at the bottom. It was her formal resignation. The word *Void* had been stamped across it in bold red letters.

"Good luck, Captain," Admiral Gates said, then stepped back from the car and saluted her. As she drove off the base, she narrowly avoided sideswiping the guardhouse. Suddenly her twenty-twenty vision wasn't all that sharp.

BAD THINGS happened in threes. Three months ago Kate had been diagnosed with acute myelogenous leukemia. Three days ago, upon being released from the hospital after her second month-long chemo treatment, she'd resigned her commission, or tried to, after getting her health insurance coverage extended through the proper channels, and just yesterday the doctors had told her that as yet no suitable match had been found for a bone marrow transplant. That made three very bad things, which meant that for a while, at least, things should go pretty smoothly.

Sure enough, the first two days of the road trip were

good. Hayden settled down, Wiggins resigned himself to riding in the pet carrier and had stopped his bloodcurdling howls, and she and her mother shared long rambling conversations about everything and nothing at all while the Sierra Nevadas fell behind and the Rockies loomed ahead. The one thing they never discussed was the reason Kate was going back home, which suited her just fine. Her mother had a tendency to become emotional when the topic came up, and emotional displays were something Kate had never been comfortable with. Her life in the Navy had protected her from that. The military discipline, male-dominated upper ranks and stern emphasis on protocol had served as her sword and shield.

It hadn't been lost on Kate that her mother had put a huge box of tissues on the seat between them, no doubt for their mutual use should the waterworks ever start. If Kate had her way, the box would still be full at the end of the trip. Tears were pointless.

On the third day, about an hour after stopping for lunch at a little diner on Interstate 15 in Idaho, her mother looked into the backseat, saw that Hayden was napping, then faced front, folded her hands in her lap and sighed. "Kate, maybe it's none of my business, but in all these years you've never volunteered much information about Hayden's father."

The subject was bound to come up sooner or later. Kate was surprised that it hadn't been sooner. A whole lot sooner. She couldn't blame her parents for wanting to learn everything they could about their grandchild. "That's because there's not much to tell. I've made a few mistakes in my life and that man was one of them. I'd rather not talk about him."

"That's been obvious ever since you told us you were

pregnant, but he is the father of your child—one of the only two parents he'll ever have."

"And the only one, once I'm gone. Is that the point you're trying to make?"

"You're going to get well, Kate. That's not what I meant at all. It's just that I know how stubborn and unyielding you can be when it comes to men. I'm not saying I blame you," Ruth was quick to add. "You've fought hard in your career and more than a few men have tried to trip you up. Nevertheless, at one time you must have felt something for this man."

Kate felt herself flush. "Mom…"

"Did he treat you badly, or abandon you when you told him you were pregnant?"

"Not exactly."

"Was he married?"

"I don't think so."

Her mother frowned at this. "Does this guy even know he has a child?"

A long silence passed between them and Kate realized her hands were cramping around the steering wheel. She forced herself to relax her grip and drew a slow breath. "I don't think so," she repeated.

"You mean, you never told him?"

"No. I never told him."

"Why not?"

"Because he was never a part of my life. In fact, I know very little about him. Our relationship was nothing more than a one-night stand. That sometimes happens between two sexually deprived individuals. You know."

"Sorry. I can't say that I do, and I'm surprised to hear that you behaved that way."

"I don't make a habit of it, Mom, but that's the reason I never told you about Hayden's father. You expect me to be perfect and I'm not. Boy, am I ever not. But in spite of how Hayden came about, he's one of the best things that's ever happened to me, and if I should die, I want to know he's with my parents, the other two most perfect things that ever happened to me. End of discussion."

There was another long silence as they both stared out the windshield, then her mother pulled a tissue out of the box and blew her nose. "I think that's very selfish of you," she said.

Kate exhaled an exasperated breath. "How so?"

"Think how much your father would have missed if he'd never known you."

"That's different. The two of you were in love. You were married. You wanted to have a child together. You planned me."

"I can't imagine you'd have slept with just anyone no matter how 'sexually deprived' you were at the time. You're too smart and independent minded. Besides, if the worst happens, what are we supposed to tell your son when he asks us about his father? This is something we need to know, Kate. It's important."

"As soon as he figured out there was suppose to be a daddy in his life, I told him his father died in a plane crash. He never asks anymore, so you don't have to worry."

"Why didn't you just tell him the truth?"

"That his mother hopped into the sack with a man she'd just met and hasn't seen since that night? What point would that serve?" Kate felt her heart rate accelerate as she fought to keep her cool. "Okay, here's the deal. You want to know who this guy is? I'll tell you. His name is Mitchell McCray. He was a major in the air force when I met him, stationed at

Eielson Air Force Base in Alaska. I have no idea where he is now, but worst-case scenario, you could contact the base and find out. Just promise me you'll never, ever hand my son over to a man you don't even know."

Her mother sat for a few moments, digesting this. "When were you in Alaska?"

"Well, Mom, we Navy types jump ship once in a while, especially when we're feeling the need for...company."

"And he never tried to contact you afterward?"

"He sent me one letter."

"What did it say?"

"I don't know. I never opened it."

"Weren't you the least bit curious?"

"No." Kate felt her stomach muscles tighten as she recalled getting that letter at mail call one month into a blue water ops and just two days before the ship's doctor had informed her she was pregnant. She'd seen the name and return address scrawled in the upper left-hand corner and felt a jolt of shock when she realized who it was from. The letter had been forwarded twice, the initial posting having been made three weeks earlier. She had stared at it for a few breathless moments, her cheeks burning as she remembered her shameless behavior with a virtual stranger, then flung it off the flight deck unopened. "It's not like we had a long-term relationship, Mom. It was just one night."

"Still, I think you should look him up."

"Just call him on the phone, ask him if he remembers me, then tell him he has a son?"

"He deserves to know. You also need to find out his medical history and that of his family. That will be important information for Hayden to have."

"What if he turns out to be a jerk?"

"I'm your mother, Kate. I know you. If this guy won your heart for even one night, he must have been something else. I suspect that's also why you ran away from him so fast and never told him about Hayden and never opened that letter. A relationship would've complicated your life and distracted you from your goals."

Kate opened her mouth to reply, then shut it again. She hated it when her mother talked to her in that tone of voice, but arguing with her would only prolong the lecture. She hesitated, then tried another approach. "It's been over four years. He could be dead, for all I know."

"I doubt that. Kate, your father is sixty-four and I'm sixty-two," her mother continued. "By the time Hayden graduates from high school, we'll be soaking our dentures in whitening solution and using canes and walkers to get around. We may not live to see him graduate from college. Then he won't have any family to cheer him on or to fall back on in tough times. He'll be all alone. Of course, we'll take care of him if, God forbid, anything ever happens to you, and we'll love him and cherish him and protect him for as long as we can, but that might not be for all that long."

Kate fought to control her emotions, but realized she'd failed when the road ahead blurred and her mother handed her a wad of tissues.

"You told me this man wasn't a part of your life, but Kate, if he hadn't cared about you, he wouldn't have written that letter. You still have the opportunity to give Hayden the father he deserves. Just think about it."

THEY SPENT the final night in a little roadside motel and ate an early supper of burgers and fries at the adjacent diner. After her mother and Hayden had fallen asleep, Kate left the room and walked beneath the overhang to where the soda machine hummed and moths dashed themselves to death against the bare lightbulb burning above. She fed coins into the machine and pushed the button for iced tea. There was a crashing thump as the can landed in the dispenser, but she left it there because iced tea wasn't what she'd really come out here for.

She'd come to think about what her mother had said about Hayden deserving a father and Mitch deserving to know he had a son. Why did mothers always have to be right?

Mitchell McCray. For years she'd tried not to think about him, but as her son grew, that became increasingly impossible. Hayden looked way too much like his father. She tried to forget how she'd behaved that night because a part of her just couldn't believe Mitch had so easily, so effortlessly, swept her off her feet.

She'd been at Midway for a week of gunnery training and was planning to refuel at Adak en route to Mirimar when the winds became so severe they actually toppled a construction crane on the base. After she'd made two unsuccessful attempts at landing with wind gusts topping one hundred knots, Adak tower told her the only chance of putting her Hornet down was at Eielson. All of Alaska was snowed in by the storm and the weather was so bad no tanker was available for her to refuel, but they told her the winds weren't quite as severe in the interior.

Good luck, they'd said.

She knew she'd need it. Eielson Air Force Base was 1,358 miles from Adak. She programmed the identifier for Eielson into her inertial navigation system and turned on the autopilot, realizing that if she made it there, it would be a miracle. A far more likely scenario was that she'd run out of fuel, eject from the plane and freeze to death before hitting the ground in her chute. Meanwhile, until that happened, she'd keep pulling the power back and climbing for altitude until it was time to start her descent to Eielson. The only thing in her favor was the wind. She was riding a jet stream of 160 miles per hour and, as it turned out, it was enough of a boost to get her to her destination just before engine flameout.

The landing was bumpy, and for a few moments after she brought the plane to a stop, she could do nothing more than slump in her seat while her heart rate slowed and the adrenaline oozed out of her. A man emerged from the nearest hangar and wrestled a yellow ladder through six inches of snow, pushing for all he was worth while twisting his upper body away from the bite of the wicked gusts. As he approached, she stirred herself back to life, popped the canopy and was unbuckling her harness when he climbed up the ladder to help her out of the cockpit. In the rapidly waning daylight she could see his dark hair whipping across his forehead.

"Welcome to the North Pole!" he called over the shriek of the wind. "You must be one of those fancy naval aviators we've heard rumors about. What happened? You lose your boat in the storm?"

He knew, of course, the reason behind her emergency landing at Eielson. He was just being a wiseass. When she pulled off her helmet and he realized he was talking to a woman, he backed away to read the name painted on the side of her canopy. "Well, Lieutenant K. C. Jones, that was one hot shit landing you just made in hurricane-force winds with zero visibility and nothing but auxiliary power. I'm Major McCray, but you can call me Mitch. Climb on down and I'll buy you a drink."

"I don't have time for socializing, Major," she said. "I'd

like to get my plane checked out before leaving. That was a rough landing and I had multiple caution lights. How soon can you have it ready to go?" she asked once her feet touched solid ground.

"This runway's closed. Hell, this air base is closed, as is every other airport in the state. Everyone's holed up for the duration."

"The duration of what? Are you telling me a little snow and wind shuts down an entire air force base? I have a schedule to keep."

"Not anymore. Don't you swabbies listen to the weather report? This Pacific howler's expected to drop upwards of three feet. Your flight log just ended here, a few miles shy of the arctic circle." When she didn't react, he added, "Don't worry—we'll get your plane checked out in time for you to catch up on your California sunbathing. I'm pretty skilled with a sledgehammer and chain saw, and the good news is you'll have time for a drink or two at the Mad Dog while you wait. I'll even drive you over there myself and introduce you around to the polar bears. They're kinda cute when they aren't hungry."

She followed him into the hangar, where several hissing and sputtering Coleman lanterns provided the only light. "Power's out and the emergency generator won't come on line, probably because this is a real emergency," he explained, slamming the door on the storm. "The lights you saw on the runway were from the plow trucks. We like to provide a little guidance for you lost pilots. Skidder! We got us a pretty little Hornet parked outside that needs to be dragged in here before the drifts get much higher. Both engines flamed out in the final approach and she had a rough landing."

A hulking giant of a man ambled across the hangar and

stared at Kate with that slack-jawed look she'd grown accustomed to over the years. "This the pilot, Major?"

"Skidder, meet Lieutenant K. C. Jones." Major Mitchell McCray gave her a brash, arrogant grin. "She wants the plane checked over and ready to go ASAP. For some reason, she prefers California sunshine to our Alaskan blizzards, but she hasn't been to the Mad Dog yet."

THAT HAD BEEN almost five years ago, but it felt like yesterday. She could still smell the jet fuel and the fresh paint scents of the hangar, feel the sting of the wind-driven snow when he escorted her out to the plow truck to ferry her the blustery mile to the Mad Dog for the promised drink. Only, as it turned out, the Mad Dog Saloon was closed due to the power outage. That didn't faze Mitch. The saloon owner tossed him the keys on his way out the door along with a brusque, "Lock 'er up when you leave."

Major McCray fixed her a drink by the soft glow of a kerosene lamp and they huddled near the woodstove in the center of the room for warmth, first sharing flying stories, the way all pilots do, then war stories the way combat pilots do. Then they had another drink and the combined effects of the alcohol, the heat from the stove and the lack of any solid food for the past twelve hours conspired against her. Kate was way beyond being seduced by an arrogant jet jock with a type A personality. She'd long since decided that men had been put on earth solely to hone an intelligent and motivated woman's desire to prove her equality, and in many cases, her superiority. She'd spent years fighting for every toehold on that precarious Navy ladder, years proving that she was a whole lot better than most of the men who looked down on her, yet she'd nearly thrown it all away in one stormy night with an air force officer in a rustic saloon called the Mad Dog.

For the past four years, she'd tried to forget how easily Mitch had seduced her, but now, standing in the harsh light of the motel, she admitted to herself that, once again, her mother was right. He'd been something else. Five minutes in his company and she'd felt like she never wanted to leave his side. Even before she'd taken the first sip of that drink he'd mixed, she'd been captivated by those dark bedroom eyes, that handsome grin and the masculine strength of him. Years of rigid discipline and unwavering focus had melted away in the heat of that passionate night. While the blizzard piled the snows up outside the Mad Dog and blew drifts beneath the door, the lone kerosene lamp gradually burned itself out, engulfing them in a darkness neither noticed.

She'd spent years trying to forget how he'd made her feel, but the memories could still make her blush. Mitchell McCray had effortlessly threatened a lifetime of dreams and visions and left her scrambling to find solid footing again in a profession that she'd fought so hard to be a part of. She'd landed on her feet after that fall from grace, but only barely. That one night had resulted in a pregnancy that nearly destroyed her career, but the only person she could blame for her actions was herself.

Kate retrieved the cold can of iced tea from the dispenser and started back to the room, stopping abruptly as the world shifted beneath her feet and tipped her off balance. She reached out for a porch post, closed her eyes and leaned against it until the dizziness passed. The fatigue gnawed at her constantly, but the dizzy spells and intermittent stomach pains were something new. She hadn't been able to swallow more than two small bites of her hamburger, in spite of her mother's

frequent glances across the Formica table in the little diner,
while Hayden smeared his fries in ketchup and in a feeding
frenzy shoved them into his hungry mouth. "Try to eat," her
mother had said. "You need to keep your strength up."

This had been so hard on her mother, and it was only going
to get worse. What had she been thinking of, agreeing to
spend the next two months in Montana? The base doctor had
urged her to stay near the Seattle hospital that had been
treating her, but her parents had argued that being home would
keep her happier and hopefully healthier until that miraculous
bone marrow donor came along. But what about Hayden?

What about Hayden!

She straightened, drew a shaky breath and wondered what
the letter had said, the one she'd so willfully destroyed. What
a fool she'd been. What an arrogant, stubborn, prideful fool.
Was Mitchell McCray married now? Did he have a family of
his own? Did Hayden have brothers and sisters he'd never
met? These were things she needed to find out, and quickly.
The bone marrow registry might come through with a good
match for her, but thus far the prospects remained bleak. Not
many people volunteered to be tested for such a donation
unless a friend or family member was stricken.

She needed to get her affairs in order—right away—just
in case.

THE NEXT DAY, two hours into the morning's journey and not
a hundred miles from home, Kate finally found the nerve to
say to her mother in a quiet voice, so Hayden couldn't
overhear, "Mom, I've been thinking about what you said and
I've decided that you're right. I need to talk to Mitch. I made
some phone calls last night. It turns out he's no longer in the

air force but he's still in Alaska, flying for an air charter service in a place called Pike's Creek. Hayden and I have a flight out of Bozeman this afternoon."

"This afternoon?" her mother exclaimed. "Don't you think you should go home and see your father first?"

She felt the twist of painful emotions and focused hard on road ahead. "I think the sooner I get this meeting over with, the better."

"But what if they find a donor? How will we contact you?"

"I'll give you my phone number so you can reach me, and I promise I'll call you every night. But I'm not going to hold my breath on a donor coming through. It might not happen, and I could be running out of time."

"Please don't talk that way."

"Mom…"

Her mother sat up straighter, preparing to deliver another maternal lecture. "You're taking Hayden? How will you take care of him? You've been so sick, you're still weak, and he's such a handful…"

"I'm not weak. I feel lots better—really, I do. But don't worry, I called Rosa last night from the pay phone in the diner. She's meeting us at the Seattle airport this evening and she's agreed to come and stay with Hayden until this is resolved one way or the other."

Her mother slumped back in her seat with a look of bewilderment. "You decided all this last night?"

"While you were sleeping." Kate heard the concern in her mother's voice, but she was resolute. "Our flight leaves at 2:00 p.m. We should be in Bozeman with an hour to spare. You can take Wiggins to the ranch, turn him loose on the mice in the barn and I'll be home in a week or two."

"What about infection? You're so vulnerable right now. Your immune system is practically nonexistent. Flying on a big commercial plane and breathing all those germs…"

"The doctors wouldn't have released me from the hospital if my blood counts hadn't been adequate, but I promise I'll hold my breath on the plane."

"Couldn't you just call this man up and ask him to come to Montana?"

"Sure I could, but how will I meet his friends and family that way? How will I see the way he really lives? How will I know what he's really like unless I see him in his own world?"

Her mother nodded slowly and sighed. "What do you want me to tell your father?"

Kate gripped the wheel tightly and had to work hard to speak the next words without breaking down. "Tell Dad I love him, and I'll be home soon."

THE MOOSEWOOD Road House was gearing up for the summer tourism season, but in early June they were still a few weeks away from being all that busy and, best of all, they were located not ten miles from the place where Mitch worked. Kate made reservations from the airport in Anchorage when their flight arrived. The helpful person at the car rental booth told her that the Moosewood was a small place with a number of cabins scattered along the edge of a river valley overlooking the mountains, and a main lodge with a restaurant and bar on the ground floor. It was a little over two hours' drive from the airport. While Rosa held the sleeping Hayden in her arms, Kate filled out the rental paperwork, got the directions to the roadhouse, and fifteen minutes later they were on their way.

It was still broad daylight at 11:00 p.m., though by the time they arrived at their lodging, twilight had fallen. They were shown to one of the larger two-bedroom cabins, which had a living room, a fireplace, a full bath and a sleeping loft.

Kate was so exhausted she had trouble mustering an obligatory "Wow" when she stood on the porch and looked toward the snowcapped mountains that appeared to glow across the violet-hued distance.

The employee set their bags inside the cabin door. "You're looking right at Denali. Believe it or not, you can't see that mountain most of the time. Big as it is, it's completely hidden in the clouds, but the past few days have been clear. You folks been here before?"

"I passed through once in the middle of a blizzard."

"Well, you're in for a real treat. Enjoy your stay and if you need anything, room service or whatever, just call the front desk. We serve in the restaurant until 1:00 a.m. and we open for breakfast at six."

Hayden barely woke as Rosa changed him into his pajamas and settled him into the queen-size bed in Kate's room. "I could sleep with him in my room, *señora,* so you can get a good rest," she'd offered, but Kate shook her head.

"That's okay, Rosa. He's so tired he won't twitch all night."

Neither did she. Even the nightmares left her in peace. A mere five hours later, she woke, feeling refreshed, much better than she had in a long time, and even better than that after taking a long hot shower. The sun was already well up when the room service breakfast was delivered. Kate drank her first cup of strong black coffee standing on the porch and staring across a vast, timbered valley toward that gigantic mountain. "Denali," she murmured, awed by the sheer magnificence of the famed peak.

While Rosa gave Hayden his morning bath, Kate phoned her mother to tell her they'd arrived safely and to give her the name and number of the Moosewood. Then she paid a visit to the office to ask where the Pike's Creek Road was. The directions were fairly straightforward. "But it gets pretty rough after the first mile," the desk clerk cautioned.

"How rough?"

"I wouldn't drive that rental car in there. The rental agencies don't like their cars being driven on gravel roads."

"Is there an airport somewhere out there?"

"I don't think I'd go so far as to call it an airport. There's a grass strip on the right-hand side just before the road gets really rough. You'll see where the road forks to the right. That leads to the landing strip. Wally's Air Charter flies out of there."

"Oh? Is it any good?"

The clerk hesitated. "I hear the pilot's great, but the plane's a derelict. We usually recommend Polar Express out of Talkeetna."

Kate considered his advice as she returned to the cabin. Hayden had eaten breakfast with Rosa and was complaining about not being able to watch his favorite TV programs because the cabin didn't have a TV. Rosa turned a practiced deaf ear. She'd grown up without the "one-eyed monster" as she referred to it. She would take him outside, she told Kate, and show him all the small wonders around their cabin.

"Thank you, Rosa. That sounds better than TV any day," Kate said. "I'll be back by dark and maybe a whole lot sooner, depending on how things go. You can order room service or eat in the restaurant when you get hungry, whichever you choose. My mom's phone number is in my bedside drawer if you should need it."

"Yes, *señora.*"

"There are lots of books for guests to read in a bookshelf in the living room of the main lodge."

Rosa smiled, seeing through Kate's stall tactics. "We'll be fine, *señora.* Good luck."

Luck was something she'd run out of several months ago, but nevertheless Kate was feeling optimistic as she climbed into the rental car. Maybe it was seeing the way the morning sunlight had illuminated the snowfields on Denali's peak an hour earlier, but she felt as if today might turn out to be pretty good. Maybe this meeting with Mitchell McCray wouldn't be so bad. Maybe it'd turn out great.

Maybe her luck was about to change.

Ten minutes later, not quite a mile down the gravel road, she felt the steering wheel pull hard to the right and knew before she stopped that she had a flat tire. She got out and stared at it for a moment, then looked down the rutted gravel track that led toward all the answers she was seeking and felt a growing sense of despair. If this was an omen of what those answers would be, she took it as a bad one.

The second bad omen was when she discovered that the rental car didn't have a spare, and because she already knew that bad things happened in threes, she figured it was only a matter of time before the hammer fell.

CHAPTER TWO

MITCHELL MCCRAY hated Mondays. For some reason, Monday seemed to be the day most of the emergency calls came in. The groups that had been flown in to base camp a week or two before would almost always have a member in trouble by Monday and be on the radio to the flying service that abandoned them there, asking for assistance. Begging, sometimes in that desperate and disbelieving way, as if the idea of failure had never occurred to them. As if illness or injury or bad weather had never figured in to any of their carefully thought-out plans.

But that wasn't why he hated Mondays. Mitch hated Mondays because it was written into Wally's secret code of work ethics: never, ever show up for work on Mondays. And because Wally was the boss, he got away with spending every Monday with Campy, who also had Mondays off and was sexy enough to make any red-blooded man forget that Monday was supposed to be the first day of the work week, not the last day of the weekend.

Therefore, all of Monday's woes fell on his own shoulders and he never had backup. He also hated Mondays because if there was one day of the week the damn plane malfunctioned it would be on a Monday. Somehow, Wally had infused his own pathetic work ethic into the very rivets of the temperamental flying machine he'd dubbed *Babe*. What kind of a mechanic/pilot/flying service owner would name a plane after a cartoon pig? Then again, maybe it was a perfect moniker. The old red-and-white Stationair sucked down aviation fuel like a factory-farmed market hog and was about as athletic. It had crash-landed twice, sustained serious structural damage both times and taken additional abuse from several bad hail storms, which was why Wally had been able to buy it so cheap.

Which was also why it was on the ground more often than it was in the air.

In the first two hours of the day, Mitch fielded a radio transmission from a bunch of German climbers who were experiencing second thoughts about one of their companion's stomach pains. "Ve sinks eet might be heez apindeezeez!" So he assured them he'd be along soon, only to discover, when he tried to fire up *Babe,* that Wally's market hog had died at the trough sometime between engine shutdown Sunday night and attempted start-up Monday morning.

Mitch now had to drive all the way into Talkeetna to pick up the part they should have replaced weeks ago, which meant he had to give the German climbers' rescue over to Polar Express, which meant they'd be the ones to reap the huge gratuity for saving the sick climber from a possibly fatal attack of "apindeezeez" because climbers, especially foreigners, tipped big when they were rescued, which was the only good thing to come out of a Monday.

All of which put him in a very ugly mood when he climbed into his truck and gunned it down the middle of the airstrip toward Pike's Creek Road, throwing up a rooster tail of gravel and dust and nearly running over Thor, who woke from his fourth boredom nap of the morning just in time to realize he was being left behind. Mitch slammed on the brakes and the big, black wolfish-looking dog leapt effortlessly into the back. He'd ride there all the way to the "big city" and back, yellow eyes staring through the rear sliding window and the windshield, watching intently for moose—a tact that was both his hobby and profession. The brute was good at it, too, especially at night. Whenever he saw one he'd let out a *woof* that never failed to get the driver's attention. Thor had saved Mitch's life many times over. Seeing a dark moose on a dark road in the dark was damn near impossible, and lots of Alaskans had lost their lives because they hadn't seen it.

He was almost out to the highway when he spotted the little tan-colored sedan with the flat tire. Why the hell anyone would try driving a city car like that on a road like this was beyond him. He slowed down. Who knows? Maybe this was a chance to pick up a few extra bucks and put some gas in the tank. Talkeetna was a long haul if you weren't a crow, and fuel was damned expensive. He pulled alongside and leaned out his window, sizing up the situation. Rental car. Young slender woman with short dark hair, dressed in blue jeans and a fleece jacket trying to put one of those little scissor jacks under the axle on the opposite side of the car. Couldn't see what she looked like, but maybe she'd be good-looking enough to turn his day around. A man could always hope.

"Need a hand?" He cut the engine and got out, slamming the truck door behind him. She abandoned her efforts and pushed to her feet to face him as he rounded the front of her car. Recognition struck a hard blow to his solar plexus, stopping him in his tracks. God almighty. K. C. Jones stood in front of him, staring him right in the eye in that proud defiant way, and she was just as dangerously gorgeous as the first time he'd set eyes on her. She'd cut her beautiful long hair, but it was her, all right. He'd thought about her from time to time over the years, more than he liked to think about any woman, but that was because of the way she'd treated him. She was the first woman he'd been intimate with who'd left him without so much as a goodbye.

"I'll be damned," he finally managed to say. "You must be one of them fancy naval aviators the government sent north to field-test rental car tires on the Pike's Creek Road."

"Hello, Mitch," she said, cool as the morning. "How are you?"

"Great. You?"

"Fine."

"Been awhile."

"Yes, it has." And then she nodded over his shoulder. "Is that your truck?"

He glanced behind him as if there might be some question. Thor was standing on the diamond-plate toolbox that spanned the bed behind the cab, ears at attention and eyes fixed on K. C. Jones. "No. It belongs to Thor. The dog. But he lets me drive it," he said, wishing the rust spots weren't so big and numerous. "Good to see you, by the way. What's it been, four, five years? What brings you this far north?"

She gave him a small smile. "I had some time off and thought I'd see what Alaska looks like without any snow on it."

"So it's just a coincidence that you happened to be driving down this particular road when you got a flat?"

"Not exactly. I was coming to see you." After an awkward pause, during which she had the decency to blush, she added, "I'm sorry, I know you must be busy. You were driving some-where in a big hurry. I probably should've called first but..."

"Not a problem," Mitch assured her. "I figured you'd show up sooner or later."

"You did? Why?"

"To apologize for not saying goodbye when you left Eielson." Her blush deepened. Good. At least she hadn't forgotten that part. "I'm on my way to pick up a part for *Babe* in Talkeetna. I'll fix the flat on your rental car, then if you want, I'll take you out for lunch."

"The rental doesn't have a spare," she said. "I discovered that just before you arrived. But lunch sounds fine. It'll give us a chance to talk."

Mitch removed her flat tire in minutes, threw it in the back of the truck to drop off at the local gas station, and in minutes they were on their way.

She'd said she wanted to talk and he was kind of curious to find out why she'd shown up from out of the blue after four plus years, especially since she'd never answered his letter, but several miles passed without her saying a word. The silence between them soon became the loudest thing he'd ever heard. He figured it was up to him to jump-start this conversation.

"So, how long have you been in Alaska?"

"I just arrived last night." She gave him a questioning glance. "Who's Babe?"

"*Babe*'s the only plane owned by Wally's Air Charter at the moment, but I have my eye on another."

"I heard you left the air force."

"Yeah. It was time. I started out on the career track, same as you, but I lost my enthusiasm for military life after they tried to court-martial me." Her eyes bore into him with such a peculiar look, he nearly drove off the highway, but he wrenched the wheel and managed to keep all four tires on the asphalt. "I wrote you right after it was over. The trial was short because they didn't have much of a case, but when the time came to reenlist, I didn't. No regrets."

"I see." She sat through another endless five-mile silence before asking, "How do you like flying for an air charter?"

"The flying's great, but business is iffy. Wally's a good mechanic—he specialized in airframe and power plant in the military—but trying to keep *Babe* in the air is costing us more than it's worth. I should be flying out to the mountain to pick up a sick German climber but instead I'm driving to Talkeetna to pick up another airplane part. Which means no groceries this week."

Six more miles of silence slipped past before she said, "Do you have a family?"

Didn't everyone? "Yeah. Three brothers, two younger, one older; a baby sister; and my dad. My mother died of cancer a few years back. They all stayed put in Maine. I'm the only escapee."

This time the silence was brief. "What I meant was, are you married?"

This wasn't quite the conversation he'd thought they'd be having. "Huh?"

"Wife, kids?"

"Happily divorced for six years, no kids." Four more miles of silence went by. With the tension screaming around the cab of the truck, he decided they were the longest four miles he'd ever traveled. He was beginning to regret asking her to come along. Why was she here anyway? "You married?" he finally asked.

"No."

He nodded. "I read about you in the September issue of

Air Force magazine. Great article, though I thought it was traitorous that they'd profile a Navy flier. It mentioned the difficulties of juggling motherhood and a career. Since it didn't include 'husband' in the mix, I figured there wasn't one."

"You guessed correctly."

"But you have a kid?"

"A son. His name is Hayden. It's an old family name."

"What does Hayden think about his mother being a Navy pilot?"

"Hayden's relaxed about everything. He's a pretty cool kid."

"I guess pretty cool women just naturally have pretty cool kids."

He thought that might get a smile but she just looked out the window, heaved a small sigh and said, "I was lucky."

"Somebody else sure was, too." The words bounced awkwardly around the cab and he cursed himself for uttering them, but it was true. Somebody was. Some Navy guy, probably. Dare he ask? Ah, what the hell. "What does Hayden think about his father?"

"I told him his father died in a plane crash."

Tragic for them both, but that explained why she wasn't married. "I'm sorry to hear that," he said, hoping his words sounded more sincere than he felt. "So, how long do you have?"

"Pardon?"

Okay, maybe the silence *was* better than talking. She was glaring at him as if he'd just insulted her. "How long are you here for? A week? Two?"

She faced front again and said, "I don't have that long. Two weeks, max."

"Where are you staying?"

"The Moosewood Road House."

"Nice place. They have a decent restaurant."

"Yes."

This conversation was going nowhere fast. He was no closer to finding out why she was here than he had been thirty miles ago, and she hadn't yet bothered to explain why she'd never said goodbye to him after the night they'd shared. He was beginning to wish she hadn't interrupted his Monday, except that, damn it all, she was just as provocative as she'd been the first time he'd set eyes on her. His hormones were already at attention as he envisioned a passionate night or two tangled up in the sheets with her. So what if she hadn't said goodbye? Maybe this time he'd be the one who flew off without a word.

Fair was fair, after all. Two could play that kind of game.

KATE REALIZED by the time they reached the tiny town of Talkeetna that she was in way over her head. While Mitch was in the aviation building at the small airport picking up his part, she sat in the truck, wondering if her erratic heartbeat had anything to do with the fevers that came and went or with the man she'd just spent the last hour with. What should she do? He was totally in the dark as to her real reasons for being here. He seemed glad to see her but he didn't know, nor could she figure out how to tell him, that she'd never read the letter he'd sent.

Court-martial? That didn't sound good. He obviously didn't make much money, and his prospects for the future didn't appear much better. He wasn't married and had no kids, just a dog named Thor and a boss named Wally who obviously owned the charter service.

How should she proceed?

He stepped out of the hangar door and she was struck again

by his sheer masculinity. It didn't matter that he was dressed in faded Levi's and an equally faded flannel shirt. It didn't matter that he hadn't shaved that morning or that his hair needed to be trimmed. He was handsome in a rugged, athletic way that matched the land he'd chosen to make his home in. Maybe he'd never be rich, maybe he'd never drive a late-model truck or fly a plane that didn't always need fixing, but she had the feeling that somehow he'd get by. He was the kind of guy that would walk away from a hard landing with that same macho swagger and arrogant grin. Nothing would ever beat him down.

He wrenched open the truck door, tossed an object wrapped in a clean rag onto the bench seat between them and hauled himself in behind the wheel. "So, what's your preference? There's a deli a little ways from here or a roadhouse that serves great burgers. Your choice."

"I'm not really that hungry."

He fired up the engine and eased the truck into gear. "Then let's grab a sandwich at the deli. It's not as fancy and it's quicker."

He was as nervous as she was, she realized as he drove to the deli; only, when she got nervous, she got quiet, whereas Mitch couldn't seem to shut up. The deli was rustic and charming with big baskets of bright flowers that hung from the porch eaves. He talked about fishing while they waited for their order to be delivered to the little picnic table on the porch, and in between bites of his sandwich he told her about salmon runs and grizzly bears that prowled the riverbank by his cabin and one instance when he'd barricaded himself inside while a bear chewed his favorite fly rod to splinters. And then came a long pause in the conversation and she glanced up and realized those disarming eyes were studying her intently.

"What?" she said, shifting under his scrutiny.

"I don't know. Why don't you tell me?"

"What do you mean?"

"Something wrong with your sandwich?"

"I told you I wasn't hungry."

"You said you wanted to talk, but this is a mighty one-sided conversation."

She averted her eyes, heart thumping painfully. "I'm enjoying listening to you describe your life here." She gave him a faint smile. "Your place sounds nice, except for the bears. Maybe you'd give me a tour while I'm here. I love log cabins."

His eyes narrowed and he sat back in his chair. "Sure. Just say when."

Kate had spent her childhood dreaming about what she was going to be when she grew up. Once she'd grown up, she'd spent every moment striving to make that dream come true, and every step of the way there had been men standing in her path, blocking her, trying to trip her up and hoping she'd fail and make a fool of herself.

Getting pregnant had been the worst setback of her career. Getting pregnant had validated all those chauvinistic remarks and those sexist attitudes. For four months she'd had to give up flying. Four whole months she'd been grounded because she'd done just what they'd expected her to do. She'd gone out and gotten herself pregnant, just like a woman.

This man had been a major player in tripping her up and almost causing her to fail, yet now she was sitting in this deli listening to him talk and his words were making her feel all warm and fuzzy inside and she caught herself thinking, *Wow, for the past four years, I could have had a man in my life that I actually liked to talk to, listen to and, yes, make love with.*

There was no denying the magnetism that had made him so impossible to resist the first time they met. It was still there. She could still feel it. Just one touch and she'd succumb again, one touch and he'd destroy all her defenses and start another fire, one neither of them could put out. Would that be such a bad thing at this stage of her life?

What was the matter with her? She must be sicker than she thought to be having such crazy ideas. She didn't need a man. She'd never needed one. She was happy being single. In fact, she preferred it. Nobody had to worry about Captain K. C. Jones. She could take care of herself. Always had and always would.

Always?

Ha! Funny how facing you own mortality cast a harsh light on everything and illuminated truths that had been so easily hidden beneath alternating layers of bravado and pride. Funny how it humbled...

"I have a confession to make," she said. "I never read the letter you sent. I threw it off the edge of the flight deck, unopened, and I'm sorry."

MITCH DIDN'T KNOW quite how to take this. All he knew was that it stung. He'd spent countless hours agonizing over each and every word, just to have her fling it off the edge of the flight deck, unopened? The letter he'd written to K. C. Jones four and a half years ago, give or take a few months, was the only one he'd ever penned to a woman. It encompassed weeks of laborious beginnings that went nowhere and awkward revisions that only made the content more stilted. He'd finally mailed it off in a kind of fatalistic coup de grâce.

"That explains why you never answered it," he said. "But why are you sorry about it now?"

"Because I think maybe I should have read it. I was so angry then. So mad at you and at myself. I know it doesn't make much sense and I'm sorry about that, too."

Mitch didn't have a clue what she was talking about. Why would she have been angry at him? Were all women born irrational?

Probably.

Even if she didn't give a damn about him, she should have read his letter and had the decency to put him out of his misery with a proper "Dear John" response, instead of leaving him wondering why she'd snuck away as she had. And now here she was, sitting across from him at his favorite deli, having told him she wanted to talk. But about what? Obviously not the fact that she'd missed him.

After watching her shred her paper napkin into smaller and smaller pieces, he finally reached out his hand to pull the remnants away. "Okay," he said, balling them up and dropping them into the center of the table. "If you're not so mad anymore, then I guess the two of us have some catching up to do."

She nodded, and a faint flush colored her cheeks. "Maybe you could take me back to your place and give me the tour. We could talk there."

"You bet." He paused in the act of rising out of his chair. "Did I mention my cabin had no indoor plumbing or electricity?"

"That seems appropriate for a cabin."

"And you're sure you want to talk there?"

She nodded again.

"Good enough." He took her uneaten sandwich, wrapped it in several napkins and stuffed it in his jacket pocket in the hopes she'd eat it later. If she didn't, Thor would. In the center of the table he left a pile of bills, enough to cover the tab and a good-sized tip, and then he escorted Kate back out to his truck and wondered if maybe, just maybe, his day hadn't just taken a big-time turn for the better.

CHEMOTHERAPY, as defined by her doctors, was the use of drugs or chemicals, often in combinations, to kill or damage cancer cells in the body. These drugs targeted not just cancer cells, but all cells that divided quickly, including those responsible for hair growth. They had been administered intravenously via a small plastic needle inserted in her forearm, delivering a mixed bag of anticancer agents into her bloodstream, a potent cocktail of life and death, of nausea and pain, of hair loss and fatigue and above all else, hope.

For Kate, those weeks spent in the hospital undergoing intensive chemotherapy had been hell. She'd kept Hayden's picture pinned to the wall by her bed, a bright icon to gaze upon in her darkest hours, and she'd requested several pieces of exercise equipment be scrubbed, sanitized and delivered to her room so she could keep fit while undergoing the most difficult physical and mental challenge of her life. She was still biking four miles each morning when her hair started to fall out, first by the strand, then by the handful. All her long, dark hair disappeared while she pedaled, and she prayed that, in the end, her love of life and for her son would triumph and prevail.

Rosa would bring Hayden to the hospital, and the medical staff would dress them both in sterile gowns and allow them into her room. The first time was hard. Hayden didn't understand why she couldn't come home. The second time was even harder. He cried when it was time for him to leave. The third time, her hair was coming out and as she tried to explain it to him he took a handful of it in his little fist and pressed it to the side of his face. "I take it for you, Mumma," he said. "Now can you come home?"

Kate clung to his precious existence and drew sustenance and strength from it. What else was there to hold on to in a life that measured everything by the yardstick of military might? She had become a weak, pale woman with no hair, retching into a toilet bowl while a nurse said soothingly from behind, "It's all right." What was all right about it? She was young and she didn't see the sense or reason in her illness. She didn't smoke or drink or do drugs. She ate a healthy diet. She jogged five miles each and every morning, rain or shine. She didn't understand how or why she'd gotten this sick and she never would, so how could she expect her son to understand when she told him she couldn't come home?

Yet somehow, Hayden did come to understand. During that first month of her treatment he came to accept her stay in the hospital and her struggle with leukemia with an optimism and resiliency that both humbled and inspired her, and made her more determined than ever to win the fight. She had to be there for him. She had to survive this for Hayden.

After her second month-long chemotherapy session at the cancer research hospital in Seattle, she'd been scheduled for two months of "rest and recovery," during which time her doctors were hoping a blood match would be found, allowing them to schedule a bone marrow transplant. Her leukemia was an aggressive type, and she'd been told the odds of finding a match were worse than the average of one in fifty thousand because of the native blood on her mother's side of the family, but the doctors seemed confident that a donor would appear. It had been her mother's suggestion to spend those two months building up her strength at the family home in

Montana, far from the large population centers Ruth was sure would compromise her daughter's weakened immune system. Her arguments were convincing, especially since Kate had just resigned her Navy commission…or tried to.

Why not go home? Her parents were there, and it would be good for both her and Hayden to be in the old ranch house in the foothills of the Rockies surrounded by millions of acres of wilderness.

Instead, she was here in Alaska, a land whose rugged beauty proved more than equal to that of Montana, sitting in the cab of a rusty old truck next to a man she didn't know anything about beyond the memories of one passionate night. A man who'd been an officer when she'd met him but was no longer in the military. A man who flew a broken-down plane and barely earned enough to survive on. A man she had to get to know as fast as possible in order to be able to decide if he'd be a fit parent for Hayden because he could end up being the only parent Hayden had.

So, how to begin?

Kate folded her hands in her lap and composed her thoughts while she studied the dramatic scenery as the truck headed north. "Tell me about the court-martial," she said, reasoning that she might as well get the worst part over with.

He drove a few moments more in silence, then blew out a breath and glanced sideways. "You really didn't read that letter?" She shook her head and he focused on the road. "I was brought up on charges of conduct unbecoming an officer, dereliction of duty and being absent without leave."

"What did you do?"

"I spent a night off base with the hottest Navy pilot in the fleet."

Kate stiffened with shock. She kept her eyes forward while waiting for her heart rate to steady. She had been the reason for his being brought up on court-martial charges? "You can't be serious."

"Remember Skidder?"

"The mechanic in phase dock?"

"When I didn't return that night he told my CO, who was convinced I was having an affair with his wife. That's all it took. He called me into his office two days after the blizzard blew itself out, threw the charges at me and said, 'Major McCray, you have just made a dire mistake and I'm going to make sure you pay for it in spades.'"

"How is it that I never heard anything about this through the liaison officer? Wouldn't Skidder have mentioned my involvement?"

"Oh, he tried. Skidder would do anything to weasel his way up the ladder." He flashed her a brash grin. "But in the end, all the prosecutor could prove was that I got stuck off base in a blizzard after delivering you to the officers' quarters."

"But you didn't deliver me there until the next morning."

"They couldn't prove that, either. The blizzard's whiteout conditions and the power outage helped out there."

"What about the owner of the saloon?"

"He testified that he locked the Mad Dog up when the power went out and went home."

"You mean, he lied under oath?"

"When the military plays hard-ass with civilians, civilians don't always play by their rules."

"Were you having an affair with your CO's wife?"

"Of course not. She was twenty years older than me. The

whole trial was a fiasco and it made my CO look like an idiot, which didn't improve our relationship much."

Kate shot him a skeptical look, then shook her head and faced front again. "I didn't know you were going through all that."

"Would you have been less mad at me if you'd known?"

She stifled a wry laugh. "No, at the time probably not. I probably would've been glad you were paying for it. Sorry."

He nodded, as if that was explanation enough for him. "I hope you like dogs," he said as he turned down Pike's Creek Road.

"I do. Why?"

"Thor's been banned from the airstrip because he chases planes, so I'll have to drop him at the cabin before bringing the part to Wally's." When they got to her rental car, he stopped just long enough to replace the repaired flat tire, then continued on. Where the road forked, he headed left and nodded to the right and said, "That way leads to the airstrip." A few miles later, after passing two somewhat ramshackle dwellings, one of which looked long abandoned, the road ended at his cabin.

Kate had prepared herself for a plywood-and-tar-paper shack with blue tarps strung everywhere and rusted fifty-five-gallon drums lying about. She was surprised by the attractive complex of log buildings. There were several sturdy outbuildings in addition to the charming cabin, including an authentic log food cache raised high on four posts. The hand-hewn main cabin had dovetailed notches, a real stone chimney and a porch that practically hung out over the creek. The clearing itself was large, and a garden space was surrounded by a rustic staked fence fashioned from alder and willow poles, but it looked as though nothing had been planted inside for several seasons. There was a wonderful view of the rugged snowcapped mountain range, including the mighty Denali, who was still showing her face to the world.

"Is that a dogsled on the porch roof?"

"Yup. A dog musher used to live here. One day his wife decided she'd had enough of living the backwoods life with a bunch of sled dogs and a guy who was always out on the trail, so she left him, and after a few years he lost heart and got rid of all his dogs except Thor, who slipped out of his collar and ran off." He wrenched open the truck door, jumped down and walked around to open her door. "He sold me the place for a song because I happened to ask him about it on the right day and then he followed his wife back to Florida. Thor reappeared a week later and decided to stay. It worked out well for me because it was so cheap and it's only seven miles from the airstrip. Plus I got a sled dog thrown in for free. Nice, huh?"

"Yes," she admitted. It wasn't at all what she'd expected.

"Will you be okay here for a little while, or do you want to help me put a fuel filter in the plane?"

"I'll be fine." Again surprised by his manners, she took his hand and let him assist her out of the truck. He'd done the same thing back at the deli.

"I'll give you the official tour when I get back, and we can talk then. Thor will keep the bears away. Help yourself to anything and everything and don't mind the mess—I wasn't expecting company. There's a satellite phone in the kitchen, if you need to use it. Here, take your sandwich." He fished her napkin-wrapped lunch of his jacket pocket and handed it to her. "Don't just look at it, eat it."

"Sir, yes, sir," she said, stepping back and giving him a mock salute.

Kate watched him drive back down the rutted gravel road and wondered when he'd realize the dog was still riding in the back. Thor obviously preferred Mitch's company, which was okay with her. She'd just have to deal with any bears that came along. Meanwhile, she'd prowl around the cabin and investigate the domestic side of Mitchell McCray.

CHAPTER THREE

MITCH WAS SURPRISED to see Wally's Harley parked outside the warming shack. He must've had a fight with Campy, but it couldn't have been a bad one because Campy's old Subaru was parked right next to the shiny bike. Wally came out when he heard the truck and the first thing he said was "Where the hell you been all day?" as if he'd been working his ass off since before sunup.

"In Talkeetna, picking up the part for your plane, which, by the way, didn't want to start this morning. Good to see you, too, boss. Didn't expect to, being as it's a Monday."

"Polar Express called to thank us for the referral of the German climbers. Said they made a great tip off that one. I came over to see what was wrong."

"Plane's broke, as usual. That's what was wrong."

Wally was fiftysomething, bald, overweight and often-times contentious, but he could work wonders with the Stationair and was a passable pilot for a guy who was mostly self-taught. "Ain't nothin' wrong with *Babe*. She started right up for me. Hand over the fuel filter."

"How'd you know that was the part I went to get?"

"I'm psychic. Thought I told you to leave that damn dog at home."

Mitch looked over his shoulder. Sure enough, Thor was

standing with his front paws on the diamond-plate toolbox wearing that sly wolfish grin. "Thor, I thought I told you to stay the hell home!" Thor's ears flattened back and he wagged his tail in response. Mitch looked back at Wally. "The bad news is, we lost a job this morning because of that clogged filter. The good news is, Raider called last night and said he's seriously considering my latest offer for the Porter."

"We can't afford that plane. Thought we already had this discussion." Wally was fishing in his pockets for a half-smoked cigar, which he stuck in his mouth and lit.

"Where's Campy?"

"Inside."

"Campy! Get out here, woman. I need you to bear witness. Wally's changing his story on me again."

The door to the airfield's warming hut opened a crack and a thin face framed by bleached blond hair stuck out, cigarette dangling from pouty red lips. She looked to be in the same kind of mood as Wally. "Go to hell, Mitch, and take that bastard with you," she snarled around the cigarette and slammed the door again.

"I told Raider I could have the money by next week," Mitch said, as he followed Wally toward the plane. "If we called Yance, he'd front us the money, and if I had it in hand I know Raider'd except my offer. We could sell the Stationair and pay back some of that loan right away."

"We ain't selling *Babe* and we ain't buying a Pilatus/Fairchild Porter. It's a good plane, I'm not arguing with you on that score, but Raider wants too much for it. Thinks its a goddamn Concorde jet. Besides, Yance'll tack a high interest on that loan if he'd even give it to us. He's a friggin' shark. Bottom line, we can't afford it."

"The price is fair and the plane's in great shape. Dependable. Flying a plane like that will boost our business a hundredfold. You know it's true and you know we need it, and I think Yance'll back us, so just bite the bullet and get it over with." Mitch jammed his hands in his jeans pockets, ducked his head and rounded his shoulders, hesitating. "Forget the plane for a minute and tell me what you think about this. This woman I knew over four years ago, Navy pilot, suddenly shows up out of the blue, and she…"

Wally stopped abruptly, turned and took the cigar out of his mouth. "K. C. Jones?"

"Yeah. How'd you know?"

"It's not rocket science. It was my saloon you wooed her in back at Eielson, and you showed us the article about her in *Air Force* magazine. She's here, in Alaska?"

"She's out at my place."

"And you're standing here, talking to me? You big dumb son of a bitch. Hey, Campy!" he bellowed toward the closed door of the warming hut. "You think I'm uncaring and heartless? Listen to how Mitch treats his women!"

"C'mon, Wally, cut me some slack," Mitch said. "I need your advice."

"Campy, you're missing out. Mitchell McCray is asking for my input on a romantic matter."

The warming hut door opened and Campy reemerged, dressed in tight hip-hugger jeans and a stretch Lycra top that barely concealed Wally's two best friends. She slouched against the doorway with a frown. "Mitchell," she drawled, "if you're desperate enough to take advice from Wally about matters of the heart, I feel real sorry for whoever your latest girlfriend is."

"It's that hot Navy pilot who was written up in that air force magazine last fall," Wally said. "Mitch showed it to us. Remember? She's out at his place even as we speak."

"No kidding?" Campy tossed her long blond hair back and took a drag of her cigarette, regarding Mitch through narrowed eyes. "If she looks as good in real life as she did on the cover of that magazine, you don't want to be making any mistakes with her."

"I just want to know why the hell she's here," he said. "Not a word of warning, she just lands on my doorstep. She must want something. I just don't know what."

"She wants you, Mitch," Wally guffawed. "A career bachelor like you should know all the signals by now."

"One thing's for sure. It's not your money she's after." Campy flicked the cigarette down and ground it out beneath one of her fancy, hand-tooled, black Tony Llama cowboy boots. "Tell you what. The two of you get that plane fixed and back in the air so we can all keep eating, and I'll take Thor back to your cabin. That woman shouldn't be there without a dog, not when the salmon are getting ready to run and the bears are walking that creek."

"I don't know if that's such a good idea," Mitch said.

"Campy's got a point," Wally said. "Might be good if she took the dog back to your place. They can meet each other and have some girl talk."

"Girl talk?"

"Trust me, they thrive on that stuff, and Campy'll find out more about where that woman's coming from than you could in a whole year of beating around the bush."

"Yeah, but…"

"Look, you wanna know why this chick showed up on

your doorstep or not? Send Campy over. You'll get the lowdown without all the dancing around."

Campy gave Mitch's arm a squeeze. "Hon, I hate more than you'll ever know to say this, but this one time, Wally's right. I'll go scope things out."

"I appreciate what you're trying to do, Campy, but…"

"Hey, what are friends for? Keys in the truck?"

"Yeah, but…"

"You like this gal, or don't you?"

Mitch ran his fingers through his hair. "I like lots of girls. I just don't know why this one's here, and I don't want you playing matchmaker on my behalf."

Campy gave him an innocent look. "What do you mean?"

"You're always trying to pair me off, but I like bachelorhood just fine."

"That's only because you haven't gotten to know the right woman yet." Campy turned and walked away. When she reached the driver's side door, she glanced back over her shoulder before hoisting herself into the cab. "Don't look so worried, Mitch. I promise I'll behave."

KATE SPENT a half an hour just browsing through Mitch's books after touring the comfortable, homey interior of the main cabin, which wasn't nearly as messy as he'd warned her it would be. Aside from some clothing tossed over various pieces of rustic furniture, it was quite neat. His kitchen sink was empty of dishes, the counters were wiped down and the floor swept. His bedroom was in the loft and consisted of a double mattress laid on the bare wood floor with a down comforter over the top and a window that was opened wide to the outside air. The downstairs was one large room, the kitchen and living area divided by a big brick chimney that hosted a woodstove on one side and a fireplace on the other. The cavernous fireplace was on the living-room side, where the bookcase was located. Most of the books were paperbacks, some were hardcovers, and there was one magazine lying flat on the shelf: the *Air Force* magazine that featured her as the cover girl. She wondered at the man who had tucked that magazine among all those books by authors as diverse as Albert Einstein, Jack London and Thor Heyerdahl.

She ran her fingers over the gilt letters embossed into an old leather bound volume of poetry printed in 1876 and carried it with her onto the porch, where the sound of rushing water lulled her senses. She lowered herself into one of the comfortable Adirondack-style chairs and sat for a few moments, wondering if this was wise. She might very well fall asleep with that beautiful creek calming her and the sun's warmth soaking into her. But what harm would a short nap do? Mitch wouldn't be back for at least an hour, and it was so peaceful here.

She could easily imagine Hayden clattering down the porch steps with his fishing rod and his dog. This place was made for little boys to grow up in, and for dogs to keep them company while they did. She sighed and opened the book to a random page, trying but not quite able to imagine Mitch reading poetry. She scanned the first line of the chosen poem and before she could finish the second, a curious lethargy soaked through her bones. On impulse she removed her wig, relishing the feel of cool air and warm sun against her scalp.

She'd worn the wig in public since she was first discharged from the hospital after losing her hair. Her mother had handed her the box and said, "I thought you might want the option of wearing this until your own grows back. The hair's real."

Kate had opened the box, sure she'd be repulsed, but to please her mother she'd taken it out and put it on. Studying herself in the bathroom mirror she'd thought, *Yes, this is much better. I like me much better this way.* With the addition of the false eyelashes and a little eyebrow pencil, she looked almost normal. Healthy.

But she was all alone here, so she dropped the wig in her lap, tipped her head back, closed her eyes and let herself drift off to the sound of the water, wondering what her little boy would look like in ten years' time….

Seconds later, it seemed, she was awakened by the sound of a truck door slamming. Kate sat bolt upright, blinking sleep from her eyes, and was still smoothing the wig into place when the stranger topped the porch steps. She'd expected Mitch and was shocked to see a very buxom bleached blonde dressed in clothes that left little to the imagination.

"Well, hey, hon," the woman said in a smoky southern drawl. "I'm real sorry to startle you. Were you sleepin'?"

"Who…?"

"I'm Campy, a friend of Mitch's, and I sure didn't mean to wake you. I brought Thor back because he chases planes down the runway and Mitch was busy helping Wally fix the plane, that's all. You just sit right where you are, all nice and relaxed, and I'll be right back." She retreated into the cabin and reappeared holding two bottles of Guinness Stout. She handed one to Kate and then dropped into the second chair. "Hope you like a bitter brew. That's all Mitch ever drinks," she said. "And I hope I didn't startle you too bad. Sorry about that."

"That's okay," Kate said, holding the cold bottle. "I must have dozed off. It's so peaceful here."

"Boring, I'd call it, but I guess it all depends on what you like. So, you're the one Mitch calls K. C. Jones."

Good God. Kate closed her eyes on the world for a few moments, wishing she could just disappear. Mitch had talked about her to this woman? "Is that what he calls me?"

She heard Campy settle herself more deeply in her chair, followed by the sharp snick of a lighter, and then smelled the acrid smoke of a cigarette. "Honey, you may not know this and I doubt he'll ever tell you, but Mitch has a real soft spot for you."

Kate opened her eyes and stared cynically at the other woman, whom she decided couldn't be one of Mitch's girlfriends if she was talking like that. She eased back in her chair and set the bottle of beer on the broad armrest. "That's a little hard to believe, considering we haven't seen each other in years."

"Oh, Mitch would never admit to it. Tough guys don't like gals to think they're so easily roped and tied, but I used to be a bartender at the Mad Dog Saloon, which was a mile or so from the base. I served up a lot of brew to Mitch while he was stationed there, and hon, nobody hears more stories told from the heart than a bartender does. He talked about you a lot."

"I can't imagine what he talked about," Kate said drily.

"Oh, he thought you were pretty special," Campy said. "He's a hard worker and a great pilot. I don't know what Wally'd do without him. Wally owned the Mad Dog 'til it burned down, then he used the insurance money to buy a six-passenger plane and start the charter service. He's a great mechanic but he can't fly so good, so he hired Mitch to do most of that. My guy Wally is your guy's boss."

"He's not my guy."

"Well, if he isn't, he oughta be. My opinion, of course. Mitchell's always been a favorite of mine. If I didn't have Wally, I'd go after Mitch myself, even though I'm a little too old for him. But he's one in a million. I guess you know that, too, hon, or you wouldn't be here, would you?"

"Oh, I'm sure he has a girlfriend. I didn't come here thinking he'd been saving himself for me all these years."

"I think he always hoped you'd show up here one day. Mitch has lots of friends, but none have come close to being serious relationships."

"I'm surprised he even remembered me."

"Remembered you? Hon, how else would I know he called you K. C. Jones?"

Kate gave her another skeptical look. "My real name's Katherine Carolyn Jones."

"Camilla Clarke," she said, giving her a crooked smile. "Everyone around here calls me Campy. You like Alaska?"

"It's beautiful."

"It's boring," she said. "I'd go back east in a minute, but Wally likes the flying here. Pilots are a crazy-ass bunch, no offense intended."

"None taken."

"I mean, I think it's pretty cool, you being a Navy pilot and all. Mitch said you were an instructor at that dogfighting school the Navy has—like in *Top Gun*. Pretty wild stuff."

"That was a good assignment. I got to be home every night with my son."

Two carefully plucked and penciled eyebrows shot up. "You have a kid? Huh. He never told us that." Campy studied her through a haze of cigarette smoke. "You married?"

"No."

"How old's your kid?"

"He'll be four next month."

"Hmm. Interesting." Campy squinted her eyes and stared

off across the river for a few moments, then glanced back at Kate with a knowing expression. "How long are you staying?"

"A week or so."

"If I'd been smarter, that's all I'd have stayed." Campy drained the last of her beer and, pushing to her feet, she dropped her cigarette into the bottle and tossed the hair out of her eyes. "Mitch means a lot to me 'n' Wally. I sure hope the two of you can work things out."

BY THE TIME Campy drove his pickup back to the airfield, Mitch was pacing around the plane amidst mechanical noises and cuss words from beneath the plane's cowling, while Wally growled for various tools to be passed to him.

Campy'd been gone a long time. What the hell could the two of them have been talking about? They had nothing in common. Campy was a fortysomething professional bartender who hadn't graduated high school, couldn't spell and liked to smoke, drink and ride on Wally's Harley. Her one ambition in life was to train circus ponies. What kind of conversation could she have possibly been having with a career captain in the United States Navy? And finally, here she was, driving up to the warming hut with Thor in the back, his front feet braced on the diamond-plate toolbox cover and wearing his sly, wolfish grin.

Campy jumped out of the cab and turned to see what Mitch was gesturing at. "Damn you, Thor! I swear, Mitch, he was standing on the porch when I left. He must've chased after the truck and jumped in." She approached the plane and tossed her hair out of her eyes. "Relax, hon, everything's cool at your place. She's reading poetry on your porch. My advice? Grill her a thick bloody steak for supper and serve it to her with red wine and hot kisses." She ducked her head under the cowling. "Hey, lover, I'm headin' to town to do a load of laundry. Can you manage here without me?"

"I'll do my best," Wally grunted.

"Hang on," Mitch said. "She told you she was staying for supper and she wanted a thick steak?"

"Don't forget the red wine and hot kisses. She's nice, Mitch. I like her. How 'bout you, Wally—what's your preference tonight?"

"Beer and burgers," came the gruff reply.

"I'm on it, sweetie. See you soon."

"Wait a sec," Mitch said. "Did you find out why she's here?"

Campy took one last fierce drag on her cigarette, tossed it down and ground it out. "She's here to see you, you imbecile. She's been missing you. How long's it been?"

"Almost five years without so much as a phone call or a letter. That's why her surprise appearance is so strange."

"Maybe not as strange as you think." Campy gave him a long, calculating stare. "Make sure that red wine comes in a bottle with a cork."

Wally peered out from under the cowling as she walked toward her rusted-out Subaru. "What'd I tell you," he said. "Girl talk. They love that stuff. Better pick up that steak at Yudy's. They have the best beef and he'll cut it nice and thick for you." He waited a few moments, then scowled. "Well, what the hell you stallin' for? Haven't you kept her waiting long enough?"

"I don't believe that's why she's here. I think there's something else going on."

"So what if there is? You gonna pass up the chance to get cozy with her? Go fix her that steak like Campy said."

"I spent all my cash on the fuel filter."

"Ah, shit." Wally dug in his wallet, peeled out two twenty-dollar bills and handed them to Mitch. "That's the last of mine. Make it count. Women are scarce in Alaska and hot ones like that are even scarcer."

YUDY'S GENERAL STORE carried everything from self-tapping sheet metal screws to wedding gowns, and had the best meat counter in the state. It also had a fairly good wine selection and a huge block of select sharp cheddar, the kind that crumbled when it was cut, and with what Mitch had left over he was able to buy half a pound along with some fancy crackers. Forty bucks didn't stretch very far at Yudy's, but the groceries were worth it and tonight he wasn't about to serve up boxed macaroni and cheese with a side of canned beans and a bottle of beer, the mainstays of his usual diet. No, tonight called for a special meal, a properly seductive prelude for what was sure to come after...otherwise she wouldn't have told Campy she was staying for supper and that she'd been missing him.

He was still kind of puzzled about the real reason she was here, but Wally was right. He'd be a fool to pass up this opportunity, and the prospect of spending another night with the sexiest pilot in the Navy was enough to send his heart rate right off the scale. It didn't matter anymore that she hadn't read his letter. The hell with it. Seize the moment and run with it.

By the time he got back to the cabin, he'd figured out just how the night should proceed. He'd light the grill first, because it took awhile for the charcoal to get just right, then he'd open the wine and get the cheese-and-cracker thing going while the meat marinaded and he fixed the vegetables. Yudy had prepped him on that. "You'll wanna grill your veggies. Ladies like that kind of stuff. Cut 'em however you like. Me, I like my peppers in quarters, some like 'em in halves. Onions the same way. Eggplant, mushrooms, potatoes, tomatoes, whatever trips your trigger. Coat 'em with olive oil and a pinch of herbs and grill 'em."

Well, scratch the eggplant and mushrooms, he hated the things, but he bought a few nice fat tomatoes and brightly colored bell peppers to supplement the vegetables he knew he already had, and he could make a salad, too, and then…?

Then they'd eat. And whatever happened after that was up to the gods and the mountain, because the mountain played a big role in his life here. He might have to fly out at the drop of a hat to pick up climbers who were calling it quits or were sick or injured. Those calls happened frequently this time of year and they certainly could use the business. But barring the climbers, who knows where the night might end? Maybe she wouldn't want to go back to the Moosewood. Maybe she'd opt to stay.

Maybe? Of course she would. That's why she was here, wasn't it? She'd spend two weeks' worth of fabulous nights with him before flying away again, back to her Navy career. What could be better than a short-term relationship with a gorgeous, sexy woman, no strings attached?

As he parked the truck, Thor jumped out of the back and Mitch heard her greeting the useless beast. He grabbed the bags of groceries and climbed the porch steps after the dog. Kate was sitting in the late afternoon sunshine, book of poetry lying open in her lap, and she smiled when she saw him. Right then and there he forgot all about how great a two-week-long, no-strings-attached affair would be because she looked like she belonged, and she looked beautiful.

"Hey," he said, caught off balance by his own reaction.

"Hey, yourself. How'd it go at the airfield?"

"Great. Got the plane fixed. What about you?"

"I didn't do a thing. I sat on this porch and read poetry and then I had a nap."

"That's what a vacation's all about. You hungry?"

"Getting there." She folded the book shut and stood. "What can I do to help?"

"You can supervise."

She followed him into the kitchen and leaned over the counter while he unpacked the bags of groceries. "It's so peaceful here. I can see why you love it."

He uncorked the bottle of wine, rummaged in the cupboard for the two wineglasses left behind by the lonesome musher and poured. "Hope you like red. It goes well with meat, or so I'm told. I'm mostly a beer drinker myself, and beer goes with everything." He handed her the glass and she smiled at him again. His heart did something that made him lose his breath and remember the night they'd had together, the night he'd spent years trying to forget.

"Thanks." She took a sip and then watched while he organized the meal, or tried to. It was hard to do anything while she stood there. "Your friend Campy stopped by in your truck to deliver the dog, but Thor chased her down the road when she left. I don't think she realized he was following her."

"No, she didn't." He unwrapped the thick tenderloin, laid it on a platter and poured the marinade Yudy had recommended over it. "Thor jumped aboard, probably in that rough section a quarter mile from here, and rode to the airstrip in the back of the truck. But it was quiet there today, not much traffic. He didn't get in any trouble or cause any crashes."

"Has he caused crashes before?"

"Yup. Two." Mitch piled all the vegetables into a colander and pumped water over them in the sink. That old-fashioned hand pump sure beat carrying water from the creek.

"What happened?"

"Both pilots tried to avoid him and went off the airstrip. One hit a bunch of willows, not much damage, just a few scratches, but the other bent a prop and we had to replace it. Wally swore he'd shoot the dog if he ever showed up at the airstrip again, but that was before Campy had the run-in with that brown bear and Thor saved her ass. Big vet bill, he was all torn up, but Campy told Wally that dog belonged here and if he shot the dog, she'd shoot him."

"This sounds like a happening place," Kate remarked with a smile.

"You betcha. Never a dull moment out here in the bush." He took a knife out of the block, laid the cutting board on the counter and began slicing up the vegetables. "You like yellow and green bell peppers, scallions, potatoes, tomatoes and carrots?"

"I love any and all vegetables. Shouldn't you start the grill?"

"Oh, yeah, forgot about that part. Here, you slice while I get that thing fired up."

"Mitch?" He glanced over his shoulder and the way she was looking at him made his heart do that weird somersault thing again and he could hardly catch his breath. Damn, was he having some kind of coronary? "Thanks for asking me to supper," she said. "And I really am sorry I never read your letter."

KATE WAS SORRY in so very many ways that her feelings of remorse nearly overwhelmed her. As she watched Mitch through the cabin door while he got the grill started, then watched him laying cheese and crackers onto a chipped china plate with little roses along its border, she knew that she'd made a terrible mistake in not reading that letter he'd sent. She'd made a terrible mistake in not telling him about Hayden the moment she'd found out herself. How was she going to right these wrongs without making them worse? What would be his reaction when he found out that he'd had a son for the past four years? How could she possibly bring the subject up in a calm and logical way?

Right after Campy had left that afternoon, she'd called the Moosewood on Mitch's satellite phone. "I'm out at Mitch's place and he's fixing a plane so I'm not sure when I'll be back," she told Rosa. "How's Hayden?"

"Oh, he's fine, *señora*. The owner of this nice place took us snipe hunting today."

"Snipe hunting? What's a snipe?"

"Some kind of bird they shoot and eat here, but it was a joke, I think. The man, he had us carry empty coffee cans and bang on them with spoons. He said the birds would fly into the cans. Of course, they didn't, but Hayden loved it."

"Did you have lunch?"

"*Sì*, a very good lunch and Hayden is napping. He has been outside all morning. This is good for him. How about you, *señora?* How does it go for you?"

"So far, so good. If I don't get back until late, don't worry. I haven't told him about Hayden yet, but I'm going to. I just have to pick the right time."

"I understand, *señora*. Good luck."

It seemed that Rosa was saying that more and more often. Was it luck Kate needed, or nerve? She had only a few days to tell Mitch he had a son and the sooner she broached the subject, the better. What if he flipped out at the idea? What if he met Hayden and didn't like him? But how could anyone not like Hayden? Besides, when Mitch saw him for the first time, he was sure to recognize himself in that little boy's grin, the mischievous flash of his eyes, the arrogant know-it-all attitude that yes, even a three-year-old can possess. He was sure to take one look at Hayden and know without her saying anything that he was looking at his own son.

She glanced up from slicing the vegetables as Mitch came back into the kitchen from checking on the grill. "This is such a great place for kids. I'm surprised you aren't married by now, with a whole bunch of them stampeding around."

He lifted his wineglass for a taste. "This cabin isn't big enough for a whole bunch. Besides, a wife and kids have never been a high priority for me. I tried that once and it didn't work. Marriage, that is. Fortunately, there were no kids."

"You don't like kids?" Kate asked with a twinge of unease.

"I think they deserve better than two parents trapped in a bad marriage. Besides, if anyone else moved in here on a permanent basis, I'd have to build an addition." He regarded her steadily for a moment, long enough for her to feel a warmth flowing through her that had nothing to do with a fever. "I suppose I could do that," he added. "I guess I'd just need the right motivation."

Kate dropped her eyes to scoop the vegetables into the bowl he'd provided. She drizzled them with olive oil and tossed them together.

"Motivation," he continued. "That's the key. A man has to be motivated in order to accomplish great things, whereas a woman self-motivates naturally. She knows what she has to do and just goes ahead and does it."

"Oh? And what does a woman know she has to do, naturally?" Kate felt herself instantly bristling at his words, the same way she'd bristled her way through ten years of Navy life.

"She knows she has to nurture and comfort and create. A woman is the heart of any home, and a man needs a woman to motivate him to build that home.

"That's a crock, McCray. I didn't join the service to nurture, comfort and create, and I don't feel obliged to motivate any man to do anything."

"No, of course not, I'm not saying you did or do or should.... I guess I'm just trying to say that the major difference between a man and a woman... That is to say, one of the major differences is..." He paused and gave her a cautious look. "I'd better go check the fire again."

Kate held up the bowl of vegetables. "Grilling basket?"

"Look under the counter. You might find something useful, but I've never grilled vegetables before. I usually just wrap them in foil and lay them in the coals."

"Nurture, comfort and create?" She couldn't resist another jab at his chauvinism.

"I take it all back, every last word, and forget I ever mentioned motivation."

"I suppose you're the type who prefers their women pregnant, barefoot and in the kitchen?"

He escaped out the door and was gone long enough for her to conclude there was nothing like a grilling basket in the kitchen. She did find the aluminum foil, however, and made do with that, carrying both the foil-wrapped vegetables and her glass of wine out onto the porch. Mitch was standing over the grill with a long-handled fork, poking occasionally at the coals. "No grilling basket, I see," he said.

"This'll work if you like soggy vegetables."

"Soggy vegetables are my favorite." He took them from her and laid the packet on the edge of the grill.

Kate leaned against the porch railing with a grudging smile. "So tell me what happened after you got out of the air force."

He narrowed his eyes, thinking back. "That'd be about three years ago. I took a job flying for a commercial carrier. Turned out to be boring as hell—passenger jet service between Anchorage and Seattle. Like driving a bus on the same route every day. I lasted only a year at that. I might have held out longer, but Wally looked me up and convinced me it was time to make the switch." He nudged the foil packet closer to the coals and it started to hiss. "After the Mad Dog burned, he held on to the insurance money, but rather than rebuild it he decided to start up an air charter service near Denali to ferry mountain climbers, hunters and sightseers around. At first I turned him down because flying for the airlines gave me a steady paycheck, but the second time he asked I jumped at the chance and here I am, borderline broke."

"But happy?"

"Oh, hell, yes. My long-term plan is to buy Wally out when he gets ready to retire and change the name of the charter to Arctic Air, but that'll only happen if we can keep the business alive, and that'll only happen if he goes along with buying this plane I have my eye on. It's a Pilatus/Fairchild Porter. Hot plane. Expensive." He turned to her. "So what was in all the letters you never sent me over the past four years?"

"There's not much to tell that wasn't in that article," Kate responded with an offhand shrug. "I was offered permanent shore duty when my son was born, I got promoted, did a lot of recruiting PR with the colleges, then got lucky and landed an instructor pilot position at the Navy Fighter Weapons School."

"Lady, in case you didn't know it, that wasn't luck. Only the best of the best end up there. The flying must've been great."

Kate took a small sip of wine, surprised that the idea of never flying like that again was still so painful to her after everything else she'd been through. "It was," she admitted. "I got to play bad guy in the air with some of the hottest young pilots in the fleet, but even better than that, I changed a lot of old-fashioned attitudes toward women in the military every time I worked with a new class."

"That had to have been the hardest lesson for them to learn."

"That women can do more than nurture, comfort and create?"

He raised both his hands in a mute gesture of surrender. "I'll get the steak. The coals are just about ready and it doesn't take long for the veggies to cook." He disappeared inside and reappeared carrying the platter with the marinating steak, Thor padding at his heels, his yellow gaze never wavering from the prize. "How do you like yours cooked?"

"Medium rare, but it looks like Thor would take his just the way it is."

"The only way he'll taste this steak is in his dreams." The meat went onto the grill with a loud hiss and savory plume of smoke. "This'll attract every bear in Alaska, but don't worry. Thor won't let 'em within a mile of the porch."

Kate glanced around, reasonably sure he was kidding, though she wouldn't have been the least bit surprised to see a grizzly hulking through the thick willows along the riverbank. She was glad Thor was with them, standing guard.

"Must've been tough for you, raising a kid and flying at the top of the curve," Mitch said, turning the packet of vegetables.

"It would've been, if I hadn't found Rosa," Kate admitted. "She was taking care of my neighbor's three kids, and when he got his transfer orders, Rosa wouldn't go with them. She didn't want to leave California. I'd just taken two months of maternity leave and wanted to get back in the swing of things, so the timing was great for both of us. I lucked out and so did Hayden. She's been wonderful with him."

Mitch poked at the steak then reached for his wineglass. He took a swallow and then lowered it, trapping her with those eyes that even after more than four years still had the power to easily seduce her. She wanted to look away but couldn't.

"Tell me why you never read my letter," he said.

"I'd rather not talk about that right now."

"I'm thinking whatever you were so mad about has to have something to do with that night at the saloon, and that's also why you snuck off on me that way. No note. No nothing. You jumped in your plane and flew back to California without so much as a goodbye. So tell me what I did that was so awful."

She shook her head. "You wouldn't understand."

"Try me."

Kate felt her heart rate instantly double as the heat of embarrassment flushed through her. How could she explain it to him when she didn't fully understand it herself? "It wasn't you. I was mad at myself for going to a bar with someone I didn't even know, and then…" Her voice faltered and she fell silent.

His gaze never wavered. "As I recall, we were properly introduced beforehand."

"I was mad at myself for going…and at you for fixing those drinks."

"As I recall, you polished off the first one without complaint and then asked me to mix you another."

Kate frowned. "I did no such thing."

"Whoa." He set his wineglass back down, his expression

wary. "Back up a step. You asked me to fix you another drink, and I did. I wasn't trying to get you drunk so I could take advantage of you. I've never done that with a woman."

"So you say."

"Is that what this is all about? You were mad at me because I mixed you two drinks and you were mad at yourself because all of a sudden your sex drive kicked into high gear after years of being repressed by life on board an aircraft carrier? That's why you never read my letter? Is that what you came back here to tell me?"

"Not exactly," Kate said, but he was too worked up to listen.

"You had me half undressed before you even finished that second drink," he said. "Remember now?"

Kate's cheeks burned. "That's because of the large amounts of alcohol you obviously put in my glass."

He shook his head. "It wasn't the alcohol that caused you to let down your hair. It was the adrenaline pumping through your system after that flight from Adak. It was the blizzard and the wind and the snow and the fire in the woodstove. It was all those things combined, but most of all, it was you and me, Kate. You and me. Call it chemistry, call it whatever you want, but you can't deny it. We were great together." He took a step closer and startled her by reaching out a hand to brush the hair back from the side of her face. "I can feel that chemistry even now. Can't you?"

She closed her fingers around his wrist to still his hand, terrified that he'd discover she was wearing a wig. "Mitch, I didn't come here to explain why I never read your letter. I came because I have something important to talk to you about."

Rebuffed, he stepped back when she released his hand and gave her a curt nod. "So, talk."

Kate was riveted by the intensity of his gaze. She knew it was now or never, and she felt a pressure building up within herself that made it hard to breathe. Her heart beat a painful cadence as she struggled to find the right words. So many unknowns loomed ahead of her. She could only hope this one turned out well, both for Hayden's sake, and for hers.

"You'd better turn the steak first," she said, taking hold of her glass of wine and damning herself for her cowardice. "This could take awhile."

CHAPTER FOUR

MITCH REALIZED that they were standing toe-to-toe like dueling partners, which wasn't what he'd had in mind when he planned this barbecue. The way things were going, she wouldn't be spending the night up in his loft, and he kind of had his heart set on that scenario. He turned away from her and gave his attention to the food cooking on the grill, fuming inwardly. Damn, but she was hard to read. What was she trying to tell him that was so vital? Was she going to accuse him of putting some kind of date rape drug in her drinks? As he turned the meat, the pager on his belt sounded. He silenced it with a muttered curse.

"Sorry. That's the boss," he explained. "Bad timing. I better call Wally and find out what's up."

Kate moved to the porch railing to watch the water rush past while he went into the kitchen to retrieve the satellite phone. He carried it back out and dialed, then, while he waited for the call to go through, he poked the steak with the tongs, taking out his frustration on the expensive piece of meat until someone picked up on the other end.

"Hey, boss, what's up?" He glanced across the creek toward the mountain range while he listened to Wally explain. Four climbers, one injured badly, winds so high on the mountain that nobody else was flying. Mitch's initial reaction to this was disappointment, then he glanced at Kate. She was standing with her back to him, and her shoulders were set in a militant line. Whatever it was she was working herself up to tell him, it wasn't going to be pretty. In retrospect, maybe now would be a good time for him to bail.

"We still have a couple hours of good daylight and the Stationair's ready to rock and roll, right? That'll be good money, especially if they want a lift into Fairbanks. We have a bank payment due on the plane and another one to buy. Radio them to hang tight, boss, I'm on my way."

He ended the call and gave Kate what he hoped was an apologetic look. "Four climbers requesting a flight out of base camp, one needs immediate medical attention. Increasing winds are predicted on the mountain through tomorrow, so it's now or never. A high-risk rescue means great money. It also means we can't share supper. Sorry about that."

"Don't be," she said with a look of ill-concealed relief. "That sounds lucrative. You go ahead. If you could drop me off at my car, I'll head back to the Moosewood."

Mitch was a little peeved that she seemed so anxious to escape his company. Women generally didn't behave like this around him. He forked the steak onto a platter, slid the foil-wrapped vegetables next to it and followed her into the kitchen. "It's really bad timing."

"Don't worry about it," she said briskly, as she set her wineglass on the counter, and reached for her purse. "You have only a couple hours of daylight. Those climbers are in trouble, and they're waiting for you. I'll come by the airstrip tomorrow morning and we can continue our conversation then." She walked out the door and headed for his truck, leaving him staring after her in bemused disbelief.

So much for the perfect seduction.

KATE WOKE at 5:00 a.m. and it was already light outside. She sat up, reached out to touch the reassuring warmth of her son's solid little body and then slipped from the bed and padded barefoot through the living room to the porch. She felt good. In fact, she felt great, in spite of the way last night had turned out. She'd eaten a big container of yogurt when she'd gotten back to the Moosewood, drunk a quart of water and slept like a rock for the second night in a row. No stomach pains had kept her awake. No nightmares had haunted her sleep. This morning, Denali was completely obscured by cloud cover. If she hadn't seen the mountain standing in that very spot the day before, she wouldn't believe it existed. She dressed in her fleece jogging outfit because the morning was chilly, then poked her head into Rosa's room.

"Rosa, I'm going for a run," she said when the older woman muttered that she was awake. "I'll be back in an hour. Hayden's still asleep."

Five minutes later she was jogging along the quiet side road, bottle of water in hand, hat pulled over her head, breathing clean, crystalline air deep into her lungs and blowing out all the residual chemicals inside of her that still burned and scorched and sickened. She thought about Mitch and last night and how four mountain climbers had spared her from having to tell him about Hayden. She didn't have to tell him, did she? All she really had to do was determine if he would be a good parent should anything ever happen to her.

No doubt about it, she was becoming an expert at avoidance.

And speaking of anything happening to her, what about Mitch? He'd flown out to the mountain last night in heavy winds. She'd lost some good friends to plane crashes during her ten years in the Navy. The plane Mitch flew had a reputation for being unreliable, something she'd never had to deal with in her flying career. Not only were Navy aircraft meticulously maintained, but the type she flew, the Hornet, was known for being so reliable it didn't require much maintenance. She'd never climbed into the cockpit wondering if the plane was going to fail her. She wondered what that must be like, especially when ferrying around a bunch of paying clients who didn't have a clue that the engine could quit at any moment.

Couldn't be much fun.

Yet he said he liked flying out here because it was seat-of-the-pants stuff.

Wing-and-a-prayer stuff...

Kind of like serious relationships, and marriage, too. Things she'd scrupulously avoided. But now she found herself wondering if she hadn't made a big mistake. She'd only been around Mitch for a day and already she felt dangerously vulnerable. Chemistry? Maybe. Whatever it was, the attraction was strong and compelling. She liked being with him. She was glad she hadn't told him about Hayden last night, yet sad the night had ended so soon. Disappointed that he hadn't kissed her goodbye...

She was getting giddy. Light-headed. Foolish. She was a young girl again, secretly writing her name in the pages of her diary, pairing it with that of every young man she'd ever had a crush on because Jones was such a plain-Jane name and she was sure she'd find someone who could change that, because she needed a far more glamorous name if she was ever going to make it in the adult world. But in fact there hadn't been that many guys in her life, and by the time she was twelve she was completely focused on stuff far more important than boys. She was going to be an astronaut. A space shuttle commander. The first woman to set foot on the moon. On Mars. And she was going to have to settle for "Jones" because she hadn't yet met a boy worth changing her name for.

When she was in college, she was completely focused on her engineering degree. No time for anything but studying. No time for guys, for parties, for any kind of frivolous activity. Sex? That was meted out carefully by girls who wanted to nab the right husband and father for their future children. K. C. Jones wasn't playing that game, and she certainly had no time for that crazy little thing called love.

Katherine Carolyn McCray. She laughed aloud in the wonderful unspoiled land she ran through, where no one could hear her and wonder why. Fantasizing was harmless, especially when her future looked so bleak, but giving substance to that fantasy?

That would be Major McCray Mistake number two.

MITCH BOUGHT the flowers at one of those all-night truck stops that had gas pumps, an ATM and, for some fortuitous reason, little bouquets of roses in a cooler next to the one crammed with beer. He bought them with some of the money the climbers had given him for a tip the night before and as he pulled back onto the main road, he felt foolish for doing it, but after last night, he thought he needed to do something to make up for having to run off as he did. Regardless of how the evening had turned out, and excepting the somber little talk she had yet to have with him, he still had hopes of another memorable interlude with K. C. Jones, and the flowers might score him a few points.

Yesterday, Kate had opened a big can of worms about the anger she'd been holding against him for the past four

years, and he'd lain awake from the time he'd gotten back at
1:00 a.m. till five this morning trying to figure out what the
real reason might be. Sure, they'd spent a memorable night
together, but she'd been ready and willing, and afterward
she'd been the one who'd run off. He'd written her, but she
never answered his letter. Hell, she hadn't even read it. She
had a kid but it couldn't be his. They'd been wild together,
but not careless.

So he bought the bouquet and hoped the reason for the
serious talk she had to have with him wasn't so awful it would
doom the future of their immediate relationship, because he
was kind of counting on two weeks' worth of nights with
K. C. Jones.

The Moosewood was a sleepy place, one of those backwater rustic lodgings that people either loved or hated. He
imagined all the hard-core city people would hate it. There was
no night life or satellite TV. No big town anywhere nearby.
Nothing really, except that killer view of Denali when the
weather was clear. And a bunch of housekeeping cabins with
kitchenettes where families could hang out and explore the surroundings without having to rack up big restaurant tabs. The
Moosewood had a decent eatery in the main lodge where those
tiny white Christmas lights burned year-round to give off what
travel writers dubbed "that redneck Alaskan ambiance." Most
road houses sported that same kind of style. He didn't mind it.
He liked Christmas lights. Why not have 'em on all year-round?

But they weren't on this morning when he pulled his truck
onto the gravel side road and drove up to the main lodge. He
thought the best he'd get was a phone connection to Kate
through the switchboard, but the clerk in the office told him
what cabin she was in, clueless as to protecting her security.

He left the bouquet on the seat of the truck because all of a sudden it didn't look nearly nice enough for her and he walked up the neatly tended path to the guest cabin at the very end of the complex. Yes, there was Kate's rental, parked in the back, and around front, facing the mountain, was a porch.

And right about here, he came to a dead stop.

A little boy was sitting on the steps, fiddling with the wings on one of those balsa wood gliders. He had blond hair and was dressed in denim coveralls, a red flannel shirt and sneakers. He was big enough to be out of diapers but still a ways from first grade, though beyond that Mitch hadn't a clue to his age. Kids weren't his area of expertise. At Mitch's approach the boy looked up from the glider, his expression changing instantly from hopeful anticipation to wariness.

"Hi," Mitch said, standing at the foot of the porch steps and wondering why Kate hadn't mentioned she'd brought her son along on this trip. "I'm guessing you must be Hayden. Your mom home?"

Hayden shook his head, studying him with dark serious eyes. "She went running."

"Looks like you have a broken wing there. Need some help fixing it? Here, let me have a look." Hayden held out the glider and Mitch took it. "I have some duct tape in my truck. If I splint the broken wing and put an equal amount of tape on the opposite wing to balance the weight, I think she'll fly okay. What do you think?"

Hayden stared at him a moment longer, then all at once he scrambled to his feet and bolted for the cabin door. He opened it and dashed inside. "Rosa!" he cried out in a young, strident voice. "There's a man looking for Mumma!"

Mitch stepped to the open door and glanced inside the

living room in time to see Hayden vanish through another doorway, and then his eye was caught by something on the coffee table. A wig lay beside an empty yogurt container holding a plastic spoon, and he felt a jolt of shock to the soles of his feet when he recognized it as Kate's short, dark, glossy hair. He was still processing this image when a stern-looking woman came from one of the bedrooms and crossed to the door. Mitch assumed this was the nanny, and hoped she was friendlier than she looked.

"Good morning, ma'am. I'm Mitchell McCray. I stopped by to see Kate."

"She's not here," Rosa said. "She went running. She should have been back a long time ago." As she spoke, Mitch realized the grim expression the women wore was one of worry. "She went up the dirt road. I told her, run out on the main road, the tarred road where people can see you if the bears come, where you can get a ride if you get too tired, but she wanted to see where the dirt road went, and so she went."

"I'm sure she's fine. I'll take a drive in my truck and see if I can find her," he offered. "That road goes clear to an abandoned mining town. Not great for vehicles, but fine for jogging. It's a nice morning. She probably just went farther than she planned."

"Yes, perhaps." Rosa nodded. "It would be good if you could look for her. She might need a ride home."

"I'll fix that broken wing just as soon as I get back," he said before he left, catching Hayden's eye peeking from behind his nanny's formidable bulk.

Mitch climbed into the truck and headed up the side road. He hadn't gone more than a mile before he saw Kate walking toward him. She was wearing a close-fitting black watch cap, a pair of gray sweatpants and a dark fleece top, and when she recognized the vehicle she stopped and waited for him to pull up beside her. He leaned out his window. "You the lady that called for the taxi?"

She walked around the front of the truck, opened the door and hauled herself in, looking pale and exhausted. "Hi," she said. "Thanks for the lift. It was so beautiful I'm afraid I got carried away and went too far." She melted back into the seat and gave him a weary smile. "I kept wondering what was around the next corner."

"If you'd gone around enough of them you'd eventually come to an abandoned mining town about ten miles out."

"Then I'm glad I turned around when I did. How'd your flight go last night?"

"Good, except the injured climber died and was frozen solid by the time I got there. Had a hell of a time getting him into the plane with all the rest of them and the gear. He had to have been over six feet tall and he wouldn't bend for anything."

She studied him for a few moments with a skeptical expression. "You're kidding, right?"

"Nope," Mitch said, turning the truck around. "It doesn't take long for a body to freeze solid at those temperatures, especially with the wind blasting the way it was. But the good news is, nobody else died and the plane ran just fine." He started back toward Kate's lodging. "I know it's early, but I wanted to apologize again for last night, and I kind of hoped we could finish up that talk we started." He cast her a questioning glance. "You feeling okay?"

"Why do you ask?" she said, instantly defensive.

"Just wondering."

"I told you, I went too far. I just need a long hot shower, that's all. You stopped by the Moosewood?"

He nodded. "Your nanny told me you were overdue and that you'd taken the road less traveled, against her advice. I think she was worried you'd been eaten by a bear."

Kate laughed. "I didn't see a bear, but that was a great road to run on, no traffic and no noise except for the birds. I've never heard so many birds. It was wonderful." She paused. "So, you've met Hayden?"

Mitch nodded again. "He broke the wing on his glider and I told him I'd fix it. Seems like a good kid. Kind of shy."

"He is, with strangers. Once he gets to know you, he won't leave you alone."

"I was kind of surprised to see him. You never mentioned you'd brought him along on your vacation."

She gave him a bemused look then glanced down at the seat between them and picked up the bundle of tiny roses. "The flowers are pretty."

He'd forgotten all about the flowers. "They're for you."

Her expression became somber as she looked down at the pitiful bouquet that rested in her lap. "Thank you."

"I'm sorry about supper last night."

"Please, stop apologizing. That wasn't your fault. I hope all that food didn't go to waste."

"Not a chance of it. Thor knocked the platter off the counter while I was gone and ate the entire shebang. He's in detention. That's why he isn't riding in the back of the truck. Anyway, I know you said you'd stop by the airstrip this morning, but I was hoping we could continue last night's conversation over breakfast. I'm guessing you haven't eaten yet."

She gave him a long, appraising stare. "Neither have Hayden and Rosa."

"Then I'll buy for all of you and we can talk afterward."

She hesitated long enough for him to wonder if she was going to refuse, then nodded. "Okay."

Since his arrival at the Moosewood this morning, Mitch had been thinking about what he'd seen back at her cabin. Kate wore a wig. Why would a woman with naturally beautiful hair have to wear a wig? On top of that, she was very thin, and, now that he was paying closer attention, he noticed she had a translucent bluish cast to her skin and dark smudges under her eyes that at first he'd attributed to exhaustion. Now he thought otherwise.

She was sick. Seriously sick. He'd been blind not to see it before.

Was that what she had wanted to talk to him about?

The moment he laid eyes on that wig, he'd given up on his fantasy of the perfect seduction. Mitch wasn't good at dealing with stuff like serious illness. His mother had died of ovarian cancer six years ago, and he'd been relieved that his air force postings at the time had kept him far from home, spared from her day-to-day downward spiral toward death that the rest of the family endured. He'd been granted emergency leave four times during the final months of her illness, and that last week spent hovering around her hospital bed, followed by the long Catholic funeral, had been a nightmare.

Kate was sick, but what did that have to do with her coming to Alaska? She certainly hadn't come to reminisce about that night at the Mad Dog.

By the time he got up the nerve to ask her directly, it was too late. They were already back at the Moosewood. He parked beside Kate's rental car. She reached for the door handle, gave him a brief smile, said, "Thanks for the lift," and disembarked before he could stop her.

The first thing he noticed when Kate led him into her lodging was that the coffee table had been neatly arranged with several magazines and the wig had vanished. Hayden still clutching the broken glider, appeared with a thunder of footsteps from a bedroom as soon as they entered. "Mumma!" The little boy plastered himself against her legs. When she knelt to hug him, the glider suffered a few more injuries in the fierce embrace. Landing gear bent, starboard wing badly fractured. He'd fix it, one way or the other. It was the least he could do for the kid.

"Hayden, have you met Mitchell McCray? Mitch, this is Hayden." Kate rose to her feet and affectionately rumpled her son's hair. "Shake hands like I taught you to," she said. "Mitch is going to take us to breakfast."

Hayden shook his hand gave him a grave stare from a pair of serious eyes. "You said you'd fix my plane."

"And I will," Mitch said. "Your mom has to take a shower, and that'll give me time to make that plane of yours fly better than ever. Come on, let's go out to my truck where my tools are, and my duct tape. Can't do much of anything without duct tape."

"What's duck tape?"

"Follow me and I'll show you. Bring your plane along."

KATE WATCHED them leave the cabin, the tall man with the little boy at his heels, and wondered how Mitch could possibly not realize that Hayden was his son...or was he just really good at hiding his reactions? She shook her head with an exasperated sigh. No. He was genuinely clueless. Behind the closed door of the bathroom, she stripped off the black watch cap, shed the jogging clothes and stepped under the hot, rejuvenating stream of water. She'd been hoping the dilemma would resolve itself the moment Mitch met Hayden, but no such luck. She was still going to have to broach the subject of paternity with Mitch.

Maybe she should wait until they'd spent some time together. Surely Mitch and Hayden would get along. So far, they seemed to be doing okay. Of course, they'd only known each other for a few minutes, and a few minutes did not a lifetime make, but...well, there was the genetic thing, right? They were blood kin. They'd automatically bond with each other.

Father. Son. Bond. Right?

Bound to happen. Lord, that water felt good. Nothing compared to a hot shower. Standing beneath the steamy spray, she could almost believe in having long hair again, in feeling strong, being healthy, in hope and sunshine and a long and happy life with a man who loved her. She still felt the chemistry simmering between them. It was impossible not to, and equally impossible not to forgive herself at least a little bit for her lapse in self-control that night at the Mad Dog. Mitchell McCray was one in a million, just like Campy had said. That night her behavior hadn't been influenced by two mixed drinks, but it had resulted in a little boy who thought his father was dead.

Only he wasn't. And now they were all here in this place, together.

Mother. Father. Son. Bonding into...

Family?

She wiped the steam from the mirror and studied her reflection long enough for the powerful and positive feelings to falter. It was hard to reconcile herself to being the stranger in the mirror, that bald sci-fi space cadet who had just endured her second round of chemo and still faced another, the last and the worst.

She dressed in blue jeans and hiking boots, T-shirt and baggy sweater. "Rosa?" She opened the bathroom door.

"*Sì?*"

Kate lowered her voice to a whisper and pointed to her head. "My wig…?"

Rosa handed her a small shopping bag. "You left it on the coffee table, *señora*. I removed it."

"Thanks."

Kate pulled it on, wishing she didn't feel like such a fake for wearing it, but reassuring herself that her own hair would grow back. This was just a temporary morale booster.

Hayden and Mitch were still outside. Good. She went to the window and peered out, hoping to catch a glimpse of their interaction, but they weren't in sight. She dropped onto the couch to pull on her hiking boots. "Rosa, Mitch is taking us all to breakfast."

Rosa shook her head emphatically. "No, no, *señora*, I think it is best if the two of you go alone and leave Hayden here with me."

Kate glanced up in the midst of tying the boot laces. "Why?"

"So the two of you can be alone together. I will fix us something here. There is plenty of food. I will make breakfast fajitas. Hayden loves them."

She straightened. "I came here to see what kind of parent Mitch would make. What better way to do that than to watch the two of them together? How else will I ever know?"

Rosa raised her hands, palms up. "What more do you need to know? Look at how they are together. Already I can see this is good. This early time should be for the two of you, alone. Then, later, with Hayden."

Before Kate could respond, the cabin door opened and Hayden ran inside, holding his plane. "Look, Mumma!" He skidded to a stop in front of the couch and flung the glider across the room. It flew just fine until it hit the far wall with considerable force and the tail snapped off. Hayden stared for a moment at this latest catastrophe, then looked crestfallen at Mitch, who was just coming through the door. "I'm sorry," he said.

"It's okay, I know you didn't mean to break it." Mitch picked up the glider and the pieces that had broken off and caught Hayden's eye. "But here's the thing. If you want to be a hotshot pilot like your mother, you better learn to fly your planes outdoors. It's a whole lot safer. I'll fix it up again after breakfast. Deal?"

Hayden nodded. "Deal."

"Good. Let's eat. I've heard the Moosewood serves the best sourdough pancakes in the state."

Rosa's well-meaning protests died a quiet death, and at breakfast, while Kate worked on a formidable stack of pancakes, Hayden asked Mitch about his real airplane and where he flew it. Mitch used the back of his paper place mat to draw a map. "I'll show you where I fly the climbers in and out. This is the park," he said, drawing a big outline. "This is the park road that comes in off the highway." Long squiggly line. "This is Denali, McKinley, the big mountain." Jagged peak. "This is the base camp where I drop the climbers off and pick them up. This is the route they climb up the mountain." He drew a series of little slashes to depict the ascent. "And this whole area inside the park is where all the wolves and grizzly bears live."

"I wanna go," Hayden announced. "I wanna see wolves and bears."

"It's a long drive from here to the heart of the park, but there's a pretty campground there. Primitive, but nice. You like to camp, Hayden?" Mitch asked.

Hayden nodded vigorously, though he'd never been camping before.

Rosa shook her head just as vigorously. "Hayden is too young to go camping."

"I wanna camp!" Hayden insisted.

"Boys are never too young to go camping," Mitch pointed out to Rosa.

"And I suppose girls are?" Kate asked, nibbling on the last of her bacon. She'd eaten every last bite of her huge breakfast. It was the first meal she'd devoured hungrily in a long time, and her stomach felt just fine.

"What I meant to say was that kids are never too young," Mitch amended.

"That's what I thought you meant to say."

Mitch pushed back in his chair. "Well, anyway, that's my flying route."

Kate took a sip of coffee and regarded him over the rim. "What kind of plane do you use?"

"A Stationair, but a better name would be Stationary." Mitch pulled his own mug toward him. "Before Wally got his hands on her, *Babe* was ground looped twice, went through the ice three winters back, weathered two major hailstorms that banged the hell out of her, and on top of that I'm convinced she was a lemon to start with. The fact that she's over forty years old is the least of that plane's problems. Everyone who flies in this neck of the woods knows all the aircraft that are in use commercially. *Babe* doesn't have a good reputation, even though she manages to pass the hundred-hour inspections."

"You mentioned getting another plane?"

"I have my eye on one, but convincing Wally to make the switch is the hard part. I thought he was on board but he got cold feet at the last minute. Says the Porter's too much money."

"I wanna go camping," Hayden interrupted.

"Hayden, it's impolite to interrupt," Kate admonished.

"But I wanna see wolves and bears."

"Mostly what you'll see are big biting bugs this time of year," Mitch cautioned.

"I like bugs!" Hayden insisted.

"Yeah, but you're a guy. What about your mother? She won't like that a bit." Mitch said, giving Kate a conspiratorial wink. "You know how girls are. They think bugs are yucky."

Kate smiled grimly over the rim of her cup. "Wrong again. I love bugs. The bigger the better."

"I'm going camping!" Hayden announced, sitting up straight to make himself look taller. "Bears and wolves, Mumma. I'm going."

CHAPTER FIVE

AFTER BREAKFAST, MITCH FIXED Hayden's plane as best he could, but it didn't glide with any of its former grace. In fact, it didn't glide at all. "Tell you what," he said after the glider's fourth abrupt nosedive off the porch. "I'll pick you up a new one at the general store. How's that? Then I better stop by the airstrip and find out what's shaking." He glanced at his watch then looked over to where Kate sat on one of the porch chairs, watching them. "I won't be that long."

She caught the meaning in his glance and nodded. "Okay. I'll be ready and waiting."

"And then can we go camping?" Hayden asked, holding the faulty glider. "Will you take us?"

"You better talk it over with your mother," Mitch advised. "I wasn't lying about the bugs. They'll eat you alive. I'll see you both in a little while."

As he left the Moosewood, Mitch realized that the way things were going, he'd have an ulcer soon. Hayden was a cute kid, but any serious conversation with Kate was impossible as long as the boy was around. And he cursed himself for mentioning camping. No way did he have any intention of taking a sick woman and a little boy out into the wilderness. A day trip, maybe, but nothing more. He stopped at Yudy's and went in to pick up another balsa glider, silently giving thanks to the generosity of the rescued climbers. It was nice having money in his wallet.

When he arrived at the airstrip, Wally and Campy were in the middle of some heated discussion inside the hut. They broke off the moment he entered. Campy tossed her hair out of her eyes and took a drag on her cigarette, studying him through curls of blue smoke. "Well?" she said. "How'd things go last night?"

"Good, until Wally called. I stopped by to ask if I could take a couple days off."

"What? That's just great, just terrific," Wally growled, heaving himself out of his battered and broken old chair. "Go ahead, abandon me here at the busiest time of year. Great. Terrific."

"Last night you told me to do just that," Mitch reminded him. "When I called you from Fairbanks to report the success-ful rescue, you told me to take a few days off. Remember?"

"That was last night. This morning I've already had three calls. Three! That's never happened before. Three calls in one morning. Hell, in one hour! What the hell am I supposed to do?"

Mitch was dumbfounded. "What do you mean? Tell 'em hell yes, we'll come."

Wally was trying to light his cigar without much success. He shook out the match with a curse when he singed his fingers. "That's what I told 'em. God knows we can't afford to turn any business away." He struck another match on the woodstove and tried to light his cigar again. "Seegar Safari," he said between puffs. "That name mean anything to you? That was one of the calls. Big-time mountaineering group based out of Seattle started by John Seegar, the Everest climbing guru. They want to set up a base camp contract.

Ow!" He shook out the second match. "Big bucks. Big-name clientele. Steady business. The kind that brings more and more business." Wally paced back and forth in the small confines of the hut, clutching his unlit cigar and waving it about for emphasis as he spoke.

Mitch shook his head, baffled. "I don't get it. Why all these calls, all at once?"

Wally stopped to face him with a triumphant expression. "Turns out that group you flew off the mountain last night were big-time climbers—famous."

"Huh. That's probably why there were a bunch of reporters waiting at the airport when I landed."

"No shit, and that's probably why they interviewed you last night, which you could've told me about, you big buffoon. Anyhow, they interviewed the climbers in the hospital this morning and they raved about how you got them out of there in that windstorm after they got into trouble. Said you saved their lives. All of the other flying services told them it was too windy and dangerous to fly, but you came. And then last night's interview with you at the airport after the climbers were taken to the hospital was spliced into the story. The phone rang three times in the hour after that newscast aired." His eyes were bright and his face flushed with excitement. "This is our big break! Maybe that fancy plane is within our reach after all."

"Mitch," Campy said, blowing smoke. "I know you want to spend some time with Kate, but you need this business to succeed as much as Wally does, and I'm sure she'll understand. When the flying's done, you can do something special with her."

Mitch rubbed the stubble on his jaw. This unexpected spate

of work was the best thing that could have happened. It provided a perfectly legitimate excuse not to have to deal with a woman who might be dying and a kid who was probably all broke up about it. "Yeah, sure, that sounds okay to me. So, when's the first job?"

"There's a group of climbers in Talkeetna who want to be dropped off at base camp tomorrow morning if the wind dies," Wally said. "Right now, nobody's flying."

Campy crossed to him and gave his arm a squeeze. "Aw, Mitch, I know the timing's not the greatest, but you might get a new plane out of it. Bring Kate out to your cabin. She likes it there, she told me she did."

"What about the kid?"

Campy's eyes widened. "Her son's here? In Alaska?"

Mitch nodded. "And the nanny's here, too."

"He has a nanny? Well, there you go. No need to worry about a babysitter while you sweep his mother off her feet. What's the boy like?"

He shrugged. "You know, a typical kid. Young, kind of shy, about three feet tall, maybe a whisker more. Look, I better get back to the Moosewood. I bought him a new glider and I told him I'd bring it right back." Mitch heaved a sigh of relief. "I'll be here bright and early tomorrow, and in the meantime I might just stop by and talk to Yance about the loan."

"You do that, Mitch," Campy said, giving him an impulsive kiss on the cheek. "Tell Kate I said hello. Maybe you could bring the both of them by. I'd like to meet her son."

KATE WAS SURPRISED at how much she was looking forward to Mitch's return, and equally surprised that he'd advised Hayden to talk to her about the camping trip. She had the distinct feeling Mitch didn't really want to take them camping, but nonetheless, a camping trip would be a good chance to see how Mitch related to Hayden. There was nothing like a journey into the back country to strip the veneer away and expose the heart wood. Throw a little rain and some biting bugs into the formula and a person's character was instantly bared for better or for worse. Camping was just the ticket to find out what kind of man Mitch really was in the shortest time frame possible. Of course, he hadn't actually offered to take them, but Hayden was convinced it was a happening thing.

Rosa was still grumbling about the idea being planted in the boy's mind. "I don't like it at all, *señora*. Hayden, he is too young to camp in a tent. The bears—they eat people. I have read articles about it."

Kate laughed. "Have you seen my bottle of vitamins?"

"It is above your bathroom sink. Does your man have a big gun, in case these bears attack?"

"Rosa, he's not my man and we're not going to be attacked by bears. I seriously doubt we'll be going camping at all. Calm down."

When the knock came at the door, Kate beat Rosa to it with a mile to spare. She couldn't suppress her smile when she saw Mitch standing on the porch, holding the balsa wood glider, but his expression gave her pause. She stepped outside and closed the door behind her. "What's wrong?"

"I have a few flying jobs lined up for tomorrow if the wind dies, and maybe more after that. Business is picking up." He delivered this announcement gravely, as if it were terrible news.

"And that's a bad thing?"

"Well, Hayden seemed pretty excited about going camping."

Kate smiled. "He's packing his things as we speak, but I

already told him it wasn't a done deal. Don't worry about it. Rosa will be delighted to hear we aren't going to be attacked by bears while sleeping in a flimsy nylon tent. Rosa?" Kate opened the cabin door and stuck her head in. "The camping trip's been canceled. Looks like the bears will have to wait for their next good meal."

At Kate's words, Hayden raced out onto the porch and fixed Mitch with that steady, somber gaze. "But I wanna go camping!"

"Maybe you could visit my place instead sometime while you're here," Mitch suggested, handing him the promised glider. "There's a big log cabin and a river and it's in the woods so it's just like camping."

"Do you have wolves and bears at your place?"

"They come around from time to time," Mitch nodded, "but Thor takes a dim view on intruders. He chases 'em off."

"Who's Thor?"

"This half-wild dog that hangs out with me. Come to think of it, maybe Thor's a wolf."

"Does he howl?"

"Sometimes."

"Can you make him howl for me?"

"I can't make that dog do anything. He keeps his own council."

"Can we go now?" Hayden pleaded.

"That's not polite, Hayden," Kate admonished gently but firmly. "You should wait for Mitch to tell us when it would be a good time to visit."

"Will you tell us to visit now?" Hayden said with youthful hope.

"You like to fish?" Mitch countered.

Hayden nodded enthusiastically, despite never having fished in his life.

Kate rumpled her son's hair with affection. "You won't even eat fish," she said.

"Salmon are great eating, Hayden," Mitch told him. "So are trout. I bet you'd like fish the way I cook 'em over the coals. Tell you what, you catch one, I'll fix it for you, and you try it. You don't like it, you get a hamburger and fries. Deal?"

Hayden nodded again. "Deal."

"Then let's go. That is, if it's okay with your mom."

"Am I invited?" Kate asked.

"You bet."

HAYDEN SAT BETWEEN them on the front seat of the truck, buckled into his car seat after a lengthy but triumphant search for the long unused seat belt that turned up all sorts of odd bits and pieces of Mitch's life. Kate cataloged it all in her quest to discover all she could about this man: a huge roll of duct tape on the floor, multiple food wrappers from various fast-food eateries, several .30 caliber rifle shells between the seat cushions, four dark brown plastic encased MREs under the seat just in case he got stuck out in the boonies long enough to get hungry, along with two half-empty cans of bug repellent in case the insects did.

"I keep meaning to clean the cab out, but since she's probably going to break down for good at any moment, the project seems kind of pointless," Mitch apologized as she delved through the layers of trash in her search for the middle seat belt.

"Probably true," Kate agreed, stuffing the MREs back under the seat.

Two miles into the journey, Hayden craned his neck to see over the truck's dash. "Are we there yet?"

"Almost. We're going right past the airstrip so you can meet Campy and Wally, my boss and his girlfriend, and see the plane I fly."

"Can we go flying?"

"That's not such a good idea. The plane's not running all that good right now. But when I get my new wings, I'll take you and your mother for a spin. Okay?"

"Okay."

Kate felt her eyes sting with dry tears and looked out the side window as she struggled with her emotions. Hayden was starved for the company of men. He didn't know what it was like to tag along with the guys because he'd never done it, but clearly, he craved male companionship. Mitch was good with him. He might not be used to being around kids, but he had an easy, laid-back manner that had alleviated Hayden's shyness almost immediately. The only thing she couldn't figure out was how Mitch could be so blind to the glaringly obvious fact that he was Hayden's father.

Mitch turned off Pike's Creek Road and headed toward the airstrip. Kate glimpsed it through the spruce. The shabby little outbuilding with wood smoke whipping from the rusted metal stovepipe, the orange wind sock standing out straight in the stiff breeze, the rough grass strip, a shiny old classic Harley and a rusted Subaru wagon nosed up to the side of the building and the big old Stationair airplane tied down near the hut, wings rocking in the wind.

"What a beautiful bike," Kate said as Mitch drove up beside the other vehicles and cut the engine.

"You're looking at the only beautiful machine at this airstrip. Just don't touch it. Wally's mighty protective and he doesn't trust pilots." He caught Kate's eye and shot her a brash, unexpected grin then opened his door and jumped down. "C'mon, pard," he said to Hayden, reaching for the passenger's side door and helping Kate first. "Unbuckle yourself and I'll introduce you to two of Alaska's finest people." He turned toward the hut and bellowed, "Campy, Wally, c'mon out here. We got company!"

"Come on," Kate urged Hayden as his shyness returned.

His sneakered feet hit the ground just as Campy came out of the warming hut, followed by a stocky man wearing jeans, T-shirt, leather vest and a biker's cap. His burly arms were completely covered with tattoos.

"Wally Gleason, meet Hayden and his mom, Kate Jones," Mitch said. "Campy, this is Hayden, Kate's son."

At Kate's gentle insistence, Hayden shook both their hands but kept his eyes fixed timidly on the ground at his feet.

"Hey, sweetie," Campy said, flinging the hair out of her eyes and bending low enough to make eye contact in spite of Hayden's evasive maneuvers. "How do you like Alaska so far?"

"Good," Hayden replied somberly, moving behind Kate.

"That's a beautiful Harley," Kate said with a nod toward the big black-and-silver machine.

"A silver anniversary Screaming Eagle," Wally said, staring first at Hayden, then at Kate and finally at Mitch. From his expression, Kate gathered he was connecting the dots. "Huh. Well, I'll be damned," he growled, then fumbled in his pockets for what looked like the remnants of a half-smoked cigar. "C'mon inside. I gotta talk to you." The group tramped into the warming shack behind him. "Got four more calls this morning after you left," he said to Mitch as he struck a match on the stove top. "One was for another flying gig next week, two more for tomorrow, the last was a film crew from a TV station based out of Seattle." He sucked hard on the stub, trying to coax life into something that should have been thrown out long before.

"They wanna do a special segment on the pilots that fly the climbers in and bring 'em back out when they get in trouble and you're the man they want to talk to. I told 'em you'd call to set up a time." He shook out the match, tossed it in the wood bin and handed Mitch a crumpled-up piece of paper. "Number's there, and the contact name. Who'd a thought one flying job could bring such a windfall?"

Mitch stared down at the paper, then shoved it into his jeans pocket. "We better get going, before we get so busy I can't leave," he said to Hayden, who willingly followed Mitch out the door. He glanced back at Kate. "You coming?"

"In a minute."

When the door banged behind them, Kate turned her attention to Wally. "Is that plane of yours safe to fly?"

Wally's face reddened at her blunt challenge. "Of course it is. We wouldn't be chartering it if it wasn't."

"This other plane Mitch wants to buy. The Porter. How much is it?"

"Too much. Raider was asking six hundred grand. Right now we can't afford it, but maybe after we pick up some new business…"

"Mitch told me about the Stationair's history," Kate said, not bothering to beat around the bush. "I don't think anyone should be flying it. I'd like to buy that other plane and lease it back to you."

"Hold on," Wally said, once he was able to move his sagging jaw. "The Stationair's safe, and even if it wasn't, any plane we charter should belong to the flying service."

"You just said the flying service couldn't afford it," Campy pointed out. "Kate says she can, and what she's offering sounds like a real reasonable option to me."

"Whose side are you on?" Wally blustered. "Mitch works for me."

"And he's flying a plane you own that shouldn't be in the air and probably won't be for much longer," Kate said. "He can't afford to be doing that. He has way too much at stake."

"That's right," Campy agreed. "Mitch needs a reliable pair of wings. All this free advertising will be for nothing if that old wreck crashes while he's flying a bunch of climbers to the mountain."

"I spent twenty-five years in the air force," Wally said, his expression dark with suspicion. "Now, maybe a Navy pilot's pay is a smidgen better than an air force mechanic's, but even at a captain's wage, ponying up six hundred grand for a plane is a big stretch of the old bank account."

"My dad's an investment analyst. He's been in charge of my money since I got my first job in grade school. He's done all right with my savings," Kate told him. "Where is this plane? I'd like to check it out without Mitch knowing. Maybe if I have a chance to negotiate the price on my own he'll sell it for less. Raider knows how much Mitch wants it, so having him around won't help."

Campy gave Kate an appraising glance. "Honey, you go on back to Mitch's place. Tell Mitch I invited you to go shopping this afternoon and get him to drop you off here, then I'll take you over to Raider's airstrip. It's not far from here, maybe fifteen miles. Raider's in the middle of a nasty divorce, so he's real anxious to sell. It's a great plane. It would put us head and shoulders above the competition. I bet Raider would have it sitting pretty at our little airstrip tomorrow morning if we went over there today."

Kate gave Campy a brief nod and smile. "Sounds good. I'll be back. And thanks."

"My pleasure, hon," Campy said. "I never liked that old red-and-white clunker, and I'll be glad to see it gone. Hey?" she added hesitantly as Kate reached for the doorknob. "I know this is none of my business, but does Mitch know Hayden's his son?"

Kate shook her head. "I haven't told him, and I don't think he has a clue."

"I'll be damned." Wally peered out the window. "That kid's a carbon copy. He'd have to be blind not to see it."

"You only saw it because I told you my suspicions earlier," Campy said. "Otherwise, you'd be just as clueless as Mitch." She gave Kate a sympathetic smile. "Good luck, hon."

Wally was still wearing that flustered look when Kate left the shack and climbed into the truck. "I was asking Campy if she knew of any good places to shop in the area," she said in response to Mitch's questioning glance.

"You want to go shopping?" Mitch started the truck.

"Why not?" Kate buckled Hayden's seat belt. "Campy said there are some good clothing stores nearby. I could use some warmer things. The nights are pretty nippy here. She offered to take me this afternoon, so I told her that sounded like fun."

"You and Campy, shopping." Mitch pulled away from the warming hut and started down the airstrip road. "You surprise me, Captain Jones."

Kate raised her eyebrows. "I rarely get to do fun stuff like that, and I'd also like to pick up a few things at the grocery store. Is there something wrong with that?"

"No." He cast her another perplexed look then shook his head. "No, nothing at all."

"I thought she was very nice to offer."

"Very nice. I'll drop you back there whenever you say. If Hayden wants, he could stay with me and we could do some fishing. Rustle up supper. You up for that, pard?"

"I wanna hear fish and wolfs howl," Hayden announced without hesitation.

AT MITCH'S CABIN, Hayden was enthralled with the river, the rustic setting and, most of all, with Thor, who, when released from being tethered to a doghouse in Mitch's absence, decided instantly that the boy belonged to him.

"Can I keep him, Mumma?" Hayden asked when the preliminary greetings were over.

"Thor belongs here, Hayden. He's Mitch's dog."

"I'm sure Thor'd go along with it," Mitch said. "He likes you, pard, no doubt about it."

"But he wouldn't like California," Kate pointed out. "He's a husky and huskies don't like hot places."

"But Mumma, you said we were gonna live in Montana. That's why we moved."

"Moved?" Mitch was climbing the porch steps with Kate and Hayden's packs and he paused to look back at her. "Since when did the Navy establish a base in Montana? Does this have anything to do with global warming?"

Kate shook her head, avoiding his eyes by watching Hayden wrestle with Thor. "I'd tell you that the west coast was about to drop into the ocean, but that's classified information. We're just going to visit my family for a while."

"But Mumma, we moved, remember?" Hayden called out to her. "All our stuff went away to Gram's and Gramp's."

"You stay away from the river, Hayden," Kate said, hoping the change of subject would be distraction enough. She glanced at Mitch. "I don't want him going near the water."

"How long are you planning to stay in Montana?"

She shrugged, trying to avoid his questioning stare. "I haven't had a vacation in years. They owe me this leave."

"I don't doubt that. How long?"

His eyes were asking for much more than a simple answer of days or weeks. She drew a painful breath, wondering how long she could sidestep and evade, and wishing she'd left Hayden back at the Moosewood with Rosa. "A month or so."

"And you moved all your furniture there so you'd be more comfortable?"

"Well, actually…" Kate tore her eyes away. "There's another reason."

"I thought as much. We never finished our conversation last night. How about we sit out on the porch and do just that?"

"But, Hayden…"

"He's on the porch. We can keep an eye on him and talk at the same time."

"But I promised Campy I'd go shopping, and…"

"How about something to drink? I have orange juice, iced tea, beer…"

"Orange juice would be great, thanks."

Kate watched him disappear inside the cabin then turned to Hayden. He was throwing a rubber ball for Thor, who ignored it and barked happily. Three months ago she never would have dreamed she'd be in Alaska, falling for the man who'd tripped up her career and fathered her son. Not in a million years. But something was definitely happening between them. She could feel the attraction, the warmth and the genuine and powerful tug at her heartstrings when she watched Mitch interact with Hayden.

But what if these feelings weren't real? She'd only been around Mitch for a day. How could she possibly be so won over by him in such a short time span? Was she just clutching at straws because she was so afraid of what might happen to Hayden if anything should happen to her?

How would she know?

And how was she going to find the courage to tell him what she *did* know?

MITCH RUMMAGED through the cupboards for a clean glass and filled it with orange juice. Then he found another and filled that one, too, just in case Hayden wanted some. He found and filled a third, finishing off the container. He tossed the empty box in the woodstove and stood for a moment, wondering what had made Kate so sick that her hair had fallen out. What else could it be but cancer?

The big *C*.

If that's what she wanted to talk about, this was going to be a grim conversation.

"It's going to be hard, prying those two apart."

Kate's voice startled him. She was leaning through the door that led out onto the porch, hands in her jeans pockets and a faint smile on her face. He could hear Hayden talking to Thor right behind her. "Now, you fetch it, Thor," the boy was saying in a stern teacher-to-student way. "Ready? Fetch!"

"No way will he ever get that dog to retrieve anything," Mitch said.

She turned toward her son and then looked back at him, her smile widening. The dog hadn't fetched. "Anything I can do to help?"

"Yeah," Mitch replied. "You could tell me the real reason you came to Alaska."

The smile faded. She straightened in the doorway, hands coming out of her pockets and arms wrapping around herself in a protective way. He heard the sound of a ball bouncing and a sudden swift scrabble of paws.

"Good boy, Thor!" Hayden cried out. "Fetch!"

Kate shot a glance over her shoulder then faced him. She bit her lower lip for a moment with an apprehensive expression. *Here it comes,* Mitch thought. But her words took him by surprise.

"Hayden'll be four years old in July."

He nodded, confused. "Yeah…?"

She was looking at him now as if she expected something more, and then she repeated, with enough significance to make him uneasy, "Four years old."

He nodded again, no closer to being enlightened. Why was she looking at him that way? Damn, this wasn't going to be easy. In fact, getting anything out of her was like pulling teeth. He was going to have to help her out.

"Okay, so Hayden's almost four and you're sick. Sick enough to have lost all your hair so you have to wear a wig." He paused as she raised a hand to her hair with a startled expression. "I saw it lying on the coffee table this morning," he explained. "So you brought Hayden to Alaska to share a good vacation with him and to make some good memories. Am I right?"

If anything, her face became paler than it already was. She glanced out the door again, watching Hayden and Thor for a long moment before looking back at him. "Partly," she admitted. "I am pretty sick and I did want to share some quality time with him. But mostly, I brought him to Alaska because I wanted you to meet him. Mitch, Hayden's your son."

CHAPTER SIX

KATE SHOULD HAVE FELT relief as she spoke those words, having finally found the courage to tell Mitch the truth, but instead she felt nothing but dread. He stared at her for an endless moment, then turned away and paced across the room to look out the window for what seemed like a very long and silent time. She heard him mutter something beneath his breath as he ran his fingers through his hair, then he turned to her, a shocked expression on his face, as if he'd just been fatally shot. "I don't understand. How can he be mine? We used protection. I mean, how…?"

"I wasn't on the pill. I wasn't seeing anyone and hadn't for a long time, and I wasn't predicting any one-night stands with an air force officer. And sometimes condoms fail."

He shook his head, in a daze. "Why didn't you tell me?"

There it was, the million-dollar question. Why hadn't she told him?

"It was just one night." Kate made a helpless gesture with her hands, abandoning the attempt to explain.

He gazed out the window at Hayden. "Obviously, it was a helluva lot more than that."

"I'm sorry."

"Jesus, Mary and Joseph. For four years you kept that a secret? Four years?"

Kate could see Hayden picking up the ball, teasing Thor with it, laughing when the dog barked, then tossing it again so Thor could chase after it. "I'm sorry," she repeated. "I don't know what else to say to you. We barely knew each other. We weren't involved in any sort of relationship. It was just one night and I honestly didn't think what happened between us meant anything to you."

He stared at the floor for a long moment, then rounded on her, his body rigid with anger. "Where the hell do you get off, passing judgment on me that way? How could you have a clue how I felt when you snuck off the next morning without so much as a goodbye? How could you know what I was thinking when you didn't even bother to read the letter I sent? Four years," he repeated, "Tell me something. How do I get those years back? How does Hayden get them back? He thinks his father died in a plane crash. Isn't that what you told him? The same thing you told me?"

Kate turned away from his accusing gaze. He already knew the answer.

"How the hell do you intend to explain me to him now? Are you planning to tell him I've come back from the dead?"

"No. I'll tell him the truth. He's old enough to understand."

"Is that why you came to Alaska now? Because he's old enough to understand that I'm not dead and never was?" He went back to pacing. "What do you want from me, Kate? What am I supposed to do? Become an instant dad? Should I be grateful that you got sick, just so I could find out I *was* a dad? Would you ever have told me, otherwise?"

Kate couldn't answer, nor could she meet his eyes. His rage and his hurt were understandable. She had no words that would possibly explain.

She felt the pain building within her and she fled onto the porch, drawing a breath of cool air into lungs that betrayed her in a fit of coughing. She'd had the nagging cough ever since the second round of chemo, but for the past few days it had been better and so had her stomach…until now. Hayden was coming back up the steps with the dog as she descended.

"Mumma…?" he said, his expression frightened.

"Stay on the porch," she choked behind her hand, not looking back. Mitch would watch him. Now that Mitch knew he was Hayden's father, he would take care of Hayden, watch over him, provide for him, love him. She knew from his reaction that Mitch would never back away from that responsibility, no matter how much he blamed her for those lost years.

She found a quiet spot by the river and collapsed there, leaning back against the trunk of a spruce tree, overwhelmed with a sense of hopelessness. She'd been wrong, so very wrong, and there was no way to make it right, no way to erase the past. Mitch's anger with her was justified. She blinked the tears from her eyes and wrapped her arms more tightly about herself. She'd told Mitch, but it wasn't over yet.

She still had to tell Hayden.

For a long time, she watched the river rush past, her mind drifting to the sound that slowly soothed and gradually washed the turmoil from her mind. After a while, she heard footsteps. Adult footsteps, measured and deliberate.

Mitch halted beside her, then crouched on his heels and plucked a stem of wild grass. She pressed the palms of her hands to her eyes and glanced sidelong at him. He should be raging at her, venting his anger and frustration, but instead he was chewing on a piece of grass with a detached expression and staring at the river.

"Is Hayden okay?" she said.

"I told him to stay inside the cabin. He's pretty upset." Mitch spoke calmly and kept his eyes fixed on the river. "He's afraid you're going to have to go back to the hospital."

Kate studied his profile and felt the pain within suddenly ebb, as if released by the swift waters of Pike's Creek. She closed her eyes and drew a deep breath that didn't make her cough. "I will to have to go back to the hospital," she said, "but not for a while."

"Why don't you try talking to me, Kate?" He turned his head. "Tell me what's really going on with you."

Those eyes of his trapped her again, and she felt her pulse beating in her veins. "I have acute myelogenous leukemia. My last round of chemotherapy put me in temporary remission, but I need a bone marrow donor and I'm waiting to hear when and if they find a match. There's a good chance I can beat this if a donor is found. There's also a good chance I won't."

Mitch looked away again, still chewing on the piece of grass. "So you came here to tell me I had a son, in case you didn't make it."

Kate sensed the tears prickling behind her eyelids. "Hayden's been through so much," she whispered around the tight cramp in her throat. "He's such a great kid. He really is. I love him so much it hurts, and I know I was wrong not to tell you about him, but please, don't hold that against him. When I found out I was pregnant, I blamed you for what happened between us that night, but it wasn't your fault, and I didn't tell you about the pregnancy because…" She hesitated, groping for the words to explain. "Because I didn't know anything about you. Nothing. Don't you see? What happened that night was so out of character for me. I don't screw around, Mitchell. I'm not like that."

He tossed the blade of grass down and lasered her with those eyes. "I know you're not. That's what I wrote in that letter you never read. Goddammit, Kate. You should've read it."

"I'm sorry." Kate drew a shaky breath. "I don't know what else to say. I'd never felt like that before. You had me so confused. I knew if I stayed around you any longer, I might never want to leave, so then I left without saying goodbye because after what we shared I couldn't say it. And that's how it is. I don't blame you for being upset. I wouldn't blame you for hating me."

He was quiet for a few moments. "God knows hating you would make this a whole lot easier, but I can't pass judgment and what's done is done. You made your decision to go it alone, but it couldn't have been easy in a close-knit military community full of officers' wives."

Kate remembered all the prying visits of the well-meaning wives at her house on the base. They'd been polite, they were verbally supportive, but they all wanted to know who the father was. They didn't come right out and ask, but she knew she had to make up something to satisfy them. The secret romance with the air force pilot who crashed seemed like a good enough story, better than a one-night stand with a complete stranger in some redneck bar called the Mad Dog Saloon in the middle of an Alaskan blizzard. Her story had appeased their appetite for the tragic and eased their insecurities about their own marriages.

"Hayden made it easy," she said. "I never thought I wanted children, but when he was born, that all changed."

"That must have changed long before then. You could've ended the pregnancy and nobody would've known."

"That's not exactly true." Kate looked away. Damn those eyes of his. She could keep no secrets from him, nor did she particularly care to anymore. "I didn't realize I was pregnant until almost two months afterward. Two days after I got your letter, to be exact."

"Would you have read it, had you known?" Mitch asked.

Kate reflected for a few moments. "I don't know," she said with a shake of her head. "Maybe. Anyhow, we were on a routine blue water ops practicing night-carrier landings when I had a low altitude engine flameout and I had to eject out of the plane."

"Whoa," Mitch interrupted. "You bailed out of a plane when you were two months pregnant?" He noted her expression and nodded. "Sorry. Go ahead."

"The ship's surgeon checked me over pretty carefully after the rescue chopper fished me out of the drink. It's routine procedure. Aside from a little hypothermia from being in the water awhile, he was afraid I'd cracked a couple of ribs and wanted to take an X-ray. He asked me if there was any chance I was pregnant and I told him no, but then all of a sudden I thought about how lousy I'd been feeling lately and how little attention I'd paid to anything personal since the ship left port, and it hit me."

"So you said yes."

Kate nodded. "When I amended my answer, the doctor ordered some tests and when they came back positive, he canceled the X-ray. He sat me down in his office and sent me into a state of shock with that news."

"I can imagine he was pretty shocked, too. It had to be a first for him."

"He was sixty years old, a grandfather of four, and tickled pink at the idea. He fussed around me like a mother hen. When I could get a word out, I brought up the subject of possible injury to the fetus because routine cat shots off the flight deck are pretty extreme in their own right, and ejecting out of a fighter is kind of like blasting off to the moon then falling into the ocean without the benefit of a spaceship. But he just told me that a woman's body was the most perfectly created vessel for protecting and nurturing the little one I was carrying, and that he'd run some tests to be certain everything was okay. He did, and it was."

"And you never thought about having an abortion?"

Kate shut her eyes. It was the only way to avoid his. "How could I? Once the ship's surgeon and medical staff knew, no matter how closemouthed they were, sooner or later the news of my pregnancy would get out."

"So that's why Hayden's out there right now? Because you were afraid of what people might think of you if you had an abortion?"

Kate felt a shiver of pain. "Not exactly," she said, her voice barely above a whisper. "There was a part of myself I was beginning to hate. I loved the flying. God, how I loved the flying, but the weapons and the death were hard to deal with. When I found out I was pregnant, I couldn't kill that baby. I just couldn't. The only thing to do was carry on as best I could and pretend I was overjoyed."

"But you weren't."

She shook her head, opening her eyes and blinking hard. The river rushed past, and she focused on the dark waters. "I was anything but. My career had been right on track and I was finally being regarded as both a great naval aviator and a top-notch officer. A baby wasn't part of my plans. I didn't want to prove all the Navy naysayers right by getting pregnant. I didn't want to be grounded because men in the upper ranks didn't think it safe for a baby to fly at Mach 2. I didn't want to swell up like I'd swallowed a beach ball, and I didn't want to be changing diapers and getting up every two hours to breast feed a hungry baby."

"You breast fed?"

She gave him a level stare. "For the first two months, until I went back on full duty. I figured I might as well do it right if I was going to do it at all. I did it right, Mitch. I wasn't excited about him at first, I'll admit that. He messed up all my plans." She gave him a wry smile. "Correction. *You* messed up all my plans. But once Hayden was born, I fell in love with him at first sight and I did the best I could by him. That's why I'm here, telling you all this. I'm trying to do the best for him because he's turned out to be the greatest thing that ever happened to me."

Mitch pushed to his feet. He stood looking into the creek for a long moment before speaking again. "When do you have to go back into the hospital?"

"Right after Hayden's birthday. I'm scheduled for readmittance to the hospital in Seattle for the bone marrow transplant, assuming they find a donor. It's a little tougher in my case because there's Crow blood on my mother's side of the family, but the doctors are optimistic."

"How optimistic?"

Kate shrugged again. "Doctors don't like to dispense gloom and doom."

"How long will you be in there?"

"Assuming the transplant's a go, up to six months, and if it's successful, for the next two years I'll be tiptoeing around trying to avoid any and all germs, which is why I tried to resign my commission."

"You quit the Navy?"

"Admiral Gates wouldn't accept my resignation. He put me on indefinite medical leave."

Mitch plucked another stem of grass and shredded it methodically. "What if they don't find a donor?"

"I'll keep undergoing chemotherapy until either I die or the leukemia goes into permanent remission, which I'm told is rare but sometimes happens."

"Other family members aren't matches? Siblings?"

"I'm an only child, and it's rare that a family member can be a donor. Mine can't."

"So that's why Hayden's looking like he just lost his best friend."

Kate nodded. "He's been through my chemo twice already. It isn't much fun for him."

Mitch moved a few steps away from her while she struggled to compose herself. He'd never forgive her. Could she blame him? No. But nonetheless, she wished he would. She wished he'd say something to release her. Something to absolve her guilt.

She heard the splash of something hitting the water. Then another splash. And another. She glanced up. Mitch was flinging stones as if trying to skip them, though none were flat. He flung them hard, putting all his strength behind each effort, and when he ran out he picked up another handful and sent them after the first. Midway through this savage, nonstop delivery, one of them skipped three times across the river.

He glanced over his shoulder at her, his eyes fierce. "You try hard enough, you can make anything happen, Kate. Anything at all. You're a fighter. You'll get through this."

She nodded, too overcome to speak.

He let the rest of the stones fall at his feet as he turned to face her. His expression was as hard and flinty as the rocks he'd been throwing. "I won't lie to you. I'm mad as hell that you wrote me out of my son's life the way you did. I don't understand why you never gave me a chance to be a part of it and I never will, but everything's different now, so I guess what we have to do is figure out where to go from here."

Kate started to speak, but he raised his hand to silence her.

"I read that article about you in the air force magazine and I think I understand the kind of woman you are, and what you're about to say," he said. "You're going to tell me you're tough enough to take on anything. You're strong enough. You're going to tell me you like going it alone. Going it alone means you might one day make fleet commander or walk on the moon. Going it alone means flying out of Eielson without saying goodbye, throwing my letter off the flight deck unread and not telling me about Hayden. You're going to tell me you don't need my help, you don't need anybody's help, but you know what? I honest to God don't think you'd be here if you didn't.

"Wait!" He held up his hand again to thwart another attempt at interruption. "Let me finish. You came here to size me up in person before telling me about Hayden, and I'm guessing I passed the test or you wouldn't have told me. Am I right? Well…" He glared at her long and hard, then turned away, shoulders set. He drew several measured breaths while looking to where the mountain would be if it weren't hidden in the clouds, then cursed softly. "I don't know what to say."

"I understand," Kate said quietly. "If you could take us back to the airstrip, I'm sure Campy will drop us back at the Moosewood when we're done shopping. That'll give you some time to sort this all out."

He nodded, rubbed the back of his neck and looked toward the porch, where Hayden waited. "Maybe that's best." His eyes caught hers with that riveting electrical jolt. "Maybe that'll give you time to tell Hayden that his father miraculously survived the crash that you thought killed him. But I'll feed you lunch first. Out here in the bush you never send anyone away hungry, least of all your own son and his mother. It's against the law."

Kate shook her head. "That's okay, Mitch, I'm not really that…"

"You're both eating before you leave here," Mitch interrupted in a voice that brooked no argument, "and that's that."

MITCH THOUGHT he knew all about suffering, but sitting through that lunch, with Hayden and Kate both looking pale and drawn, he realized he didn't have a clue. He also didn't know how to conduct himself, for that matter. He was a father now, and being a father wasn't as easy as making soup. He couldn't just add water and stir himself into something warm and paternal. But that's why he'd forced her to stay. He'd been hoping some divine transformation would occur within him, and that suddenly the first and foremost thing he'd want to be in this whole wide world was a good father to this kid.

In retrospect, perhaps he should just be grateful he hadn't already suffered a nervous breakdown. He really didn't have a clue how to deal with any of this.

"Good soup, huh?" he said to Hayden. Most of the boy's soup was still in the bowl; his toasted peanut butter sandwich was untouched. "How about you eat your sandwich, pard. You're a growing boy and peanut butter's good stuff. Full of protein and…whatever else is in peanuts." He glanced at Kate, who was pushing noodles through the broth with her spoon—as uninterested in the meal as her son.

Their son.

"Okay," he said, leaning across the table with a surge of frustration. Kate was sick. She was too thin. She needed to eat. He wrested the spoon from her hand as she raised startled eyes. "Watch this, Hayden. This is how my mom used to feed me when I wouldn't eat. She'd scoop up the soup, like this, with the noodles dangling off the sides of the spoon, and then she'd pretend it was an airplane like this. Ready, Kate?"

She intercepted his hand with her own and reclaimed her spoon with a look that would've struck him dead, if looks could, but she downed the spoonful and ate another for good measure. "You're right," she said, forcing a tight smile in his direction. "This is delicious. Definitely the best soup I've ever had. Hayden, eat your soup."

"You heard your mother," Mitch said. "Eat your lunch." The intonation of his words disturbed him. He definitely didn't like sounding like his own dad. Fatherhood wasn't something he'd even remotely imagined, and now his almost four-year-old son was sitting here at his table, being scolded by a man he didn't even know was his father. This was, without a doubt, the toughest challenge he'd ever faced. Forget the combat pilot fly-and-fight, life-or-death stuff. All that paled in comparison to finding out that a woman he had definite feelings for was battling cancer…and her little boy just happened to be his son.

Minutes that felt like hours later, Mitch pushed back in his chair. "Good job, pard. And your mom did great, too." He gathered up the dishes and deposited them in the sink. "I'll take care of these later. Let's get you headed out on your shopping trip."

Coward.

That was the word that crossed his mind as he shepherded Kate and Hayden out to his truck. Thor tried to jump in the front seat with Hayden. "In the back!" Mitch snapped, and the black beast flattened its ears and reluctantly obeyed.

He couldn't help it. He couldn't wait to be rid of them. He couldn't deal with any of this. Not Kate's awful sickness nor the fact that Hayden was his son. He was a coward, and his first instinct was to run far, run fast and not look back.

WALLY WAS POLISHING his already gleaming Harley and Campy was sunning herself outside the shack when they arrived. She stood up and stubbed out the cigarette she was smoking. "Hey," she said as Kate and Hayden climbed out of the truck. "Thought maybe you'd changed your mind about our shopping trip."

"Of course not," Kate replied. She unfastened Hayden's car seat then walked around to the driver's side. "Thanks for lunch," she said to Mitch.

"Have a good time," he said politely, but there was no sincerity in it. Both his words and his eyes were cool. He was obviously distancing himself from her, from his son. She'd dreaded this moment, and now here it was, staring her in the face.

Retribution.

"We will." Her reply sounded as hollow as his.

"I'll call you," he said, but she knew he wouldn't. "See you, Hayden." Hayden looked at him but said nothing. Mitch sat for a few moments, staring back at Hayden, then sighed. "Look, I'm sorry we didn't get a chance to go fishing. Maybe later?" He glanced at Kate and she caught a glimpse of uncertainty that overrode the anger he clearly felt toward her. "Why don't you let me give Hayden a ride back to the Moosewood? It'll give you girls a chance to do your thing and we can talk more about fishing, and stuff like that. Guy stuff."

Kate hesitated. Mitch was trying to make a connection with Hayden. She had to give him credit for that. "Okay, if he wants."

Hayden didn't waste any time climbing back into the truck, which surprised her. She buckled him back into the car seat and kissed him goodbye. Mitch gave her a cool nod, put the truck in Reverse and had started to back up when Campy sauntered toward his window, tossing her hair out of her eyes. "The phone's been ringing off the hook, Mitch. You're going to be the busiest pilot in Alaska pretty quick here, so enjoy your afternoon off. Wally wants to know if you called the news station back about the interview."

"Not yet."

"You'd better. They're giving Wally holy old hell because they can't get in touch with you. They're hot to trot for this flying story, and it'll only help us out. Free advertising is the best advertising, especially when you don't have any advertising budget."

"I'll call them this afternoon," he promised before driving off.

Kate watched the battered old pickup truck bounce down the airstrip road, Thor riding in the back, and felt an ache of loneliness deep inside. The ride to the airstrip had been made in complete silence, and she'd felt the tension and hostility radiating from him. She just hoped none of it trickled down to Hayden. Tonight, somehow, she'd find the words to tell her son that his father hadn't died in a plane crash after all. Meanwhile, she'd look at that fancy plane and if it was halfway decent, she'd buy it to make sure Mitch wouldn't suffer that fate. Whatever the cost, it was a small price to pay to ensure Hayden's security in the event she didn't survive her illness.

"You sure you're up for this, hon? You look tuckered out," Campy said, coming up beside her.

"It's been a rough morning." Kate glanced at the other woman. "I told Mitch about Hayden. I'd hoped he'd figure it out himself, but he didn't."

"He's a man." Campy shrugged. "Sometimes you gotta hit 'em over the head with a baseball bat to get 'em to clue in. So, how'd he take it?"

"Not all that well, but I can't blame him for that."

Campy led Kate to the old Subaru. "So. You sure you want to buy this plane?"

"It's a good plane, right?"

Campy shrugged again. "I guess so. I'm no expert, but if Wally looked it over and says it is, and Mitch flew it and says it is, then I guess it is."

"It has to be better than the Stationair."

"How do you want to play this scene? Raider's a shark. He gets the scent of blood, he closes in for the kill. But since we know Raider needs the money to settle things in this divorce he's going through, I'm thinking he'll take less than what he's asking if we catch him at the right moment…and if you play your cards right."

"Meaning?"

"Raider likes pretty women, and hon, you're not only gorgeous, you're also a top gun pilot. He'll think he's died and gone to heaven the minute he sets eyes on you. If you promised to go out with him, he might even give you the plane."

Kate uttered an abrupt laugh. "I'll pay full freight and be glad to do so. It'll be a whole lot cheaper in the long run, not to mention easier."

MITCH STOPPED BY the general store on his way back to the Moosewood. It wasn't exactly on the way back. In fact, it was six miles out of his way, but he needed a few essentials. "Okay, pard," he said, parking in front of Yudy's, which looked as if it still catered to patrons driving buckboards hauled by swaybacked horses. "C'mon inside with me and meet Yudy."

"I don't feel so good," Hayden said in a subdued voice.

"This won't take long, then we'll get you home. I need a bag of dog food. Can't let Thor go hungry, can we?" He unbuckled Hayden's seat belt as he talked and helped him out of the truck. Hayden grudgingly tagged along. Inside the store, Yudy and a handful of locals were seated around the barrel stove shooting the breeze. They seemed to do nothing else but hang out there most of the day, chewing over every bit of news long after it was news. The men eyeballed Hayden with considerable interest.

"Wal, howdy, son. You must be Hayden," Yudy said, pushing out of his chair. "I bet you'd like some penny candy."

"I don't feel good," Hayden repeated.

"No?" Yudy frowned. "Well, now, that's too bad. I got just the thing for a kid that doesn't feel too good. How 'bout I fix you a little soda water and bitters?"

"I dunno about that treatment, Yudy," Mitch said. "My mom used to give me ginger ale and dry salty crackers."

"Naw. Soda water and bitters'll do the trick. I'll get it. You set here, son, right here by the stove where it's nice and warm, but don't let these old fools talk your ear off. They will, you know," he said as he departed for the rear of the store in his leisurely shuffle.

The old-timers studied Hayden somberly as the boy took Yudy's chair. "So," one of them said. "You like Alaska?"

Hayden nodded.

"You like to fish?" another asked.

Hayden nodded.

"You like Mitch?" a third asked.

Hayden paused and looked up at Mitch. "I like Thor," he said.

They all guffawed and slapped their knees. One of them got up and stuffed another stick of wood into the stove even though the store had to be ninety degrees and rising. "Well, that's a start, huh, Mitch?"

Seeing Hayden was fine on his own, Mitch left him to his own devices and found Yudy at the back of the store, rummaging through some boxes of dry goods. "I know I got some bitters in here," he muttered as Mitch approached. "This is my odds-and-ends box. I keep meaning to put this stuff out on the shelf, but…" He paused, then lifted a small bottle. "Bitters!"

"Yudy, you know that steak you sold me yesterday?"

"It was good, wasn't it? Damn, didn't I tell you? Feed 'em right and you can go anywhere and get anything."

"Thor ate it and I need to buy another one."

Yudy's pleased expression vanished. "No! That damned useless dog."

"I had to leave just as supper was ready. There was this bunch of mountain climbers that had to be flown off the mountain, and…"

"Jeez, yeah, I saw that on the news! The wife watches that interview this morning and says to me, 'Yudy, did you see that? That was our Mitch,' like she was personally responsible for creating you and teaching you good from evil. Too bad about that steak! I'll fix you up with another good cut of meat. First, though, I'm gonna fix the kid a bitters and tonic to settle his stomach."

Yudy proceeded to mix up a vile-looking fizzy concoction in a stained coffee mug and carried it back to the barrel stove while Mitch followed and watched, frowning. Hayden took the proffered cure and drank about half of it obediently. "Good boy. You'll feel better soon," Yudy said. "C'mon, Mitch. Let's round you up some gourmet ingredients so you can do the Emeril thing tonight and wow the pretty lady's socks off."

CHAPTER SEVEN

THE PORTER WAS A bold and beautiful plane and Kate understood instantly why Mitch wanted it. It was the kind of aircraft a bush pilot could rely on come hell or high water and enjoy flying at the same time, the ultimate performance plane for a rugged wilderness like Alaska. Raider, on the other hand, was forty-nine going on seventeen, smiled way too much and talked even more, but in spite of his raging hormones, Kate could find no fault whatsoever with the plane, especially after the rigorous test flight. The maintenance records were faultless, the flight hours dutifully logged and the asking price more than fair.

"I'll give you five for it," she said, stone-faced.

"Five?" Raider tipped his head back and uttered an incredulous laugh. "Get real. It's worth every cent I'm asking, and then some. This was Fairchild's demonstrator model for years. Its got all the add-ons, has low time and has been well taken care of. Even Mitch said the price was fair."

"Mitch might have said that, but he doesn't have the money," Campy interjected. "Yance won't lend it to him and Wally won't back him. He thinks you're asking too much."

"Well, no way in hell am I giving that plane away for five hundred grand." He puffed his chest out and crossed his arms.

"That's your prerogative," Kate said. "I have a few more

planes to look at. The Porter's nice, but it's overpriced and I didn't like that rotational vibration in the engine. Thanks, anyway." She was halfway to the car before Raider rose to the bait.

"Rotational vibration? That plane is mint!"

"Where'd you say our next stop was, Campy?" Kate said.

Campy never batted an eyelash. "Lake Hood. That's down in Anchorage. There's a real beauty of a one-eight-five with all the trimmings that's a whole lot cheaper than Raider's Concorde jet."

"Now hold on a minute, ladies. Let me think about this before you do something you might regret." Raider tugged on the earlobe with the diamond stud, eyed Kate lustfully up and down for the tenth time and said, "Ah, what the hell. Either I sell it to you right now and save Mitch's sorry ass from crashing in that Stationair, or my soon-to-be ex-wife gets her claws into it and takes me all the way to the cleaners. I'll take five for her, but I want a certified bank check or money order or cash. I don't take personal checks or credit cards."

"Is there a bank handy?"

"Alaska Federal Credit Union in Talkeetna," Campy said. "We can be there and back in less than an hour."

"I'll have the bill of sale ready and waiting. You'll need to get the insurance transferred from the Stationair before anyone flies it, and by the time you get back here with the money and we get the papers signed, the insurance office'll be closed."

"That doesn't work for me," Kate said. "Mitch has three flights tomorrow."

"If they're after 9:00 a.m., he'll be all set. You can call first thing in the morning and get the coverage he needs. Otherwise he'll have to take the Stationair. What the hell. He's been lucky so far," Raider shrugged. "Nobody else could've kept that damn thing in the air so long. Hey, did you see him on TV this morning?"

"He was good, wasn't he?" Campy said.

"He was great, but don't tell the arrogant bastard I said that."

"Oh, don't worry, Raider, we won't," Campy said, tossing her hair out of her eyes. "Come on, Kate. Let's go rob that bank before it closes."

Campy hadn't driven a hundred yards down the road before she let out an earsplitting rebel whoop. "Hon, you just got the bargain of the century!" she burst out, ebullient. "Five hundred grand for that plane? Wally'll be floored. In his wildest dreams he never envisioned having a plane as fancy as that. Is that rotational vibration serious?"

"It's not Wally's plane," Kate reminded her. "And there was no vibration. I made that up. I'd like an official name painted on it. The new name of the flying service."

Campy cast her a puzzled look. "New name?"

"I'd like Arctic Air painted on it in big blue letters."

"Arctic Air," Campy echoed. She thought about it for a while, then nodded with a perplexed smile. "I like it, hon, but Wally sure as hell won't."

HAYDEN THREW UP not a mile from the Moosewood. He didn't say much before doing it. Never gave Mitch a chance to pull over and get him out. He just leaned forward and upchucked onto the floor at his feet, and since Mitch had a weak stomach for stuff like that, it was a wonder he didn't immediately follow suit. Instead, he stuck his head out the driver's side window to avoid breathing the curdled air and said, keeping his eyes averted, "You okay?"

The boy wiped his mouth on his shirtsleeve and nodded. "You sure?"

Hayden nodded again.

"Okay then, we're almost there. Hang tight."

Five minutes later, he braked to a stop beside Kate's rental and jumped out of the truck, taking great lungfuls of fresh air. What if Rosa wasn't there? What if he had to take care of a sick kid? He couldn't do it. No way. He wasn't even sure how he'd clean up the truck. Hayden dropped to the ground on the passenger's side and plodded toward the cabin. As they rounded the corner, Mitch was relieved to see Rosa sitting on the porch, reading. She stood at their approach, her broad maternal face radiating concern.

"Ay, what is wrong with you, little one!" she said, closing the distance between her and Hayden more rapidly than Mitch would have thought possible for such a large woman. She felt the boy's forehead. "You have a fever. You must get to bed at once," she said to him. Then she raised her dark eyes to Mitch and they transformed instantly from pity to suspicion. "Where is the *señora?*"

"Kate went shopping with a friend of mine to pick up some warm clothes for our camping trip," Mitch explained. "Hayden threw up on the way back here."

"I'm okay," Hayden said.

"You are sick. Go and get into bed," Rosa said in a stern but compassionate voice. When Hayden didn't comply, her brow furrowed in an indignant scowl. "Did you not hear me?"

But Hayden was looking at Mitch with those disturbingly somber eyes. "When are we going camping?"

"Just as soon as I can get some time off from work," Mitch said.

"Promise?"

"I'll start packing our gear this afternoon."

"Young man, you go to bed, right now," Rosa said.

But at that moment Mitch heard something else and so did Hayden; out of the blue Thor leapt onto the porch. "Thor!" Hayden said, wrapping his arms around the big black dog. "Can he stay?"

"Nope," Mitch said. "But he can go camping with us once you're better, so you better listen to Rosa and get to bed." There it was again; his own father's stern voice coming back to haunt him. And what the hell was he doing, promising a camping trip to this kid? That was the last thing he wanted to do.

Mitch dragged the reluctant Thor back to the truck, drove down the old dirt road that led to the abandoned mining town until he came to a small creek, where he pulled over and spent ten minutes alternately cleaning Hayden's mess out of the cab of the truck and gagging with dry heaves. Task accomplished, he washed his face and hands in the creek, squatted on his heels for a few moments at the water's edge debating his next move, then decided to talk to Raider one more time about the plane. Wally wasn't going to do anything. It was up to him to get the ball rolling. If they were going to buy the Porter, he'd have to first get Raider to accept his offer, then convince Yance to lend them the money. Most might do it in the opposite order, go the pre-approval route, but why bother haggling with Yance over the loan if Raider wasn't going to sell at a price they could afford? One way or the other, it was more important than ever for them to get that plane, get serious and start making some real money. He might very well have a son to support.

What the hell. He did have a son to support! If Kate lived

to be ninety-nine and counting, Hayden was still going to be his son, too. And there was college, and dentists, and doctors, and sports and stuff, and clothes….

His stomach was still roiling as he climbed back into the cab, but it wasn't just because of cleaning up Hayden's mess. He was a father now, and that changed everything in a big way. Huge. Was he up to the challenge? Could he handle all that responsibility? He wasn't sure. Did he have any choice in the matter? No. The first stages of panic began to take hold. The cold sweat had passed but his heart was still pounding when he arrived at Raider's place. The big white-and-black plane was parked on the tarmac, waiting for him. Damn, that plane was hot.

He fed some coins into the soda machine outside the hut then downed the entire can of iced tea to chase the dryness from his mouth so he could talk. He had to be clever about this. Whittle the price down somehow. They couldn't afford six hundred grand. Five hundred? That was a stretch, but it was a little easier to swallow. And the Porter was easily worth that and more.

Raider was inside, schmoozing some potential clients and signing them up for a sightseeing tour of Denali as soon as the wind died. He caught Mitch's eye and excused himself from the two older women.

"If you're here about the plane, you're twenty minutes too late. I just sold it."

Mitch felt his heart skip a few important beats and his knees went a little weak. "What?"

"Sorry, Mitch. I know you wanted it, but you were a tad too late. Hey, that was a pretty good interview you gave them Anchorage reporters, by the way. Must've boosted your business, huh? Hey, where're you goin'…?"

Back in his truck Mitch started the engine, spun his tires

and headed for Brock's Bar and Grill because he suddenly felt the need for something a little stronger than iced tea.

KATE AND CAMPY had made it to the bank in time, and by five-thirty they were back at Raider's place, where Kate signed all the proper papers, handed over the bank check and became the owner of a Pilatus/Fairchild Porter, registration number N352F.

An hour later, they were back in Pike's Creek at Wally's airstrip, making out all the lease papers. Wally was excited about the plane but less so about the lease agreement. He was also quite put out at the idea of painting a different name on the fuselage, but Kate held firm.

"It's my plane. I could have purple flowers painted all over it if I wanted," she told him. "No offense intended, but Arctic Air is a better name than Wally's Air Charter. The phone book listings are alphabetical. You'll get more business."

Wally also didn't like the terms of the lease, which specified Kate would get a percentage of the profits as her lease payment.

"Five percent is peanuts," Campy pointed out. "Out of the goodness of her heart she's basically giving you and Mitch the use of that plane 'cause she knows you can't afford anything more than that right now. Quit your grumbling and sign the papers before she changes her mind. She could very well be saving your lives, getting you out of that Stationair. I'm taking Kate out for a bottle of champagne to celebrate."

Scowling and red-faced, Wally reluctantly bent over his desk and signed. Campy patted his shoulder consolingly. "Thank you, sweetie. I'll be home when I get there. Keep the light on for me." She kissed his cheek and five minutes later she and Kate were back on the road, heading for a bar called Brock's. "I work there," Campy explained. "It's a real redneck kind of place, serves up beer and burgers, has a couple of pool tables and lots of fights."

"Sounds great," Kate said, glad that Hayden was back at the Moosewood.

"Truckers love it. On Saturdays we have a live band. That's when most of the fights are. It should be kinda quiet, now, being as it's midweek." Kate tried to hide her relief. "You know, Wally never would've bought that plane, no way could he afford it, and honey, you don't know how many sleepless nights I've passed, worrying about him if he was out flying. Oh, I worried about Mitch, too, but Mitch, he's a phenomenal pilot. Wally…?" She shook her head. "He never flies clients, just gear. That's the arrangement they have. But lately, Mitch wouldn't even let him do that. Said the plane had developed too many quirks."

She slowed as they approached a long, low log building off to the right with a big sign out front that pronounced it to be Brock's Bar and Grill, with lots of vehicles in the parking area. Campy pulled in and parked. "C'mon, hon, I'm buying, seeing as you just spent half a mil." She had a cigarette lit before her feet touched the ground and it was half smoked by the time they entered the building and managed to find an unoccupied table in the bustling establishment. "You set yourself down and I'll be right back," she said and sauntered off toward the bar.

Kate didn't think there could be that many people in the entire town. The interior of the bar was dimly lit and smoky. Most of the patrons were men but there were a few women. A jukebox belted out tunes and the noise level was high since people had to raise their voices to be heard over it. At the pool table, two guys played while half a dozen others coached. The smoke made the air quality terrible and knowing she shouldn't be exposing herself to it, Kate hoped this champagne celebration of Campy's didn't take too long.

Campy returned to the table triumphantly, bearing a galvanized metal pail full of ice that contained a bottle of cheap champagne and several bottles of beer. In her other hand she had a basket of mixed nuts and two tall beer glasses. She plunked all of it down in the middle of the table and pushed the hair out of her eyes. "Brock says it's on the house. Half his business comes from Mitch and he's glad the Stationair became history before Mitch did."

"Mitch must drink an awful lot," Kate commented uneasily as Campy popped the cork.

"Nope. He's the best damned pool player in the state. Folks come from Anchorage and Fairbanks and Dutch Harbor to play against him. Once, a whole slew of 'em flew in from Seattle. The women come in by the score just to watch him play. He's one sexy guy, in case you haven't noticed. He brings a lot of business to this little backwater bar." She poured the champagne into the beer glasses and stuffed the bottle back into the bucket of ice. "Brock didn't have any champagne flutes, so these'll have to do."

Kate picked up her glass. "To a successful charter enterprise for Arctic Air," she said.

"Amen," Campy replied as they touched rims. "I'm glad you pulled it off. Must be nice having such a financially smart dad. Mine's a dairy farmer. He's smart, too, but in a different way. He told me when I moved way out here that I'd miss the farm. I laughed at him then, but now, you know, I really do miss that place. I miss the horses the most. We had two draft horses. Daddy worked 'em in the fields and he hauled logs with them in winter. Ben and Buddy. They were great."

"Why don't you get one? They have horses in Alaska."

"I'd love to have a horse here, but Wally says the winters'd kill 'em if a hungry bear didn't get 'em first, and besides, Wally doesn't trust anything that doesn't leak oil. But my lifelong dream has been to train ponies for the circus. I just think that would be the neatest thing."

"I like horses, too," Kate said, trying to envision Campy training circus ponies and deciding she'd probably be pretty good at it. She was a straight shooter, and animals liked honesty. "I grew up with them in Montana." Just as she was about to take a sip of her champagne, she saw Mitch walk through the door and head for the bar. She froze, and Campy followed her gaze.

"Hey, talk about good timing," she said, starting to rise out of her chair. "I'll go invite him to join us."

Kate's hand shot out and closed on Campy's forearm. "Not such a good idea. He's still pretty upset that I didn't tell him about Hayden. I think he'd rather avoid my company right now."

"Too late. He's heading this way. Brock must've told him we're here." Campy sat back down and Kate tried to read Mitch's expression as he approached the table but she couldn't. He grabbed a chair, spun it around and dropped into it, leaning his forearms over the backrest.

"Evening, ladies. I see you're celebrating."

"We had a very successful shopping spree," Kate said. "Would you care for some champagne?"

"No, thanks. I'm not exactly in a partying mood." He said this looking directly at Kate, who dropped her eyes and studied the golden bubbles in her glass. "Hayden got sick on the ride back to the Moosewood," he added, and her eyes shot back to his face. "I guess that lunch didn't agree with him. He's okay. Rosa put him to bed. So what did you buy that warrants a bottle of Brock's bubbly?"

"A plane," Kate said.

"A plane," he echoed in a flat voice.

"The Porter," Campy said. "The plane of your dreams. C'mon Mitch, join us for the celebration."

"You're telling me you bought Raider's plane." He was speaking far too carefully, and Kate felt herself tightening up.

"Yes."

"The Navy planes aren't hot enough for you, K.C.?"

"I didn't want you flying the Stationair anymore, and you couldn't afford to buy it right now."

"So you went out and bought a six-hundred-thousand-dollar plane for me."

"She got it for five," Campy interjected. "Kate's pretty good at wheeling and dealing."

"I just bet she is."

He pushed to his feet, spun the chair back to its original position and walked to the bar without another word. Within moments he was fraternizing with a good-looking woman and pulling on a beer. Kate released a pent-up breath and took a big swallow of champagne. The fizz burned her nose and made her eyes water. Champagne was terrible stuff. Why was she drinking it? Besides, she felt more like crying than partying.

"Wow, I sure didn't expect that reaction," Campy said. "Don't worry, hon. I'll be right back." She pushed out of her chair, walked up to the bar and wriggled in right between Mitch and the other woman, where no doubt she'd do her best to smooth things over and make the world right again. Kate groaned and took another swallow of champagne. She was beyond ready for this day to end. While she waited for Campy to return, a man broke away from the huddle around the pool table and approached her table, beer bottle in hand.

"Hey, beautiful," he said. "Mind if I join you?"

"I'm with someone."

"Yeah, I know. I saw you come in with Campy." He dropped into the seat Mitch had vacated. "You're new around here, aren't you? I'm Bud Wilson and I'm the man you need if you're looking for a good time."

"I'm not."

"Of course you are. Every woman is." He leaned toward her, gave her a long, knowing leer and the tone of his voice became way too intimate. "My guess is your flavor is strawberry."

For a moment Kate was too shocked to respond. Had he just made a crude sexual remark to her? Anger flooded through her and without further thought, she picked up her glass and flung the rest of her champagne into Bud Wilson's face. "Wrong," she snapped, pushing out of her chair, snatching up her purse and making for the door.

She heard Bud call her a very bad name as he jumped out of his own chair, but she didn't look back until a commotion stopped her. Through the milling crowd she could see that Mitch had Bud pinned up against the wall. Campy was two steps behind, apparently trying to thwart a beating. Kate watched for a moment more, long enough to see Campy grab Mitch's arm, Mitch reluctantly let go of Bud, and Bud breathe a sigh of relief.

She turned and pushed her way through the onlookers toward the door, feeling sick at heart and wanting nothing more than to go home. But where was home? Montana? California? An aircraft carrier cruising the Gulf? The truth was she didn't have a home anymore, and might never need another one. She started walking swiftly down the road, needing to move, needing to get away, to be anywhere but here. When she heard Campy call her name, she waited for her to catch up.

"Hey, hon, I'm real sorry about that," she said, breathless, as she came to a stop beside Kate. "Bud's a jerk. He runs the seasonal ice-cream shop here in town and thinks he can guess everyone's favorite flavor by looking at 'em. He says he's sorry you misunderstood. Mitch heard what he called you and was ready to kill him. Maybe I should've let him." She reached out and touched Kate's arm in apology. "Listen, hon, Mitch is sore because he thinks you should've told him you were planning to buy the plane."

"Why? We're not married. Not even dating. I don't have to report my activities to him, or ask him how to spend my own money."

"He was just taken by surprise, that's all. That's why he's so grumpy." She glanced over Kate's shoulder. "Here he comes. Doesn't look like his mood's improved any."

Mitch came to a stop beside them and Kate could feel the tension crackling in the air.

"You okay?" he asked her in a cool, detached way.

"Fine," Kate replied in the same tone of voice. "You shouldn't have attacked that man. I can take care of myself."

"I'm taking you back to the Moosewood," he said. "Thanks for everything, Campy."

Campy took his curt dismissal with an easy nod and sauntered back toward her car. Kate felt a flush of anger.

"That was rude and presumptuous. What if I don't want to go back just yet?"

He gave her a flinty stare. "I suppose you could hang out here for a while. Drink some beer. Shoot some pool. Flirt with Bud Wilson, if that's what you'd rather do."

She turned away abruptly and walked back toward his truck, climbed into the passenger's seat and slammed the door as hard as she could, hoping it would fall off in a shower of rust. She felt instantly better and thought about doing it again for good measure, but he was already climbing into the cab. They drove the short distance to the Moosewood in silence. As he cut the engine, hot metal ticked and antifreeze gurgled through the ancient hoses. A cool gust of wind blew through the open windows. Kate reached for the door handle but kept her eyes carefully averted.

"Thanks for the lift, I think."

"You shouldn't have bought that plane. I could've managed it myself."

She slammed the truck door again and didn't look back as she headed around the corner of the cabin. It wasn't until she reached the porch that she realized she'd forgotten to ask him when his first flight was in the morning, but by the time she ran back around the corner, he was gone.

CHAPTER EIGHT

MITCH COULDN'T EAT AND he couldn't sleep. All night long he lay in the cabin loft, listening to the wind blow in big gusts across the mountain valley and thinking about Hayden and Kate and that damn Raider selling the plane to her instead of him. Thinking about that lousy, foul-mouthed creep Bud Wilson and what he'd called Kate. He should've flattened the bastard. Would've, if Campy hadn't grabbed his arm. Thinking about how Kate had glared at him and slammed the door of the truck when she left him at the Moosewood. Thinking about the big silence that was building between them, the little boy that was their son and the gourmet dinner he hadn't prepared for a seduction that would never happen.

He laced his hands behind his head and thought about the camping trip Hayden wanted to take. Hayden. Where did she come up with a name like that? She'd said it was an old family name. He thought and tossed and turned and got up at 3:00 a.m. to make a pot of coffee and drank it black, sitting on the porch in the cool duskiness of the hour, watching the sky in the east turn the snowfields the color of melted butter and wondering if she'd told Hayden yet that he was his father.

By the time he got to the airstrip the sun was well up and so was Wally, already tinkering on the Stationair. The first batch of clients hadn't arrived yet. Mitch tossed his pack into the rear compartment and drank a second cup of coffee inside the warming shack, exchanging surly grunts with his equally surly boss. He looked over the log book. There were two flights listed. One departing at 9:00 a.m. with three climbers to be flown to base camp, and another with a group of four at 2:00 p.m., ditto. Too bad they weren't busy enough to be flying one load in and another out in the same trip. It would save a ton of gas and generate twice the money.

"Raider sold the Porter yesterday," Mitch told Wally when his boss came inside. "That should make you happy."

"It should make you happy, too." Wally poured himself a cup. "Think of the half-million bucks we don't have that we just saved."

"Kate bought it."

"I know. She stopped here afterward. She's leasing it back to the charter for five percent of the profit."

"That's charity," Mitch said curtly. "I won't accept charity, especially from her. We'll find another plane, and in the meantime we'll make do with the Stationair."

Wally raised bushy eyebrows in question, but decided to leave this one alone.

Thirty minutes later the clients arrived. There were two more passengers than were logged in the book. "Got another call yesterday," Wally explained as Mitch looked out the warming shack's window and did verbal head count. "Those reporters from the Seattle TV station that wanted to interview you are riding along on this trip."

"No way," Mitch said. "You really want them to see that plane in action?"

"*Babe*'s good to go. I got here at 4:00 a.m. to make sure

of it. You dump the climbers off at base camp and they can interview you on the way back."

"How? There's only one headset and I don't know sign language."

"Then talk to 'em when you get back. They wanted to get a feel for what you do and they're paying full freight. Quit arguing and go weigh their gear. You don't want to be overloaded on this flight. It wouldn't look too good on the evening news if you didn't even make it off the ground."

KATE'S MORNING JOG was more of a long walk, which was all she felt up to after a troubled night plagued with nightmares. She'd fully intended to talk to Hayden about Mitch the evening before, but he was cranky and feverish and in the end she let him spend one more night as a fatherless child. She'd tell him this morning, after her shower.

Better yet, after breakfast.

Or maybe she should wait until after calling the insurance company about getting commercial coverage on the new plane....

Sooner or later she'd have to tell him. She'd put it off for a little while longer and deal with it after calling the insurance company. She'd sit Hayden down out on the porch and tell him the truth, and handle whatever consequences came of it. And then, finally, it would be done. Hayden would have some time to get to know his father, and then he could spend the next few months getting to know his grandparents in Montana.

That plan firmly in place, she finished her walk, took her shower, ate breakfast with Rosa and Hayden, who was completely recovered from his upset stomach of the day before, then called the insurance company at exactly 9:00 a.m. That's when she hit the first big glitch.

"Commercial coverage?" the woman's voice said. "We'll need a copy of the most recent FAA inspection reports on the plane. Who's insuring the plane now? I can't seem to find that registration number in our files."

"I'm not sure but I can find out from the previous owner. What's your fax number?" Kate jotted it down, hoping the Moosewood had a fax machine. She then called Raider. The phone rang and rang until his answering machine picked up. Kate left a brief message after the beep but was fuming with impatience when she hung up. Then she dialed Wally's Air Charter, and Wally himself answered.

"Do you know who Raider insured the Porter with?" she asked.

"Nope. I assumed he used the same carrier we did."

"He doesn't, he's not answering his phone, and without all the background info on the plane this could take some time. I wanted to get the insurance taken care of as soon as possible so Mitch wouldn't have to fly the Stationair today. What time is his first flight?"

"You're too late. He just left with a batch of climbers for base camp, but maybe you can get the plane insured in time for his afternoon trip."

"I'll do my best, but there are a lot of insurance agencies in Anchorage." Kate hung up, doubly frustrated, and pulled the phone book toward her. This might take a while, but it gave her yet another good excuse to put off her talk with Hayden.

Twenty minutes and four phone calls later, after finding Raider's carrier and getting the plane's insurance straightened out, she decided she'd better ferry the newly insured purchase to Wally's airstrip before Mitch got back, and then the deed would be done.

Then she'd talk to Hayden.

Kate gave Rosa the directions to Wally's Air Charter when they arrived at Raider's airstrip. Raider had just returned from flying some clients to Fairbanks in his Cessna 185 and Hayden was excited about the prospect of going aloft. "Can I go with you, Mumma?" he begged when everything was all set to go.

"Not this time. You and Rosa are going to meet me at Wally's airstrip. But maybe later we can take it for a spin. Okay?"

Hayden's face fell but he nodded and let Kate buckle him back into his car seat. She watched until Rosa had driven the sedan out of sight at her usual sedate pace, then climbed aboard the Porter, did a quick preflight check and five minutes later was airborne.

It didn't take long to cover the distance between the two airstrips in this speedy bird, and she touched down and taxied the plane right up to the warming hut where the Stationair had been parked. Wally was all over the plane before she could even disembark. His prior disapproval over the lease agreement and new charter name was replaced by sheer admiration for the aircraft.

"Beautiful!" he proclaimed around his unlit cigar when his inspection was done. He gave Kate a grudging nod. "You done damned good, getting it for that price."

"Thanks. She's a nice plane. Mitch seems to think I shouldn't have bought it, but I'm hoping he comes to terms with the arrangement."

"First time he flies her, he'll come to terms." Wally chewed on his cigar with a perplexed expression, then his face cracked into a broad smile. "I think I'll name her Lulu," he said. "She looks like a Lulu."

"Over my dead body," Kate said, relieved to see a trail of dust approaching up the airfield road. "Here comes my ride. Take good care of her, Wally."

"Don't you wanna wait and see Mitch's reaction?"

"Nope," Kate replied as Rosa gently brought the sedan to a stop beside her, and climbed out of the driver's seat. "Just find another home for that Stationair—the sooner the better."

"That might be a little difficult."

Kate slid into the driver's seat and said, "Try the Smithsonian. They have an interesting air-and-space museum."

THE TRIP OUT to base camp with the three climbers and two reporters was uneventful. Boring, even. But then, that pretty much defined most routine flights. Boring, just as driving a farm tractor was, unless you were burning trail in an F-16. But the thing about flying in Alaska was that the scenery was pretty goddamn magnificent. Mitch never tired of it. He could drone around aloft all day and never tire of studying the craggy mountain ranges and the broad river valleys or scouting for wildlife on the taiga. And those early morning or twilight flights were pure magic, the way the sun reflected symphonies of light against the glaciers and snowfields. There were times when he felt like bursting into song, except he couldn't find the words or the music to define such staggering beauty.

And besides that, the clients would think him strange.

Would Kate?

He didn't think so. Somehow, even though he didn't know her all that well, he sensed that she shared the same sensitivity toward the natural world. The same connection. She'd been raised in Montana. Maybe that was it, or maybe it was just wishful thinking on his part. But a part of him hoped. And what about Hayden? He wanted to go camping. Wanted to see grizzly bears and hear wolves howl. He was almost four years old and his life was just beginning. Handsome kid. Stoic, except when it came to his mom being sick...and maybe dying.

"McCray!"

A blustery shout interrupted his thoughts and he watched as one of the reporters who'd helped the climbers unload their gear inched toward the side door of the plane, crabbing along like the hunchback of Notre Dame and wearing a pair of thick rubber boots that made every step sound as if he were tramping on indignant ducks. "Is it always this windy here?"

"Pretty much," Mitch replied, handing out the last of the duffel bags. "Big mountain range, big wind."

"Will it be as rough taking off as it was landing?"

"We'll be lighter so it'll be a lot bumpier."

"And you do this every day?"

"If we're lucky enough to get the business."

"What will happen to them?" he asked with a jerk of his head to indicate the group of climbers.

"They'll try for the summit. Some make it, some don't. When they're done doing what they came to do, they'll call us and we'll come pick 'em up. That's the last of their gear. You about ready?" Mitch was anxious to conclude this trip. He didn't much care for all the questions, most of which seemed sophomoric to him, and he didn't like the look of the clouds that were building up around the peaks.

Airborne again after the predictably bumpy takeoff, he

headed the Stationair south-southeast and began the turbulent traverse of the Alaska Range.

KATE HAD PROCRASTINATED telling Hayden about Mitch for as long as she could. After lunch, she took her son into town to pick up a few groceries, and on the way back to the Moosewood, she took a deep breath and dove in.

"Hayden, we need to talk about something important. It has to do with your father." She glanced at him in the rearview mirror to gauge his response, but he was gazing out the side window at the craggy mountains, hoping to spot an eagle or a mountain goat or a grizzly. "I told you he died in a plane crash, but that wasn't true."

Hayden redirected his attention and sat up straighter in his seat.

Kate tightened her grip on the wheel. "The truth is, your father's not dead. I never told you about him because I wasn't sure I'd ever see him again, but I was wrong."

Long silence. She looked at him and caught him studying her with a confused expression. "He's alive?"

Kate nodded. "Yes, and I believe he's a good man, so yesterday I told him about you, and now I'm telling you about him, and I hope both of you can get to know each other." She hesitated, drew a sharp breath and spoke aloud the words she'd practiced. "Hayden, Mitch is your dad."

She felt Hayden's eyes on her for a moment longer before he stared out the window again. In a serious voice he asked, "Does he like me?"

"He likes you very much."

"Do you like him?"

"Yes, I do."

Hayden turned to look at her. "Does he like you?"

"I don't know. Right now he's pretty mad at me for not telling him about you before."

"Is he going to stay mad?"

"I don't know," Kate repeated. "But he's not mad at you. Do you like him?" Another long silence followed. "Hayden?" she prodded.

"If he's mad at you, I don't like him," he announced.

Damn, Kate thought. "I'm sure he'll get over being mad and I really don't blame him for it. Everything's going to be okay, you'll see."

But as she drove back toward the Moosewood, she couldn't help but wonder if she was telling Hayden another lie.

AT 2:00 P.M. the cabin phone rang. Rosa answered it.

"It is for you, *señora*. Someone named Wally."

No doubt Wally wanted to tell her about Mitch's reaction to seeing the plane parked and waiting for him at the airstrip. She took the phone from Rosa. "Well, has he come to terms with it yet?"

There was a brief silence, and when he spoke, Wally's voice was somber. "Mitch radioed in at eleven to say the weather had taken a turn after he dropped off the three climbers and was heading for home. Heavy hail, high winds. He'd lost visibility and was hoping to climb out of it. He gave his coordinates and that's the last we've heard from him," Wally said. "That was three hours ago."

Kate's heart constricted. "Have you contacted the proper authorities?"

"All the Talkeetna air services are keeping an eye out and the park service has sent two choppers to search the area."

"Top up the Porter's fuel and have his flight plan and last coordinates ready for me. I'm on my way." Kate hung up and caught Rosa's eye across the room. "There's been some trouble with Mitch's plane. I'm going out to the airfield."

Hayden intercepted her before she could get out the door. "Can I come, Mumma?"

She knelt and gripped his shoulders. "No, honey, you can't. You stay here with Rosa."

"Did Mitch's plane crash?"

Kate felt a jolt to her core as her son spoke these words. "I'm sure everything's fine. You be a good boy for Rosa. I'll be back as soon as I can."

By the time she reached the car, her hands were shaking. Could this really be happening? And could the timing be any worse? She'd only just told Hayden his father hadn't died in a plane crash. Had she lied to her son again?

WALLY WAS PACING back and forth just outside the warming shack when she arrived, and Campy came out, shrugging into a windbreaker, wearing a pair of dark sunglasses and smoking a cigarette. "Hey, hon," she said as Kate threw her day pack into the plane. "I'm coming along as a spotter. My eyesight's a whole lot better than Wally's."

"Good," Kate said, grateful for the offer. "Two pairs of eyes are better than one. Climb aboard."

Wally handed her a chart with the flight plan drawn in and Mitch's last coordinates circled. Kate felt her heart sink when she saw the expanse of mountain range he'd been flying over. "How long have the other aircraft been searching?"

"An hour, maybe less. An Alaskan State Trooper helicopter's been dispatched out of Fairbanks and the civil air patrol is getting some aircraft up, as well. The Talkeetna pilots are reporting bad flying conditions around the mountain. Zero visibility, severe winds, whiteouts and downdrafts, and most've turned back. The radio transmission from the base camp reported the same heavy hail that Mitch did. They said it was big stuff. Fist-sized."

Kate couldn't have described her feelings as she took off from that little airfield that encompassed all of Mitch's dreams. She was badly shaken, but didn't want Campy to guess at her mental state. She was grateful for the big engine in the Porter because she knew she might need every last ounce of horse-power and grit it could give her. She wished that she and Mitch had parted on better terms. And more than anything she wished she'd never told Hayden that his father was still alive because these Alaskan mountain ranges were formidable, and if Mitch's plane had gone down in the Alaska Range, the odds of him surviving such a crash weren't all that good.

Campy had obviously flown enough to know how to put on the copilot's headset and key the intercom. "I gotta tell you, hon, I'm scared shitless."

"Don't worry, he'll be fine," Kate said, knowing her words were unconvincing. "Mitch is an excellent pilot."

"Oh, I know that. That's not what I'm talking about," she said as she matter-of-factly organized the air charts on her lap, draped the binoculars around her neck and readjusted her headset. "I'm scared shitless of flying."

IT TOOK NEARLY forty-five minutes for them to reach the coordinates Wally had penciled in on the air charts, and during that time, Kate made contact with all the other aircraft in the search and worked out grid plans and respective search areas.

They had nearly four hours of daylight left, but the weather was proving problematic. The Porter was bounced all over the place by the fickle winds once they got over the Alaska Range and Campy started turning green, though she never once complained. She kept the binoculars to her eyes and scanned the mountain slopes through breaks in the cloud cover while Kate flew the grid and tried to give Campy as smooth a ride as was possible under the circumstances. She came to understand fairly quickly what Mitch had meant by kick-ass, seat-of-the-pants flying. She just hoped the wings held fast. The sudden downdrafts were incredible. Throw in zero visibility and a bad hailstorm like Mitch had been flying through and Kate wondered if anyone could have kept it all together, especially piloting that Stationair.

She worked her grid pattern religiously in spite of the turbulence, staying in radio contact with the other aircraft, but three hours passed without any of them spotting anything, and the sun, when it showed itself in brief glimpses, was low on the horizon. It was a big, wild, rugged area to search, and the odds of finding them quickly, when there was no signal from the emergency location transmitter on the plane, were next to nil. Seconds seemed like minutes, minutes like hours and the hours like an eternity stretching toward darkness. She heard the chopper pilots discussing how much longer they could search before calling it quits for the night. Too soon they'd have to head back because the deepening twilight would prevent any effective search, and at this altitude, in such high winds, the bitter temperatures would finish off anyone who might have survived the crash.

Desperation took firm hold as time passed and the sun set behind the mountains. Kate had finished her grid, but there was one area she wanted to double back over, try to get closer to. Then after a particularly rough spate of flying on an upwind leg that paralleled a spiny ridge, she heard Campy draw a sharp breath.

"I see smoke," she said—three electrifying words—pointing with one hand and holding the binoculars to her eyes with the other.

Kate had to top the ridge before she saw it, and for a few moments she forgot to breathe. The minute the plane cleared the bare knife-edge of rock, a downdraft nearly sucked them into oblivion. At full throttle she kicked the rudder hard, clearing a jagged outcropping before sliding through the air over a narrow snowfield that serpentined between two sheer walls of rock for maybe a hundred yards, then dropped off the side of the mountain into a deep crevasse.

"I see the plane," Campy said, her words taut with emotion.

So did Kate. She radioed their position in a calm and controlled voice, verbally detached from the tragedy of the moment even while her heart raced and her eyes struggled to pick out some signs of life in the wreckage of what had once been Wally Gleason's Stationair. The plane's nose was buried in the glacial scree, completely obscuring the cockpit's windshield. The left wing had caught a rock outcropping and snapped off, spilling fuel and igniting the plane, which still plumed black, oily smoke. The fuselage was intact but crumpled and blackened from the fire.

"I'm going to make another pass," she said, and Campy nodded tersely, binoculars at the ready.

It was a bumpy pass, and lower than the first. She knew she was erasing her margin for safety, but she was hoping beyond all rational hope that Campy would spot something other than charred bodies in the wreckage.

"I see something moving!" she shouted so loudly that Kate quickly adjusted the volume on her headset. "There! In those rocks! See?"

"I'll try to make another pass, but it's pretty rough."

Kate didn't see what Campy had. She was too busy flying the plane and trying to avoid the mountainside. How could anyone have survived that crash? Dare she hope? She racked the plane around and came back at the crash site from behind while the downdrafts tried to rip them out of the sky. She felt her heart leap when she saw a human form step away from the rocks and raise his arms in a motion that made her feel instantly light-headed.

"They're okay," she said, weak with relief. She pulled the plane up over the ridge and fought to control both the aircraft and her emotions. "They're okay."

"How do you know?"

"That's what his signal meant, that they're all okay."

Campy's rebel yell nearly busted Kate's eardrums.

They made one more pass while Kate radioed the coordinates to the helicopters and reported that all three men who'd been on board had been spotted. Then she radioed Wally on the airstrip's frequency. "They're alive. The park service choppers are ten minutes from the crash site. I'll fly high cover and guide them in. It's a pretty tight spot and the weather's dicey."

She fully understood Wally's inability to speak because after the choppers had arrived, after the rescue had been made and after the second park service chopper had radioed that they were transporting the men directly to the Fairbanks hospital, Kate had no idea how she managed to fly the Porter. Campy was equally quiet on the way in, and after landing at the Fairbanks airport, both women sat in silence for a long moment in the arctic twilight.

"I'm not the least little bit religious, hon," Campy said, pulling off her headset with hands that shook visibly, "but seeing that plane all burnt and broken apart, I gotta say it's a true miracle any of them survived. Let's keep our fingers crossed that Mitch really is okay. That they're all okay."

They took a taxi to the hospital and collapsed on hard plastic seats outside the E.R. while two state troopers, having been alerted by the park service pilots, took their statements and the crash survivors were tended to by the medical staff. Information as to their status was something that wasn't dispensed freely in the long hour that followed. Finally, Campy lost her patience and stalked over to the desk.

"Listen," she said to the charge nurse. "All we want to know is, are those boys going to make it?"

Before any answer was forthcoming, Kate heard the E.R. doors swing open and turned to see Mitch walking through them. He came to an abrupt stop when he saw her. Kate would have stood but she didn't have the strength. Seeing him standing there, bruised and bandaged but very much alive, sapped the last of her reserves. She could only stare as if he were an apparition.

"I didn't know you were here," he said, looking as dazed and exhausted as Kate felt.

"My God, Mitch, you gave us quite the scare," Campy said as she crossed the distance between them and gave him a tender hug. "I guess that's the end of *Babe*. She's finally crashed her last. Are you all right? Are they letting you walk out of here? Your face is all cut up, hon. Are you sure you're okay?"

"I'm fine. John has a busted leg. Mike has a concussion and some fractured ribs. They're being admitted." His eyes caught Kate's over Campy's shoulder. "The chopper pilot said you found us."

"Kate had a hunch. She'd already flown over that area but she wanted to take another look, and she was right," Campy said. "It was pretty nasty up there, but she did great."

Mitch was watching Kate with those keen eyes as she studied the crisscrossing of cuts on his face, one that had required stitches. He dropped into the chair beside her. "I'm sorry I put you through that."

And at his words, and the surprisingly tender way he spoke them, Kate lost it. In front of the hospital staff, in front of Campy, in front of Mitch, she curled over and buried her face in her hands, shaking all over. She felt his arms go around her and pull her near.

"It's okay," he said in that same rough yet tender way.

She lifted her head and pulled away from him. "How can you say it's okay? What was so okay about it?"

"Well, the landing was a little rough, but we walked away from it, and we're all right, thanks to you finding us. We were getting damn cold about the time you flew over and was that the Porter you were flying? How'd she handle the downdrafts?"

"How can you ask about stuff like that now?" Kate said. She tried to stand but a wave of dizziness overwhelmed her and she sat back down and doubled over, breaking out in a cold sweat. She closed her eyes and drew several deep breaths, hoping she didn't make a fool of herself and pass out.

"Easy, take it easy," Mitch said, his hand on her shoulder. "Campy, get a doctor? Kate's sick."

"I'm just tired, that's all," Kate muttered, wrapping her arms around herself.

"No doubt. I had to get checked out, now it's your turn. Afterward, we'll go home. Don't waste energy arguing with me, K.C., you won't win this one."

Campy led a doctor and nurse, complete with wheelchair, back to the waiting area.

"Kate has leukemia and she's not feeling well," Mitch told them. "She was being treated at the cancer research hospital in Seattle. Can you check her out?"

"Leukemia?" Campy's expression betrayed her shock.

"I'm fine," Kate said, irritated that Mitch would mention her illness. "Just a little tired…as any*one* would be."

The E.R. doctor backed Mitch. "We'll run some tests, just to make sure," he said.

Mitch helped Kate into the wheelchair and she was whisked into the E.R., where they took her temperature, blood pressure and pulse. After several painful needle pricks in an arm already scarred and bruised from chemotherapy treatments, enough blood was drawn to satisfy the doctor. "The lab'll call with the results in a little while," he said. "Meanwhile, I'll touch base with the Seattle hospital."

The E.R. doctor left the cubicle and Mitch dropped into a chair. He cast her a weary look. "That wasn't so bad, was it?"

Bad? It was awful. Kate felt sick all over, but it wasn't from the leukemia. She was shaky and weak and wrung out and she wanted nothing more than to tell Hayden his father was okay and weep her relief in a private place.

Campy ducked through the curtain, handed Kate the bottle of water and Mitch the cup of coffee they'd each requested, then gave Kate the same kind of sisterly hug she'd given

Mitch. "You poor thing, being so sick and doing all that tough flying. No wonder you're done in. I made reservations at the hotel near the airport. No way are we going back to Pike's Creek tonight. I called Wally, too. He's been sitting by the phone at the airstrip since we last called in. He said to tell you he'd fed Thor and the dog won't get out of the back of your truck. I asked him to call the Moosewood and tell your nanny everything is okay."

"Thank you. They'll be worried." She should have done that herself, an hour ago. Kate uncapped her water and drank half the bottle. It was the fourth she'd drunk since arriving at the hospital and she was still thirsty, but feeling a little better. She glanced at Mitch, who was watching her carefully. "What happened after you left the climbers at the base camp?" she asked.

"The weather closed in. The winds got squirrelly and the downdrafts were strong, but then it started to hail. The hail blew out the windshield and pushed the plane down. Beat it right into the side of the mountain. I found the best landing strip I could. End of story."

Kate guessed there was a lot more to it than that. Somehow he'd managed to set that plane down on the only patch of reasonably level snowfield within miles. Not all of it was pure luck, though luck had surely worked in his favor.

Twenty minutes later, the doctor ducked back into the cubicle. "Your blood work looks okay. The values aren't what I'd like to see, but according to the doctor I spoke with at the Seattle hospital, they're in the ballpark for what you're going through. He asked if you were having any stomach pains."

Kate hesitated. "A few. Not too bad."

"If they get worse, he wants you to come back for more

tests. Meanwhile, I think you're long overdue for some rest and relaxation. No more search-and-rescue missions while you're in Alaska."

"No camping trips, either, I suppose?" Mitch asked.

"She's a very sick young woman, and you're lucky I didn't make you stay overnight for observation. You were banged up pretty good. I'd advise complete bed rest for both of you for the next couple of days, and no flying for either one of you for the next week. You're both officially grounded."

Campy stood. "Come on, hon," she said, slipping her arm around Kate, "there's a taxi waiting outside to take us to the hotel. I think we could all use some shut-eye."

CAMPY DREW Kate a hot bath after they checked into the two rooms she'd reserved. "Trust me, you'll sleep better after a long soak," she said. "I told Mitch to do the same, but being as he's a man I doubt he'll take my advice." Kate was too weary to put up much of a protest. Besides, a hot bath sounded good, even if it was nearly 3:00 a.m. She soaked in the tub of hot water, immersed to her chin, eyes closed, trying to push away all the what-ifs.

What if Mitch had been killed?

What if she'd had to tell Hayden that his father really had been killed in a plane crash?

What if Mitch had been killed and she didn't get a bone marrow donor and she died, too?

What if…?

The dark thoughts were overpowering. Once upon a time, Navy Captain K. C. Jones had been invincible, but now she struggled through a quagmire of fears and doubts, fueled by Mitch's close brush with death and Hayden's increased vulnerability. She should never have told Hayden about Mitch. She should never have told Mitch about Hayden. She should never have come here in the first place, foolishly trying to undo all the mistakes she'd made. In the end, all she'd done was create more opportunities for heartbreak for Hayden.

Kate left the tub when the water cooled, dried herself off, pulled on her underwear and the T-shirt she'd worn under her sweater and, leaving the wig on the bathroom counter, she crawled into the bed Campy wasn't already sound asleep in. She turned out the bedside lamp and finally allowed herself the private release of all her emotions. Drained, she fell asleep with her cheek pressed against the wet pillow.

CHAPTER NINE

MITCH LAY on his back in his hotel bed and stared up into the dark and kept seeing that plane, that white-and-black Porter, side-slipping through the mountain pass with inches to spare and skimming right above the three of them, who were huddled down in the rocks to escape the brunt of the bitter winds. He kept thinking about the fact that Kate had been flying that plane, that the flying conditions had been terrible, that she might have been killed trying to locate him, that they might both have died and left Hayden without any parents at all.

He kept thinking about those last few airborne minutes of that vicious hailstorm, when the plane's windshield blew out and he knew, he *knew* they weren't going to make it out of the mountains, that they were going to crash and burn and become yet another of McKinley's statistics. Three more names added to the already lengthy fatalities list.

He thought about the reporter and cameraman from Seattle, Mike and John, good enough guys who'd been looking for a story and had become part of a whopper. They were going to do a documentary, they'd told him that morning when they first boarded the Stationair. A story about bush pilots and mountain climbers and mountain flying and how hazardous it all was. They'd gotten their story and their film footage.

They had everything they needed to rivet their television audience, and then some. John even got footage of Kate flying overhead, finding them, and the park service chopper that hauled their sorry asses out of the mountains.

Kate would be a part of Mike and John's story. A big part, since both reporters were in shock and becoming seriously hypothermic by the time they'd been rescued. They wouldn't have survived the night out on that glacier in the shape they were in, so it was safe to say they owed their lives to Kate's superb flying and Campy's sharp eyesight.

Helluva story.

At 4:00 a.m., Mitch got up and made a pot of coffee in the little in-room pot. He hurt all over. The stitches across his cheekbone burned, his head ached, his gut was sore and his hands and face were bruised and covered with cuts from the hail that had slashed through the open cockpit. He'd never seen hail that size before. Incredible. He drank his coffee and pondered the fact that he was still alive when by all rights he shouldn't be standing here at the window of a Fairbanks hotel room, watching the sunrise over the city.

By 7:00 a.m. he'd showered and dressed. He tapped lightly on the door to Kate and Campy's room just across the hall from his own. After a few moments the door swung inward and a sleepy-eyed Campy peered around it and blinked at him. "Damn. I was hoping it was room service with steak and eggs and a gallon of coffee," she muttered. "I could eat a horse. We never did get any supper last night."

"Kate awake?"

Campy shook her head. "Not yet, but if she's half as hungry as me, the smell of food might do it. I saw a McDonald's on the corner."

"I'm on my way."

"Mitch? She mentioned yogurt last night. She said it helps her stomach. Can you get her some?"

He walked two blocks and cleaned out his wallet on a big bag of breakfast food, including two fruit-and-yogurt parfaits. By the time he returned, Kate was up and dressed. When their eyes met across the room he felt a swift, sudden stab of fear. She looked terrible.

"You look a lot better," he lied.

She gave him a wry smile. "So do you."

"We're all extremely beautiful," Campy said. "Let's eat. I'm starving."

He emptied the fast-food breakfast onto the desk and handed Kate a large orange juice and one of the yogurts. They sat together on one bed and devoured the food. Kate finished her first yogurt, half of the second and one of Mitch's four hash browns.

"Delicious," she proclaimed after draining the last of her orange juice.

"Ditto," Campy agreed.

Mitch crumpled all the wrappers back into the bag and tossed it into the trash. "In an hour we'll probably be paying for that greasy meal for a second time."

"Speak for yourself. I thrive on the stuff," Campy retorted. "By the way, I called the hospital while you were picking up breakfast. Mike and John are doing fine. They'll be released later today and they'd like us to stop by before leaving. I told them we'd be by around eight-thirty." Campy gave him a long, significant look and Mitch guessed that Mike and John had taken Campy into their confidence about wanting to interview Kate for their story.

"You two go ahead," Kate said as if reading his mind. "I'll head out to the airport, get the plane gassed up and file our flight plan."

"Hon, it's you they want to meet," Campy said. "You're the gal who saved their asses."

"You're the one who spotted the smoke," Kate reminded her. "Besides, I've spent way too much time in hospitals lately. I'll pass."

"I promised them last night I'd introduce you," Mitch said. "They want to ask you a few questions for their story. It won't take long."

"I'll go check us out of the hotel and have them call a taxi." Campy picked up her purse and left the room to avoid the wrangling and move things along in the proper direction. As soon as the door closed behind her, Kate shook her head.

"I'm serious, Mitch. A hospital's the last place I want to be right now, and I don't want to be interviewed."

"Did you see the sunrise this morning?"

Kate hesitated, then said, "No."

"It was beautiful, but I wouldn't have seen it if it weren't for you."

"You could have been killed yesterday," Kate said.

"So could you. Where would that have left Hayden?"

"I told him about you just before Wally called to say your plane had gone missing. I told him you were alive, that you hadn't died in a plane crash, and then you go and nearly get yourself killed in one."

"I didn't plan it that way."

"What if you *had* died?" She was staring at him as if he'd just committed cold-blooded murder, or was thinking about it.

"I didn't, and I can't stop living just because you're afraid you might. Not even for Hayden's sake. I am what I am, and I do what I do. I'm not going to stop. Now let's go."

"I am not going to the hospital. I'll meet them later, somewhere else. Anywhere else."

Mitch decided to drop it for the moment and ask about the other thing bothering him.

"Tell me about the blood test last night and the stomach pains the doctor mentioned," he said. "What was that all about?"

"There's nothing to worry about."

"Tell me anyway."

She sighed impatiently and paced to the window. "My blood has to be checked regularly to make sure my immune system is holding up and the leukemia's still in remission. As for my stomach, chemotherapy is hard on the intestines. The pains come and go. They were pretty bad during my last chemo treatment. They ran all kinds of tests to check for perforation or hemorrhaging but couldn't find anything. The ones I had last night were probably due to stress. No big deal."

"Right. No big deal." The bedside phone rang and Mitch picked it up. It was Campy.

"The cab's waiting," she said.

"We're on our way." He hung up the phone.

"I'm not going," Kate repeated. "I only went last night because that's where they brought you and we didn't know what shape you were in."

"Dammit all, Kate, they're nice guys. I told them all about you on the chopper flight to Fairbanks. Come on. Just say hello. You saved their lives. They want to meet you and ask you a few questions, that's all. Ten minutes and it's over and we're out of there."

She looked at him and he was sure she was going to say no for the fourth time, but to his relief she gave a reluctant nod. "Okay. Ten minutes."

KATE DIDN'T WANT to go to the hospital. She wanted to go back to the Moosewood and wrap her arms around her sweet little boy and kiss his soft warm cheek and breathe his youthful innocence. Yet she was in the backseat of a taxi, Mitch on one side, Campy on the other. Campy had said nothing when she'd seen Kate emerge from the bathroom without her wig that morning and had given her a sisterly hug that somehow had made Kate feel better.

It was a short trip to the hospital.

Then they were out of the cab, Campy was paying the driver and Mitch was escorting her through the hospital doors. Down the corridor. Down another corridor. Gleaming corridors, clean and polished, awash with fluorescent lights, still quiet in the early hour with the big metal breakfast carts still making the rounds.

Kate had a flashback to her first days at the cancer research center in Seattle, undergoing the first round of chemo, opening her eyes to see a human figure in full Hazmat gear adding more of the chemical cocktail to her IV bag. "Now that's a reassuring sight," she'd said.

"We have to wear this suit because these chemicals will burn right through our skin if we accidentally spill any," the man apologized.

She still had nightmares about that technician in the Hazmat suit.

And then the second hospital stay. By then she knew the ropes. She'd lost her hair and could recognize the different stages of hell other cancer patients were going through: the

new arrivals with their full heads of hair, scared and apprehensive and surrounded by stunned family members trying to
be cheerful; the ones who'd already lost their hair along with
their eyelashes and eyebrows and wore that same introverted
expression that she did; the ones who were getting ready to
go back home…and the ones who went upstairs into intensive care and never came back down again.

She became immersed in the study of hematology,
spending long, bedridden hours researching her disease and
questioning the teams of doctors so intensively when they
came into her room that, after a while, they started holding
previsitation huddles outside the door to prepare themselves
for her cross-examination. Knowledge was power, but it came
at a price. The dark uncertainties she'd learned about loomed
alongside the cautious optimism voiced by the medical per-
sonnel, and all of it came rushing back while Mitch escorted
her down the hospital corridor. She wanted to turn and flee,
but instead lifted her chin and drew calming breaths.

Ten minutes and counting.

Kate put the brakes on and very nearly turned around
when Mitch guided her into the nurses' station on the second
floor. The first thing she saw was the group of reporters sur-
rounding the two patients in wheelchairs. Big video cameras
with their red recording lights flashing; pens scribbling notes
onto little flip pads; doctors, nurses and patients alike answering questions into microphones and tape recorders. All
activity paused when they arrived. All eyes and camera
lenses turned toward them. Kate felt Mitch's hand in the
small of her back as he guided her toward the men in the
wheelchairs.

"Kate, Campy, I'd like you to meet John Kelly and Mike

Lane, two wounded warriors from Seattle. Gentlemen, these are the ladies who spotted us yesterday and got us rescued."

Both men looked a little worse for wear, but they grinned and shook Kate's and Campy's hands and voiced their thanks repeatedly while the reporters and news crews took footage of the introductions.

"You boys are lucky Kate played a hunch and searched that area again," Campy told them in her smoky drawl, tossing her hair out of her eyes. "Otherwise you might still be up there. We're heading back to Pike's Creek and if the hospital plans to spring you this morning, you're more than welcome to fly back with us."

"Oh, no thanks," Mike said with a chuckle. "Right now we're a little leery of anything with wings. Matter of fact, we've been talking about driving or taking the boat back to Seattle."

"Mitch told us all about the two of you yesterday, on the flight to Fairbanks. I hope you don't mind if we ask you ladies a few questions." John said. "Mitch saved us twice over when he somehow managed a landing that didn't kill us outright, then pulled both of us out of the burning wreckage, but you found us before we froze to death, so that makes you a big part of this whole story."

"There's not much to tell that you don't already know," Kate said. "Several aircraft were up searching. We were one of them. Campy spotted the crash site and I radioed your position to the rescue choppers."

"Well, there's a little more to it than that, hon," Campy prompted. "For one thing, the flying was terrible. Three other planes turned back instead of joining the search, and if you had, too, things might've turned out a little different for these boys."

Kate was startled to feel Mitch's arm settle over her

shoulders and pull her close. "That's right. If she'd turned back, we wouldn't be having this little chat," he said.

"Mitch tells us you're a captain in the Navy?" John prompted.

"Yes," Kate said, silently damning Mitch for talking her into this interview. "I'm glad we were able to help."

"I understand you're a top gun instructor and you've flown combat in the Gulf," Mike said. "According to Mitch, you've received numerous citations and medals during your career, and he says you're a mother, to boot."

"That's right, she is," Mitch said. "Our son Hayden will be four in another month."

"We came here to do a story on the hazards of a bush pilot's life and I guess we got it," John said. "We want to thank both of you for risking your own lives to save ours. If there's anything we can do to repay you, anything at all—"

"As a matter of fact, there is," Mitch interrupted. "Kate's a great mother and great pilot, but right now she's fighting the biggest fight of her life. She has acute myelogenous leukemia, she needs a bone marrow transplant, and she needs help to find a donor."

MITCH KNEW he was going to pay big-time for this. Even as he spoke he felt Kate's body become completely rigid. She was taut with anger when he paused his little speech, but he held firm when she tried to twist out of his embrace. "Without a bone marrow transplant, she might die, and her odds of finding a donor are a little longer than most. There's some native American blood on her mother's side of the family, and that makes finding a good match even harder, but I know…Alaskans have big hearts, and maybe if more people know about this critical need, they'll get tested. They'll sign up to be on the bone marrow registry because they'll want to help. I'm proposing we hold a statewide bone marrow drive, and I'm offering free flights to the medical centers for villagers in remote locations who want to get tested."

Kate gave him a look he couldn't quite fathom, then pried herself free of his encircling arm and stepped forward to shake Mike's and John's hands one last time. "It was nice to meet you, but I'm afraid I really have to be going." She nodded to the cluster of reporters, ducked through the crowd and vanished down the hallway.

Gone.

"Oh, boy," Campy muttered at his elbow. "I'll go catch up with her and try to smooth things over."

Mitch watched Campy head down the same corridor, not holding out much hope for her conciliatory efforts, then turned back to the reporters. "That extraordinary woman saved our lives. We have the opportunity to do the same for her, and for others in the same situation. I happen to think her story's a whole lot more important than a story about bush pilots, and that's all I have to say about that."

After he'd said his goodbyes to Mike and John, Mitch headed for the lobby, hoping Kate would still be there and hoping Campy had somehow managed to calm her down.

KATE HAD NEVER been so humiliated in all her life. Mitch had stood there bold as brass and aired her private medical problems to the world. All those reporters with their blinking camcorders and all those gawking bystanders. All those pitying looks. She'd never forgive him for that.

Ever.

Not even for Hayden's sake.

She was feeding coins into a vending machine off the main lobby when Campy caught up to her. She made her selection and picked the bottled water out of the dispenser with a hand that trembled. Avoiding Campy's eyes, she said, "Ten minutes? They just wanted to meet me? That was a dirty trick." Her voice quivered as much as the rest of her body.

Campy reached out and in a conciliatory gesture, stroked her arm. "I'm sorry about that, hon, I really am, but Mitch just wants to help. So do I. When those boys asked if they could interview you for the documentary, Mitch thought it was a good way to get people to care about what you're going through."

"He had no right to do that. He deceived me," Kate burst out.

Campy nodded her bleached-blond head. "Maybe he did, hon, but he did it because he loves you, and that has to count for something."

"You call that love?" Kate clutched her bottle of water, blinked her eyes and began walking toward the main doors. "Let's just get a cab to the airport."

Mitch and the taxi arrived at about the same time, and when Mitch tried to apologize, Kate cut him off. The silence between them was awkward on the ride to the airport and only intensified as Mitch refueled the plane and did the preflight. When the time for departure came, Kate boarded the plane and sat in the passenger section, buckling herself in and keeping her eyes averted. She was aware of Mitch's long hesitation before taking the pilot's seat.

"You sure? The doctor said we were grounded for a week," he said. She nodded, keeping her eyes on the tarmac outside the passenger window. "Then take the co. I want to talk to you."

Grudgingly, Kate moved into the copilot's seat. Campy boarded, and after they were airborne, Mitch handed her the headset, which she donned with equal reluctance. She didn't want to talk. She didn't want to listen. She was completely exhausted. She wanted to sleep. She wanted to forget all about everything. Mitch, the crash, her illness, everything.

But Mitch had other plans.

"I'm sorry you're mad about the interview," he began.

"It sounded like you spent all night rehearsing that. You tricked me into going there. You lied to me," Kate accused.

"I'm sorry. I thought it was important, and I knew you'd bail if you so much as suspected anything that public," Mitch said, keeping his eyes fixed straight ahead. "This isn't just about you, Kate. A lot of people who are diagnosed with serious blood diseases could be helped by getting more bone marrow donors listed in that registry. It just so happens you're the one most important to me."

"You should have been upfront with me. You knew all those reporters would be there."

"I want to help you, Kate. That's all."

"Right back at you with this plane, Mitch," she said heatedly. "I want to help *you*. That's why I bought it."

"Now that you mention it," Mitch said, his voice tightening. "I called Wally this morning. He agreed to put the insurance money he gets from the Stationair toward purchasing the Porter. He said the Stationair was insured for two hundred thousand, so we'll get a loan from Yance for the balance."

"The plane's not for sale. I'm leasing it to your company."

"We won't lease it. Either you sell it to us, or we'll look for another plane."

"That's foolish. This is a great plane. And if the business buys it, you'll have no stake in it. You don't own any part of that charter."

"Eventually, I'll own the entire business," Mitch stated stubbornly.

Shivering with cold, Kate pulled her jacket more closely around her. "That doesn't cut it with me. I didn't buy that plane for Wally to own. I bought the Porter because it was a safe plane for you to fly and because you couldn't afford it."

"Thanks just the same, but I don't need your money to keep me afloat."

His voice was full of a thousand kinds of egotistical indignations. Just like a man. Kate shook her head and uttered a humorless laugh. "The truth is, you do need help staying afloat, as well as aloft, and the Porter will do both and then some. It came with wheel skis, floats and wheels. It's loaded with all the options. And bottom line, I bought that plane for Hayden as much as I did for you. I'm leasing it to your air charter and when you can afford to buy it from me, I'll sell it to you at fair market value."

"Fair market value for that plane is way more than I could ever pay. And while we're on that subject, how the hell could you afford it on a captain's salary?"

"My father's an investment analyst, and he's invested my savings quite successfully for years. Thanks to him, I'm doing quite well, which is more than you can say. I don't see how you could offer to give free plane rides to potential marrow donors when you can't even buy groceries."

"I make enough to get by, and I'll honor the offer I made. Wally'll get the insurance money for the Stationair and we'll buy a plane we can afford with it. I won't take charity from you."

She felt a rush of anger at his words. The Porter was a great plane. He should be grateful she'd bought it before someone else had. As soon as they got back to Pike's Creek, she was leaving. She would take Hayden and head for Montana on the first commercial flight and to hell with Mitchell McCray. "Fine, then. Get another plane, if you want, but you might not have much business after that crash of yours gets publicized. Reporters love plane crashes. Smoke and flames and bloody, burnt, mangled bodies. Stories like that sell papers but they aren't much good for drumming up future customers."

"Most of those reporters just happened to be there because they know Mike and John. They flew with me yesterday to do a documentary on bush pilots and how hazardous their jobs sometimes are."

"Maybe it wouldn't be such a hazardous occupation if you had a decent plane."

"That crash wasn't the fault of the plane I was flying, not that I was a great fan of the Stationair. Mountains make their own weather and we ran into some of it, that's all."

"That's all," she echoed in a bitter voice. "Well, that's reassuring."

"I suppose you're going to tell me that being a Navy pilot is a whole lot safer."

She didn't reply to this barb, just gazed out the window, hugging herself against the chills even though Mitch had boosted the heater and the cockpit was warm. She sounded like a nagging shrew. She'd come here to make sure Mitch was up to the responsibility of parenthood if it should ever fall on his shoulders, and now she was arguing with him about how dangerous his job was, when hers was just as dangerous.

Mitch was right. He couldn't stop living his own life just because she might die.

And she shouldn't be feeling the things she was feeling for him because there were no guarantees that there would be a future for her, and yet, did anyone have that guarantee? Why couldn't she accept the miracle of Mitch's survival, be grateful for his presence and give up the fight for her own independence? Why couldn't she let herself fall in love with him? Why couldn't she let him help her, and why wouldn't he let her help him? Were they both so bullheaded that they could find no common road, no path wide enough that they could walk side by side?

"How did Hayden take the news about me being his dad?" Mitch said changing the subject and interrupting her thoughts.

"As well as could be expected. We didn't have a lot of time to talk about it. I told him just before Wally called to tell me you went missing."

"Bad timing."

"It could have been much worse," Kate said.

"Maybe he could spend tomorrow over at my place. That'd give you some time to rest."

Kate looked at him, surprised by his thoughtfulness. "What about that camping trip to Denali?"

"You should probably crawl into bed and stay there awhile, like that doctor told you to do. A couple of days, at least."

"If I'd listened to what every doctor told me, I'd have died after the first round of chemo. Bed rest might work for some, but for me, getting outside is the best kind of medicine. I don't want bed rest. As long as I'm alive, I intend to live. And if you really want to take Hayden camping, I'd like to go along."

He thought about this for a moment before nodding. "Okay then, Denali it is. It may be against doctor's orders, but my guess is that doctor doesn't know how relaxing and therapeutic a camping trip can be, especially after a plane crash. If he did, he might have written the prescription himself."

CHAPTER TEN

HAYDEN ANXIOUSLY AWAITED his mother's return. He ran to meet Kate before she'd even gotten out of the truck and wrapped his arms tightly around her when she knelt to hug him. "I missed you, too," she murmured.

He pulled away from her to stare at Mitch with a grave expression. "Did you crash your plane?"

"I prefer to call it a rough landing."

Those young eyes studied every visible bruise and cut and stitch. "Did you get hurt?"

"Hardly a scratch. I was lucky. And it was even luckier that your mom found me."

"Are you still mad at her?"

Mitch glanced at Kate. "Who said I was mad?"

Kate rose to her feet and gave him an apologetic glance. "I told Hayden you were mad at me because I never told you about him," she admitted.

Mitch looked down at the boy. "I wish your mother had told me about you, but I'm not mad at her. She was trying to do what she thought was the right thing." He smiled at Kate before turning back to Hayden. "You still want to go camping and hear the wolves and see the bears?"

Hayden nodded, his eyes lighting up.

"Then let's load up and go. It was a beautiful sunrise this

morning, and with any luck, we'll be watching the sunset from Wonder Lake."

"Señora?" Rosa's voice came from the porch. "Your mother called this morning. She asked that you call her back. She was worried when you didn't call her yesterday."

Kate excused herself, and while Mitch loaded their duffels into the truck, she placed a call to Montana. He heard snatches of the brief conversation and guessed from the discouraged slump of Kate's shoulders when she hung up the phone that the news from her doctors hadn't been good. "I was hoping maybe the hospital had called, but apparently they haven't found a donor yet," she told Rosa.

"I do not think you should go camping, *señora.* You are too tired. It would not be good."

"Actually, Rosa, I think it's just what I need. And you could use a couple of days of rest yourself. Why don't you take a drive down to Anchorage? You said you wanted to see the Native Heritage Museum."

On the drive to his cabin with Hayden and Kate to pick up the rest of the gear, Mitch boosted the truck's heater to thwart Kate's chills and made unsuccessful attempts to engage her in conversation. She answered in monotones and her thoughts were clearly a million miles away. He thought about the beauty of the sunrise on a morning he never thought he'd see and the confusion of discovering he was a father and the frustration of trying to communicate with Kate on some level, any level, and in the end he gave up thinking about anything at all and just drove.

WHEN THEY REACHED Mitch's cabin, Hayden clambered out of the truck but Kate remained in her seat. "I'll wait here," she said in response to Mitch's questioning glance.

"You sure you're up for this?"

"Of course. I'm fine."

He nodded and shut the truck door.

"C'mon, pard," he said, resting a hand on Hayden's shoulder as they started toward the cabin, Thor at Hayden's heel. "Let's rustle up the rest of our camping gear and get headed north."

As they disappeared inside the cabin, Kate released her breath, dropped her head into her trembling hands and fought back a painful sob. The stomach pains she'd suffered last night had eased, but the pain in her heart had worsened. Seeing Mitch and Hayden together and getting along so well, father and son, should be a good thing. A positive thing. She should be glad that Mitch seemed to be a natural at parenting. So why did it hurt her so much? Why did she feel this way? What was the matter with her?

Was it because she was looking into Hayden's future and not seeing herself in it?

She had to put her personal feelings aside and concentrate on what was best for Hayden. She had to focus on this camping trip, on giving Hayden what might become the only two-parent experience of his childhood. She had to make sure this was a meaningful time for him, and that the memories he took away from it would last forever in the best of ways. Mitch was offering Hayden the chance to see a grizzly bear, to hear a wolf howl, to watch the sunset over Wonder Lake. She hadn't seen the same sunrise Mitch had that morning in Fairbanks, but she'd seen it two mornings before. She'd watched the sky brighten and the snowfields on the highest peaks glow violet and pink and then the clearest shade of pale, ethereal yellow as the sun's early rays illuminated the stunning splendor of Denali at dawn. Some people never saw anything that beautiful in their entire life.

Kate knew there were no guarantees of a tomorrow or a day after. There was only the here and now, and each moment was a precious gift. Something about the wild, harsh beauty of the Alaskan wilderness had triggered a poignant loneliness within her, and the need for something more in her life, however short it might be. Given the choice, she'd take a weeklong camping trip with Hayden and Mitch over a life of ninety-nine years and counting, if she had to live those years all by herself.

So why was she sitting here feeling sorry for herself when she should be helping Mitch and Hayden get the camping gear together? Kate swiped her palms over her cheeks and wrenched open the truck's rusted door.

Time was on the wing, and she, of all people, should know not to be wasting it.

"YOU KNOW HOW to use a compass?" Mitch asked Hayden as he dangled the old Silva on its leather thong in front of the boy, who shook his head solemnly. "Then I'll teach you," he said. "It's an important skill, especially out here. A lot of people use electronics now, but it still pays to know map and compass. They're basic skills that don't rely on batteries and satellites. Know what I mean?"

Hayden nodded, concentrating hard on his every word.

"This compass is pretty old." He opened it and held it in the palm of his hand so the boy could see the magnetic needle trembling within its glass-and-nickel housing. "It belonged to my father. Your grandfather. He got it when he joined the Army, and after the war he took a job cruising timber for a lumber mill in Maine. He carried this compass with him every day of his life. Wouldn't go into the woods without it. One day, it'll be yours." He saw a shadow in the doorway and glanced up, surprised to see Kate standing there, watching them. He closed the compass up and slipped it into his pocket. "We're almost ready."

Her gaze was inscrutable. Was she still mad? Depressed? Exhausted? Hard to say.

"We should stop at Yudy's and get a few more groceries before heading up," he suggested. "It's a five-hour trip from the park entrance to Wonder Lake. We'll be getting to the camping area around nine or so, but there'll be plenty of daylight left. All we need to load is the tent and the canoe and we're good to go."

Kate nodded.

"The canoe's not fancy. It's an old aluminum clunker the dog musher left behind, but it doesn't leak and it came with two paddles and a couple life jackets. He used to canoe in the river right here. You can get down to the Tanana pretty easy, but coming back up's a real struggle in high water."

She nodded again.

"The tent's an old canvas job," Mitch continued, feeling borderline foolish for trying to bridge the gap between them with too many words. "Has a few holes in it but I patched the worst of them, and there are a couple of air mattresses. They didn't leak the last time I used them."

"I'm sure they'll be fine," she said.

Good. At least she could still talk.

"I have a camp kit with all the pans and utensils we'll need. It's in a big bearproof metal foot locker that'll hold most of our groceries, and a stove and enough fuel to last three, four days."

Another nod.

"Hayden said he'd help me set up the tent."

They were staring at each other across the room, Kate in the doorway with her arms crossed, he standing by the fireplace, yet it felt as if an entire ocean separated them, an ocean so vast and uncharted they'd never be able to find each other across it, not even with a GPS. He felt a growing sense of frustration and dropped his eyes to Hayden. "You ready?"

"Ready," Hayden said.

"Then let's roll."

It didn't take long for Mitch to toss the tent, tarp and cook kit into the back of the truck and lash the canoe to the cab and bed. Thor jumped into the back as they started down the gravel road, grinning from ear to ear at the prospect of going on a camping adventure.

He and Hayden were the only two who were.

AT YUDY'S, the usual crowd was hanging out around the barrel stove and all conversation came to a screaming halt when Mitch stepped through the door. He held it open for Kate and Hayden, who were one step behind, and was unprepared for the scraping back of chairs as all the old-timers lurched to their feet.

"Hello, Captain Jones," one of them said gravely, pulling off his baseball cap.

"We saw you on the morning news, while you were being interviewed at the hospital in Fairbanks," Yudy explained, nodding to Kate. "It's quite an honor to have you here, ma'am, and I want you to know, anything you need, anything at all, you just sing out. I carry just about everything here in the store and what I don't have, I can sure enough get. You just name it."

"Thank you," Kate said. "All we need are a few groceries."

"And we all of us want you to know we're pulling for you, one hundred percent. Ain't we, boys?"

The old-timers rang out their agreement.

"And we're all getting tested as potential donors, just in case we can help you out."

Kate felt her heart squeeze as she looked among them, none under seventy years of age and some a lot older. Tough men who'd lived tough lives, all of them too old to be bone marrow donors but they didn't know it and she wasn't about to tell them. No one wants to be told they're too old to help out. "I appreciate that very much," she said with as big a smile as she could muster.

"Mitch, you lucky son, you cheated the devil yesterday, crashing on that mountain and living to tell about it," Yudy said.

"It wasn't a crash, it was a short landing," Mitch corrected.

"That right? They showed pictures of the plane on the news and it sure looked crashed to me. There ain't no way in hell Wally's going to put Humpty Dumpty back together again this time. I guess that's the end of Wally's Air Charter."

"Not exactly," Mitch said. "We'll get another plane with the insurance money."

"Hopefully one that'll stay in the air," Yudy said, his remark eliciting a few guffaws from the group around the stove. "What can I get you for groceries?"

"We're heading up to Denali to camp out at Wonder Lake," Mitch said, with a glance in Hayden's direction. "I think we'd better start with a couple of bags of marshmallows, some chocolate bars and a box of graham crackers."

IN SPITE OF her determination not to miss a moment of the journey to Denali, Kate fell asleep on the drive up the George

Parks Highway to the park entrance. It was Hayden who woke her. "Mumma, we're here," he piped up when Mitch turned onto the gravel road.

She had no idea how long she'd been sleeping, only that she was stiff, sore, thirsty and glad when Mitch pulled into the park headquarters and announced a break. "We have another five hours of travel time ahead of us," he said. "Let's stretch our legs and eat."

They had the place pretty much to themselves, and after a brief tour of the visitors' center and the restrooms, they sat outside, sharing the sandwiches Yudy had made them. Fresh crusty French bread and deli cold cuts, complete with crunchy dills and big bottles of lemony iced tea. Delicious. Both Kate and Hayden finished their sandwiches. Mitch ate two. Afterward, only Hayden was inspired to move. Kate could have lain back in the grass and fallen asleep in the next breath, but napping wouldn't get them to Wonder Lake. "Five more hours?" she murmured as the warmth of the sun turned her muscles to butter.

Mitch was propped on his elbows, hat brim pulled low to shield his eyes from the strong afternoon light, watching Hayden and Thor play tug-of-war with a stick. "It's a real pretty drive, but we don't have to do it all in one fell swoop today, if you'd rather camp someplace in between. It's four o'clock now. The Savage River checkpoint's another twenty miles in. That's where Rick hangs out. He's the ranger I'm counting on to let us through the gate. Most folks have to park there and take the bus in."

"What if he's not there?"

"I'll bribe whoever is."

Kate cocked her head to catch his eye. "With what? You couldn't even pay for the groceries."

"Easy," he cautioned. "A man has his ego."

"If little else."

Mitch flopped down flat on the grass with a real moan of pain. "Have mercy."

"I'm just trying to figure out how you'd feed this kid, buy him clothes, educate him."

He moved his head slightly to stare at her from beneath his hat brim. "Oh, that's right. I forgot to tell you about the gold mine that's located directly under my cabin. Whenever I feel the need for money I just dig a couple buckets of gravel and pan out the bigger nuggets."

"Mitch, I'm serious. If I don't get a donor—"

"You will," he interrupted, pushing back onto his elbows while stifling another moan brought on by the movement. "Hayden, you about ready to get back on the road?"

Forty minutes later they were at the Savage River checkpoint, and Ranger Rick himself greeted Mitch with a broad grin and an enthusiastic handshake. He was young and handsome in his park uniform. "You kidding? 'Course you can drive through," he said after the introductions were made along with the request, then he leaned in the open window and caught Kate's eye. "This guy saved my hide last summer, in fire season. He flew into this little squint of a pond nobody else dared land in and somehow managed to fly four of us rangers back out without clipping more than three trees."

"Two," Mitch corrected.

"He's just naturally heroic," Kate said.

"Glad you didn't crash and burn along with your plane yesterday, dude. I followed that pretty close on the radio. You had us worried." He glanced at Thor. "Don't let your dog run loose or he's apt to get eaten by a grizzly."

"That's not a dog, Rick, that's Thor. He's a wolf."

Rick grinned. "I thought he looked kind of wolfish. In that case, he'll have lots of company. The Kantishna pack was spotted near the Toklat two days ago. You might get lucky and see them along the way. That weather we got yesterday dumped a foot of snow on the road up near Stony Hill, but the crews've been plowing since sunup. You shouldn't have any trouble getting to the lake. The road's in real good shape otherwise." He looked at Kate. "Nice meeting you, Captain Jones. Hope you have a good campout. You both look like you could use a little R & R."

With Ranger Rick's blessing, they passed through the gate and continued on. "Is Thor really a wolf?" Kate asked.

"I think so," Mitch said. "What do you think, Hayden? Is Thor a wolf?"

"Yup," Hayden said.

AT 9:20 P.M. the sun was just sinking behind the mountains and Mitch had to wake both Hayden and Kate when he cut the truck's ignition at the primitive camping area. Kate woke first, her eyes fluttering open, then widening as she sat up. "Wow," she said.

Wonder Lake spread out before them, a vast molten shimmer reflecting all the colors of sunset, as well as the rugged, majestic heights of a snow-clad McKinley, which topped an imposing horizon made up of the Alaska Range. For a moment they sat listening to the wind that hissed through a grove of stunted spruce near the truck, then Kate glanced down at Hayden. "Wake up," she said softly, brushing the hair back from his forehead. "We're here." As he roused, she lifted her eyes to Mitch. "And you're right. It's beautiful."

"Looks like we have it pretty much to ourselves, too," he said, opening his door and dropping to the ground. His entire body protested the hard jolt and he hung on to the door for a moment, catching his breath and bracing against all the residual pains from the day before. No doubt about it, he was getting old. "I'll get the tent set up," he said, straightening. "You and Hayden just take it easy."

"Are you kidding? That's all I've done all day," Kate replied, opening her own door and sliding out. She helped Hayden down and stood for a moment, absorbing the quiet beauty of their wilderness surroundings. "I'll get supper started. Believe it or not, I'm hungry even after a whole day of doing absolutely nothing."

Mitch was, too. It took him longer to erect the tent than he anticipated because he kept stopping to help Kate unload the cooking gear from the back of the truck and then get it set up on the picnic table. He directed Hayden to start collecting small sticks around the campsite for a small fire in the fire pit to toast their marshmallows on after supper, scrounged a bottle of wine out of the groceries and opened it using the corkscrew on his jackknife. He poured some into a tin cup and handed it to Kate, then snagged a beer out of the cooler and twisted off the top. "To the sunset."

"To the sunset," she echoed, touching the rim of her cup to the neck of his beer bottle.

They watched for a few moments more before returning to their tasks, standing side by side in companionable silence while Hayden and Thor wrestled over a piece of kindling. By the time Mitch had the big canvas wall tent reasonably squared up and tied off, Kate was preparing a salad in a big blue plastic bowl at the weathered picnic table and Hayden had collected three small pieces of bleached driftwood, two of which Thor promptly chewed up. Mitch tossed their sleeping bags inside the tent and began inflating the air mattresses, taking frequent pauses to keep track of Hayden and Thor. By the time he was done he could smell something great cooking on the stove and his stomach was growling with anticipation.

"You're getting potluck tonight," she informed him with a bemused smile when he bent over the pot to have a peek. "Vegetarian chili. It's fast and easy, and we'll have a salad with it and s'mores for dessert. Tomorrow you can wow me with one of your gastronomic tours de force."

"I'll try, but I doubt I'll come close to what you're making right now. I don't know when I've smelled anything that good. I better go hunt up some wood. Hayden doesn't have enough yet to toast one marshmallow. How long until supper?"

"Ten minutes."

"Call out when it's ready."

He carried his beer down to the lake's edge and stood for moment, the waves lapping against the gravel at his feet. He felt full of something he couldn't even put a name to, as he looked out across the still beauty of the water and the soaring heights of the mountains and realized that he was closer to happiness right now, at this very moment, than he'd ever been in his life. Which didn't make any sense at all, because the past few days had dealt out a series of traumatic events. Finding out he was a father, finding out Kate was battling cancer and then on top of all that, crashing the Stationair. He should be suffering an ulcer or a high-stress tension headache, but instead he was filled with a kind of peace and contentment like he'd never known.

He glanced back to where Kate was sorting through the cook kit for eating utensils and plates, and he watched her for a long moment, long enough to believe that she wouldn't die. She couldn't. She was too vibrant and beautiful and intelligent and alive. No way was she ever going to die. And then he watched the little boy who was trying to wrest a skinny stick of driftwood away from Thor and he felt a kick of pride that such a cute and well-behaved kid could be his.

His and Kate's.

Their son.

How humbling was that? He'd been telling Hayden the truth when he said he wasn't mad at Kate anymore for not telling him he had a son. He wasn't. Given the circumstances of their first meeting, her focus on her career and her stubborn, prideful self-reliance, he understood why she hadn't.

What he still didn't understand was why she hadn't read his letter, and he didn't think he ever would.

"Supper's ready," he heard Kate call, and he gathered an armload of driftwood on his way back to the campsite.

AFTER SUPPER, Mitch cut willow switches to toast the marshmallows on. He went out into the twilight with his jackknife after lighting the little campfire and returned with three peeled sticks, handing one to each of them with a ceremonious air.

"It isn't a real campout if you don't toast marshmallows and make smores," he informed them.

Kate took her willow branch and examined it critically.

"This isn't thick enough and it's too smooth," she pronounced. "When the marshmallow heats up, it's going to slide right off."

He gave her a playfully offended stare. "Woman, you're

deluded. That's a perfect toasting stick. Hayden? Watch and learn."

Kate had to squelch a smile as she watched Hayden and Mitch huddle close to the little campfire with their willow toasting sticks and the bag of marshmallows. Hayden was in his element, thriving in Mitch's company, reveling in the outdoors, in having a wolf-dog to pal with and a man, his very own father, to take him under his wing.

Soon, marshmallows were catching fire and slipping off the sticks and into the flames, but enough survived to sate the sweet tooths of all. Between the three of them, they put a good dent in the first bag.

"I can't believe it's past midnight," Kate said in a hushed voice as they watched the embers glow the same color as the sky had just before full dusk.

"You must be pretty tired," Mitch said.

"Mmm. It's a good kind of tired."

Hayden was so groggy he barely protested the bedtime ritual of washing up and brushing his teeth and was asleep, with Thor sprawled next to him, before Kate could fold his blue jeans and shirt and tuck them into his duffel.

She rejoined Mitch at the fire pit and had no sooner settled back into her place and picked up the tin cup of wine, nearly empty now, when she heard the mournful wail of a loon out on the lake. The beautiful, bittersweet sound echoed into the arctic twilight, amplifying all the feelings churning within her and vocalizing them aloud to the wilderness. She felt a surge of emotion and was glad that it was dark enough to hide the tears that suddenly flooded her eyes.

"Thank you for bringing us here," she said, when she could manage the words past the painful tightness in her throat.

Mitch caught her gaze across the dying fire. "Hayden's a good kid," he said after a long while.

"Yes, he is," she murmured, wishing she could turn back time and steal just one more night with Mitch like the one they'd shared at the Mad Dog Saloon all those years ago. She was so tired, so drugged and dreamy with exhaustion, that the memories no longer triggered that impenetrable wall of self-defense. She no longer cared about being independent. She liked being with him, and the sound of his deep, reassuring voice. She liked feeling safe and secure and protected.

"You did a good job with him," he added after another long while of contemplating the bed of coals. The night was so quiet, so still, that she could hear his heart beating…or was it hers? They were going to share a tent together for several days. Sleep together, eat together and take care of Hayden together for the first time as parents…and maybe the last. She wondered why she had ever felt anger toward him, because right now she couldn't feel anything but enormous gratitude and respect. He was like no other man she'd ever known, and she'd known a lot of men throughout her career. Worked with them, flown with them, commanded them and been commanded by them.

But none had been like Mitchell McCray.

Some had been as heroic, some had been as tough, some had been humorous, some opinionated, some arrogant and brash, some brilliant and some had been chauvinistic. Mitch was all those things, but he was something else, too. He was good-hearted.

And even more than that, he seemed to genuinely care about her.

Kate wished she had the nerve to move closer to him, to sit

beside him and rest her head on his shoulder. Let the wine and her own exhaustion break down the last of her barriers. Right now she'd be perfectly content to let him protect and defend and be the strong one. She wanted to lean into the warm, solid strength of him and let him shoulder the load for a while. She was so tired. So very, very tired. She glanced across the fire and was startled to see that he was watching her.

"Tell me why you won't use my plane," she said.

For a long time, for the longest time, she thought he wasn't going to respond. The loon called again, a lonely, haunting wail that pierced her heart with a pain like she'd never felt before. And then, finally, after an aching eternity, he spoke.

"I already told you why. You of all people should understand the independence thing. I don't need to ride on your coattails and I'm not going to. I appreciate what you're trying to do, Kate, but I'm a big boy. I can take care of myself. I've been doing it for years."

"Yourself, yes, but what about Hayden?"

"It won't come down to that, but if it does I'll do right by him. Now, before you say another word, why don't you try moving a little closer? It's getting cold. I promise I won't bite, and you're way too good-looking to be sitting there all by yourself, brooding about a plane."

"AND THE FOURTH star to the left of Antares is called Pleiades, and it's where all the Sky Dragons go to play after they've saved the universe from the scourge of the Magogs," Mitch said, concluding his narrative of the night sky.

The fire was out and the arctic night was as dark as it was going to get. The wind had died, the lake was still, and the sound of the waves against the shore had died to a faint whisper. Kate's breathing had become even and regular. He could feel the moist flutter of her breath against his neck and the pliant warmth of her body pressed against him. Was she asleep? Would she wake when he moved? Had she heard any of what he'd said?

He shifted slightly and she nestled against him with a soft sound, her arms curling around his neck. He scooped her up with him as he rose, lifting her effortlessly, not because he was so enormously strong, but because she was so light.

Too light.

He carried her through the door of the tent and she roused as he tried to position her as gently as he could on the bed. She made another soft noise as he untied her running shoes, slid them from her feet and wrapped her in the warm cocoon of her sleeping bag. It was dark enough inside the tent that he couldn't tell if her eyes were open or not. He shucked out of his boots and pants and dropped into his own bed, glad the air mattress hadn't sprung a leak because he was still sore as hell and didn't feel like sleeping on the cold, hard ground.

"Mitch?" she murmured ever so quietly just before he drifted off. "Pleiades isn't a single star, it's a group of stars representing the seven daughters of Atlas, but I loved your story about the Sky Dragons."

CHAPTER ELEVEN

BACON FRYING. Coffee brewing. The fragrant tang of wood smoke. All these savory, pleasing aromas mingling together in the cool arctic air roused Kate from a blissfully dreamless sleep. She lay with her sleeping bag drawn up to her chin and came awake slowly, reluctant to leave that place she'd drifted off to in Mitch's arms the night before…or had that just been a dream after all? She turned her head on the pillow. No, his mattress was right beside hers. He'd moved it there when she'd asked him to. Small-voiced. Reluctant. Needy. Pleading. He'd let her fall asleep in his arms, and his presence had banished the nightmares that had plagued her ever since she'd been diagnosed with cancer. She hadn't slept as well in over three months and she hadn't felt so at peace ever before in her life.

Hayden was still dozing. She could see the tawny thatch of his hair poking out of the sleeping bag laid out along the tent's far wall. She heard a stealthy pad of paws just before Thor poked his wolfish head through the tent door, yellow eyes studying the place where Hayden slept for a long moment before the dog backed out again. Thor was waiting for Hayden to get up and go outside to play.

Mitch was cooking breakfast.

The wind picked up, causing the tent door to flap and sunlight to stream through the opening, laying a band of warmth across her legs. She could hear birds singing in the stunted spruce trees around the tent site, waves breaking against the shore, Mitch's voice saying something to Thor. It was time to get up, but it was so very sweet lying here, absorbing the morning this way, taking it into her soul little by little, committing to memory all the sounds and the smells and the feelings, secreting them in a special place where she could draw on them later to help get her through the hard times to come.

Footsteps approached and Kate closed her eyes, feigning sleep, as Mitch did what Thor had just done, pausing outside the tent door, peering inside to see who was up, then retreating silently. She wondered how many times he'd already done that in the course of the morning. She also wondered what time it was. The sun was well up in the sky. Kate drew a deep slow breath and released it, stretching as she did. She felt so good it was almost possible to believe she wasn't sick at all, and that the past three months had all been a bad dream.

Maybe the doctors had been wrong.

Getting dressed was a simple matter of pulling on her sneakers and lacing them up. She reached a hand up to adjust her wig, marveling that she'd managed to keep it on all night. Although she hadn't even considered what might happen if it came off while she slept, she was grateful it hadn't. Her hair was no more than a fuzzy dark shadow, growing back slowly after that last round of chemo.

When she went outside, Mitch wasn't at the Coleman stove. The bacon was draining on a paper towel, the flame under the frying pan had been extinguished and he was standing down on the lakeshore with a cup of coffee looking across at the mountain. Kate washed up, poured herself a cup and joined him there.

"It seems I missed the sunrise for the second morning in a row," she said. "You should have woken me."

"You can catch it tomorrow. You needed the sleep." He gave her a slow up-and-down. "Looks like it helped. Not that you looked anything but beautiful yesterday, but yesterday was a damn long day."

"Preceded by an even longer day," Kate said, startled by his unexpected compliment. "How are you feeling?"

"Like I crashed an old Stationair into the side of a tall mountain two days ago. The air mattress could've been thicker and the bath I took this morning was a little chilly."

Kate took a sip of the strong black coffee and regarded him over the rim of her cup. He hadn't shaved and with all the cuts and bruises on his face, she doubted he would for a few days, but the shadow of stubble only enhanced his virility. "You swam in the lake?"

"Very briefly. I'm surprised the ice is out. Feels like that water should be frozen solid."

"How long have you been up?"

"Long enough to drink nearly two pots of coffee and get the canoe ready to go." He nodded up the shoreline and she spotted the old aluminum boat and a pile of gear next to it. "Thought Hayden might want to try his hand at fishing."

"What about Hayden's mother?"

"Does she like to fish?"

"She used to, when she was a young girl." She smiled at the memory. "There was a creek that came out of the mountains and flowed through a high, pretty meadow and sometimes I'd ride up there on my horse Gunner with an old cow dog named Tootch. I'd catch a slew of cutthroat trout with my grandfather's fly rod."

"Then what would you do?"

"Sometimes I'd build a little fire in the gravel beside the creek and cook a trout or two in the frying pan I always carried in my saddlebag. Other times I'd bring a few home for my parents, but most of the time I let them all go because they were just too beautiful to kill."

"That meadow sounds like a nice place."

"It's a glorious place. The Crow used to winter there. You can still see the rings of stone that anchored the bottom edges of their teepees, and there's an old line camp on the creek, too, built in the early nineteen hundreds, back when Colt Drummond ranched that whole valley, but the logs are mostly rotted away now."

"So this place you grew up was part of an old cattle ranch?"

Kate nodded. "I had a great childhood. Idyllic. I was outside all the time. When I was twelve I got a job working for the Drummonds taking care of their horses. There aren't many cattle left on that ranch, but they raise great quarter horses, some of the best in the country. I loved that job and those horses."

Mitch watched her while she spoke, slowly sipping his coffee. "If you liked it so much, why didn't you stay in Montana and become a horse rancher?"

"Because I'd spent most of my childhood working on bigger dreams than that. Katherine Jones was going to be a pilot. An astronaut. A space shuttle commander and the first woman to step foot on Mars." She shook her head with a wry smile, remembering. "What about you? Why did you join the air force?"

"It was the cheapest way to get the flight training I wanted and I thought the lifestyle would be glamorous and romantic."

"Funny how dreams and reality duke it out with each other."

"Sometimes it isn't funny at all," Mitch said. "You ready for breakfast?"

IN EARLY June, the summer tourist stampede had yet to begin, and thanks to Ranger Rick's nod through the gate at the Savage River checkpoint, Wonder Lake belonged to them that day. The fish, if there were any, weren't biting, but that didn't seem to faze Mitch, who was intent on teaching Hayden how to use a fly rod while the wind blew the aluminum canoe like a leaf across the choppy surface of the lake. Kate spent an hour on the water with them, then opted for land and poked along the shore with Thor at her heels, looking for fossil stones and gathering an assortment of geological wonders, then wandered onto the taiga to pick a handful of wildflowers. She returned to the campsite, put the flowers in an empty beer bottle filled with water, set the bottle on the picnic table and then arranged around its base all the different stones she'd picked up along the shore.

Never in her strictly regimented and ladder-climbing military life had she spent so much time doing nothing at all and enjoying every precious moment. She thought about fixing lunch and having it ready when Mitch and Hayden tired of fishing, then thought about a nap, and the nap won out. The interior of the tent was warm from the sun and smelled of canvas and wood smoke. She curled up on Mitch's sleeping bag because it smelled like him, which she found comforting. Thor lay down beside her, and with two deep breaths she was sound asleep.

It was Thor's low growl that woke her.

She opened her eyes and watched the dog stand, hackles

raised. She heard the footsteps and knew it wasn't Mitch or Hayden, not the way Thor was behaving. She pushed to her knees and stood, cautiously peering out the door and coming face-to-face with Ranger Rick, who stopped dead in his tracks. He was carrying a cardboard box and gave her a sheepish look.

"Sorry," he said. "Didn't think anyone was home. I was just going to leave this and go. Didn't want to bother you."

"That's okay," Kate responded, realizing she must look as if she'd just been woken up from a nap, since she had. "Mitch and Hayden are out fishing."

"I saw them out there. Me and the guys got a bunch of stuff together for you. That's what's in this box, along with a phone message from the governor and another from the head of the park service offering you the run of his private lodge. The messages were still coming in when I went off duty. There's a few here and I guess by now there are probably at least that many more. I hope you can read my writing. Anyhow, I thought you'd want to know. The news coverage of Mitch's plane crash and the fact that you were the one to find the crash site went national. We don't have TV at the checkpoint so I wasn't privy to the broadcasts. Seems the whole world somehow knows you're hiding out at Wonder Lake though, and someone named Wally gave them the satellite phone number to the ranger station."

Kate nodded. "Thank you, Rick. Sorry about that. We gave Wally that number in case of an emergency. I didn't realize he'd hand it out to anyone trying to get hold of Mitch."

"Oh, I think it's you these callers wanted to talk to. Anyway, it's no problem. I was glad to help out." Rick set the box down just outside the tent door. "Tell Mitch he'd have better luck fishing out on the tundra. He might snag a caribou."

"I will. And thanks again for coming by. It's a long haul from your checkpoint."

Rick grinned. "Not nearly as long or as risky a road as Mitch took the day he hauled us rangers out of that fire. You take care, ma'am, and good luck to you. For what it's worth, I'm going to sign up for the donor registry and so are the rest of the rangers."

After he'd departed in the park service truck, Kate carried the cardboard box to the picnic table. The messages he'd spoken of were handwritten on phone message sheets, stuffed into an envelope that was on top of what appeared to be an eclectic mix of food and alcohol. The alcohol was mostly home brew, stuff Rick and his friends had concocted. The food, ditto. Kate unwrapped a package of smoked salmon and broke off a piece, smelling it first before sampling. It smelled great and tasted even better. Cold smoked and delicious. So good she'd eaten half of it before she heard the scrape of metal on stone and glanced up to see Mitch beaching the canoe and Hayden jumping into the ankle deep water with a satisfying little-boy splash, wet sneakers be damned. Thor bounded down to meet them and Kate wiped her greasy hands on a paper towel, hoping she didn't look too much like the cat that ate the canary.

"Catch anything?" she asked.

"Nope," Mitch replied, "but it looks like you did."

"As a matter of fact, I caught a salmon and smoked it while you were out on the lake. Here. Try some."

Mitch broke off a piece and put it in his mouth. "That's mighty tasty. Guess we'll have to keep your mother on as camp cook, huh, Hayden? Take a taste of that."

Hayden crinkled up his nose at the offering but took it from

Mitch and bravely took a tiny bite. Kate had to squelch her smile. He never would have done that for her.

"Well?" Mitch said as Hayden chewed with solemn concentration.

"Yuck."

"Yuck's okay with me as long as you try it first," Mitch said. He broke off another piece and ate it with great relish. "Did I see Ranger Rick skulking about?"

"He caught me napping. He left this offering and some phone messages." Kate delved into the cardboard box and began setting the contents onto the picnic table. "Apparently, your ranger friends like to ferment things. There's birch beer and salmonberry brandy…. And look, another package of smoked salmon."

"This must be our lucky day. We don't catch a fish or even get a nibble, but a smoked salmon lands on the picnic table. Who were the messages from?"

Kate shook her head and pushed the envelopes toward him. "I haven't read them and I'm not sure I want to. The interview at the hospital was televised and Wally gave our contact number to every caller. Let's eat lunch first. Hayden, are you hungry?"

Hayden nodded. Mitch sifted through the envelope of messages. Kate pushed to her feet and opened the cooler, inside of which were enough sandwich makings to last a week in the bush. She selected a package of sliced turkey breast from Yudy's deli, a head of lettuce and some mayo.

"Jeez, this one's from the governor," Mitch muttered, scanning the first of the messages. "He saw the newscast and now he's pushing for a statewide drive for bone marrow testing. The local chapters of the American Red Cross and

Blood Bank of Alaska are on board to conduct the testing and provide the test kits. Everything's set to begin next week. He wants you to agree to a press release to kick the whole thing off."

Kate got the loaf of bread out of the metal foot locker and began making the sandwiches. She heard Mitch rustle through the stack of messages.

"This one's from the chief of the village of Umiak. It's in Ranger Rick shorthand, but it says his young nephew died of leukemia because they couldn't find a donor in time. Only the Blood Bank of Alaska carries the Tepnel kits and they would have to go to Anchorage to pick them up. He says Alaskan native families are huge, but few are on the registry because they can't afford to be. The travel expenses from isolated villages keep most natives from being tested. He says the bone marrow needs to be waiting for Kate, not Kate waiting for a donor to be found, and because Kate is in the news now, she can bring more awareness to this problem and help save lives."

Kate spread the mayo and laid the slices of turkey breast on the bread while Mitch studied the next message.

"Here's another one, but the writing is hard to decipher. 'I have forty-three-year-old friend Tuttu, native of Kotzebue, has the same leukemia. Tuttu had twin brother, would make the perfect bone marrow donor, but separated at birth. She thinks he is already dead, but others have been searching. Tuttu's grandfather raised winning sled dogs for the Iditarod in the 1960s." Mitch turned the piece of paper over and continued reading slowly, squinting with concentration. "His name may have been Kikikagruk and he may have been the first Eskimo ever to own an airplane, a Beechcraft Bonanza. If we could find some other family who might know where Tuttu's brother is, she might find the will to live. We are all praying for you, Kate, and hope you can help us to help Tuttu.'"

Mitch glanced up at her as he folded the message and returned it to the envelope. "Heavy stuff."

He opened the next and read for a moment in silence. "Hey, this one sounds right up our alley. The head honcho of the park service is offering us the exclusive use of his 'rustic' lodge in Kantishna. Rustic! It comes with a hot tub, a full bath and a private airstrip." He held up a key that was inside the envelope and shook it enticingly. "He's serious. Says it's empty and will be until the end of the month. All ours, if we want it."

"No doubt all of it funded by taxpayer dollars," Kate interjected, glancing up from distributing lettuce atop the turkey. "I like where we are just fine."

"So do I, but a hot shower would be nice, not to mention a hot tub. And by the way, it's privately owned, not government property." He looked at the letter again. "It's just another seven miles from here at the end of the road. If we took him up on it, we could invite the governor there for lunch, the chief of Umiak and Tuttu's friend. It'd make a pretty powerful press release and, who knows, maybe someone would come forward with information about Tuttu's brother." He glanced up. "Remind me to thank Ranger Rick for taking shorthand. These are mighty long phone messages."

Kate put the top slices of bread on the sandwiches and cut each one in half, then arranged them on paper plates and added the huge crunchy dills from the pickle crock at Yudy's and a handful of crispy, kettle-cooked potato chips. Mitch was scanning the last phone message as she slid the paper plates into place and retrieved two bottles of iced tea and a container of milk from the cooler. She poured Hayden a cup of milk and sat down, wondering why Mitch wasn't narrating this one aloud. Perhaps he didn't dare.

"Eat," she said to Hayden.

She took a sip of iced tea and waited. At length, Mitch folded the final message, pulled his sandwich toward him and glanced up, catching her eye. "That one was from your boss," he said. "The big boss, Ransom Gates. It's kind of cryptic. Bottom line, he's flogging all the Navy brass to put on a big donor drive, courtesy of Uncle Sam. Not bad behavior for that rough old cob. There must be a soft heart in there somewhere." He tapped the envelope with his fingers. "The president's will probably be in the next batch." He picked up his iced tea and took a swig. "What do you say we check out that lodge after lunch? On the way over, we could take a walk out on the tundra and look for wolves and grizzlies."

Kate knew she should be grateful for the offer of the lodge, but it no doubt had multiple bedrooms. What then? Would they all be sequestered in their own little rooms at the end of the day? Would she once again be facing her nightmares alone in the dark?

"Wolves, Mumma!" Hayden said around a mouthful of turkey sandwich.

"All right," Kate conceded. "Remember not to talk when your mouth is full. It's not polite."

THE WIND on the tundra was fierce, thundering across the vast land, the rounded swales flushed with spring greenery reaching toward the abrupt upheaval of the mountain range and the towering peaks. Wildflowers bloomed in protected hollows, lichens and mosses carpeted the tundra itself, and low-growing shrubs provided scant cover, making it ideal for wildlife viewing. From where they parked the truck, Dall sheep could be spotted on the lower mountain flanks, their creamy white coats making them easy to pick out.

"Sheeps!" Hayden said, pointing.

"Dall sheep," Mitch said, unslinging the binoculars and raising them to his eyes. "Wolves sometimes hang out pretty close to where the big game roams." After a few moments he lowered the glasses and shook his head. "Don't see any wolves, but there are some mighty cute lambs. You know how to use binoculars, Hayden?"

Kate watched while Mitch gave yet another patient lesson to his son. She wasn't sure how much of the techno-talk Hayden was really absorbing, but he clearly loved being with Mitch. Hayden dogged his heels like a puppy, anxious to keep up, to get noticed, to be talked to and instructed, and to have his constant questions answered. Mitch seemed okay with all of this, juggling the multiple roles of teacher, disciplinarian, buddy and father as if he'd spent years with Hayden instead of just days.

While Hayden held the binoculars to his frowning face, Mitch straightened and gave Kate an inquisitive look. "Tired?"

"Me? I had a nap before lunch, remember?"

"If we walk up on that ridge, we'll be able to see for miles. There's bound to be caribou down in the valley, and maybe a wolf or two, but it's close to a mile of hiking, or better."

"Then we better get walking."

Kate enjoyed the push of the wind, the smell of the cool clean air and the magnificence of the wilderness itself. The land was charged with energy, every living thing packing as much regeneration into each summer moment as it could. The same energy flowed through her, like a current that connected her to the network of life, the same web that linked all of them together on this planet. She watched Hayden struggling manfully after Mitch as Thor ran tireless circles around all of them. As if sensing when the moment of exhaustion had been reached, Mitch stopped and swept Hayden up onto his shoulders for the final half-mile hike up the side of the hill.

When they crested the summit, the wind tore her breath away. Mitch set Hayden down and pointed, and following his arm Kate saw the small band of caribou ranging in the broad, undulating valley below. There was a narrow body of water, and they were edging along it, grazing on ground cover as they went.

Mitch scanned the valley with the binoculars. "I see wolves," he said, his words setting Hayden to jumping up and down. "There. Just on the north edge of that water. See those bushes? Just on the other side of them. They're watching the caribou the same as we are. Use the binoculars like I showed you and tell me what you see." He handed Hayden the binoculars but the boy was so excited he couldn't find the pond, let alone the bushes.

"Nothing!" he wailed, close to tears.

"Okay then, lower the glasses and look where I'm pointing. Can you see the little pond and the bushes on the left? Just above them, see those three spots? Those are wolves."

"Wolves, Mumma!"

Kate saw them at the same time Hayden did and felt a tingling thrill. Even as distant dots, dark against the tundra, it was something to spot wolves in the wild. Hayden lifted the binoculars again, but it was no easy feat to focus them across the distance on such a small target. His frustration only added to the difficulty of holding the binoculars steady, and Mitch rose to his feet. "Never mind, pard. We might get lucky and see them a little closer up."

Hayden lowered the glasses, eyes wide. "Down there?"

Mitch shook his head. "Thor would start chasing caribou if we got too close. Besides, we have to check out that lodge before the sun sets."

Kate took one long last look at the primitive scene below and was turning to follow Mitch and Hayden when a sudden and strong gust of wind struck her from behind and knocked her off her feet. She fell to her knees and cried out as she felt the wig flip neatly off her head, landing in front of her and tumbling away in a wind-borne sprint down the hillside. The appearance of what he perceived to be a dark, fast moving animal kicked Thor into high gear. He lunged snatching the wig out of midair and shaking it fiercely in his jaw before tossing it down and pouncing on it again. Before Kate could stand she had witnessed the swift destruction of what had been a very expensive head of hair.

When Mitch figured out what it was that Thor was attempting to shred, he spun around and met her shocked gaze with his own. Too late, he regained his wits. "Thor, no! Leave it!"

Kate watched as Thor dodged out of reach, wig in his jaws, and Mitch took up the chase. It didn't last long. Thor smartly realized that although he could run circles around the man all day long, the man was mad, and so, because he respected the man's anger, the dog dropped the wig and retreated up the slope to where Hayden stood. Mitch lifted the remains of Kate's wig off the tundra. He held it aloft, clearly and literally at loose ends as to what his next action should be, so Kate helped him out. She took a breath, lifted her chin and marched down to take the wig out of his hand. A closer examination proved that Thor had effectively disposed of the threat, so she stuffed the remnants into her jacket pocket and heaved a philosophical sigh.

"Good thing I brought along a warm hat."

THE PARK SERVICE director's lodge was beautiful, tucked into a secluded setting high on a timbered knoll overlooking Canyon Creek. No expense had been spared in the design and construction of the log building. Huge windows let the wilderness vistas inside and a big fieldstone fireplace dominated the living room. There was a four-person wood-fired hot tub sunk into the corner of the cedar deck, four spacious bedrooms, a modern kitchen complete with a microwave and a garden bath with a two-person Jacuzzi-jetted tub overlooking what had to be the best bathroom view in America. Native American art and artifacts adorned the rooms and woven wool rugs covered the gleaming hardwood floors. Kate wandered through the rooms and imagined what it must be like to have a second home like this. She decided that for her, at least, it would make facing the day-to-day rat race of city life far more difficult, knowing that on the edge of the wilderness a place of peace and beauty sat empty.

"It's nice," she said in response to Mitch's questioning look when she finally joined him and Hayden out on the deck. "Then again, so is our lakeside tent."

"But there's no shower at the campground and it's a Friday night. The park bus'll come through and the place is sure to be crowded with campers by suppertime," Mitch pointed out.

She studied his bruised face. A hot shower would undoubtedly help to ease his aches and pains. "Maybe we could shower here and sleep back at the tent."

"Or we could pack up our gear at the campsite and be back

here in an hour, living in rustic luxury. You could stay here and have another nap or sit in the sun out on the porch. Hayden and I'll go back and do all the packing up."

Kate felt a stab of pain. The wig had been a vanity, true, but already she sensed a detachment from Mitch, as if the sight of her without it brought the reality of her cancer too close for comfort. He was backing away from her, and it hurt. "If you'd rather I stay behind, I will."

"I wouldn't rather you stayed behind. I just thought…"

"It's okay. I'll stay. You and Hayden go."

She sat down on one of the deck chairs to make her point, but his expression remained uncertain. "Are you sure?"

"Yes," she said, fairly snapping the word, then she softened her tone. "The two of you go ahead. I'll enjoy some quiet time by myself. Maybe I will have another nap."

"Okay then, we'll be back soon and I'll fix supper, the gastronomic tour de force I promised you. C'mon, Hayden. You can help me take down the tent. Who knows, maybe those wolves will cross the road in front of us on the drive."

Kate tipped her head back and closed her eyes. She listened to their receding footsteps, heard the doors slam shut and the old truck sputter to life, then the engine noise slowly faded into the distance and the silence blew in on the wind, along with the unbearable loneliness. She'd never minded being alone before. In fact, except for Hayden's company, she preferred it most of the time. Or at least she had, until very recently. But it was different now. Everything was changing.

Mitch walked away, and she yearned to follow.

She was turning into the weak, clinging and dependent sort of woman she'd always despised.

CHAPTER TWELVE

MITCH WAS DISTURBED BY Kate's change of mood. As he drove back toward the campground, he tried to figure it out. He knew it had something to do with that damn wig. She was upset about losing it and didn't like to be seen without it. She had no idea how exotically beautiful she looked without hair. Not many women could pull that off, but she could, and did. Hell, if she walked down any city street looking like that, half the women would go home and shave their heads and the other half would wish they had the nerve.

Last night she'd asked if he'd mind very much if she moved her bed next to his. At first he wasn't sure he'd heard her correctly, but he'd pushed fatigue away, propped himself on his elbows, and said hell no, he wouldn't mind a bit, and then as she started to move he beat her to it and moved his own bed next to hers. He thought that would be it, but no. She'd cuddled up next to him in her sleeping bag, as close as she could get.

"I'm afraid of the nightmares," she'd confessed.

K. C. Jones wasn't afraid of anything she could face down, but bad dreams snuck up in the night and caught a person at their most vulnerable. So he'd pulled her into his arms and she'd fallen asleep with her head on his chest. Her head with its glossy, short-haired wig. Now that she'd lost that prop, he guessed she'd probably never snuggle with him again. That was that. Everything would be at arm's length with averted eyes from this point onward, all because of a damned wig!

"I guess your mom's upset because Thor ate her wig," he said to Hayden.

"When Mumma got sick her hair fell out," Hayden informed Mitch in his serious way. "It made her sad."

"Well, I think your mom's beautiful just the way she is, but her hair's going to grow back."

"Even if she stays sick?"

Mitch hesitated. He was now facing his first truly difficult question as a father. How to respond? "I don't know," he said, deciding honesty was the best policy. "I don't know enough about that stuff. But I think your mom's going to get better. She's a pretty tough gal."

Wolves didn't cross the road in front of them on the way back to Wonder Lake, but while Mitch was taking down the tent a moose waded out into a cove across the lake from them, galvanizing Hayden to race down to the water's edge with Thor and watch, transfixed, until most of the camp gear had been stowed in the back of the truck. Mitch had been right about the Friday night crowd. The shuttle bus had delivered enough young backpacking campers to fill all the sites and destroy the illusion that he, Kate and Hayden had the whole park to themselves. Still, they'd had last night, and last night had been pretty special.

A little under two hours after leaving, they were back at the Kantishna lodge. The sun had set and the clouds were moving in from the south, cloaking the Alaska Range and the mighty Denali in a shroud of dark gray. Kate was still sitting on the porch, awaiting their return. It was getting chilly, and she had pulled on her black hat and zipped up her parka.

"Mumma! We saw a big moose!" Hayden raced up the steps and plastered himself against her. Kate gave him a hug and raised her eyes to Mitch, who was ascending the steps at a more sedate pace carrying their duffel bags.

"It was big," he agreed, relieved that her mood seemed to have improved enough to allow a smile. "Sorry it took us so long but moose watching slowed things down a little. I'll get a fire going in the fireplace and start our gourmet meal. I don't suppose you checked to see if there was any hot water?"

Now that she was wearing the hat, she could look him in the eye again. "I already took a shower, but there's plenty left. Why don't you take one now and I'll get things started here. Hayden can give me a hand unpacking the groceries. We have a refrigerator, we might as well use it." She gave him a gentle push when he didn't move fast enough to suit her. "Go on. That hot water will make you feel like a new man."

Mitch deposited the duffel bags on the living-room floor and retreated to the bathroom with his kit. He didn't argue with her logic. A shower would feel pretty good about now.

IT STARTED TO RAIN even before Mitch emerged from his shower. Kate had barely retrieved the food out of the back of the truck by the time the wind picked up and the clouds let loose. She put all the perishables into the propane refrigerator and lit a couple of gas lamps against the gloom. Then she laid a fire in the fireplace and found a book of matches on the mantel and, within minutes, the warm cheery flames made the idea of a rainy night spent inside the snug log lodge seem wonderful. She was glad they weren't in the canvas wall tent, as much as she had liked it. This was far more pleasant.

She was cutting vegetables when Mitch appeared, hair

damp, wearing a fresh pair of jeans and flannel shirt. "Couldn't shave around all the cuts yet," he apologized, padding into the kitchen in stocking feet into the kitchen to peer over her shoulder.

"I'm fixing the salad." She gave him a pointed look. "You're doing the gastronomic entrée, right?"

"Right after I pour you some wine. Or would you prefer Ranger Rick's baked apple brandy?"

"I'm sure the home brew is delicious, but it might be a little strong for my stomach."

She continued making the salad while Mitch found a genuine wineglass in a cupboard and worked the cork out of the bottle. "I'm sorry about the wig," he said as he handed her the glass.

His words took her by surprise. "It wasn't your fault."

"Thor wrecked it, and he's kind of my dog, which makes me responsible. I'll buy you another one to replace it. There's a place in Fairbanks right across the street from a pool hall I sometimes play at. It's called Big Wigs. When we leave here, I'll take you there, if you want."

Kate stared at him for a few moments to see if he was pulling her leg. "Big Wigs?"

He nodded. "I've never been inside, but they have all kinds of wigs in the window."

She felt the laughter building inside of her. "Are they all big?"

"I don't know how to judge something like that," he responded tactfully. "I mean, I don't know all that much about wigs."

He was so serious and sincere that the laughter won out. Kate laughed so hard she spilled some of her wine and had to set her glass on the counter. When she could finally catch her breath, she wiped her eyes on her shirttail and assessed him cautiously, the same way he was looking at her.

"I thought you were upset about it," he said.

"I was. Believe me, I never wanted anyone to see me like this, bald and sick and ugly, struggling with cancer. I wanted to hide it from everyone else and from myself, too, but when I saw Thor shaking that wig and ripping it apart like it was a live animal..." Kate swallowed another eruption of laughter. "I don't know. It put everything into a different perspective. It took me a while to come to terms with it, but I am sick. I am struggling with cancer. I am ugly, and that wig was a farce, and—"

"Whoa," Mitch interrupted, setting down his beer bottle and closing his hands on her shoulders. "You are so off base here. You might be sick right now, but you're going to get better. And you couldn't be ugly if you worked full-time at it." His voice unexpectedly lowered a notch and became husky with emotion. "You're beautiful, Captain Katherine Carolyn Jones, with hair or without. I'd take you either way, and gladly."

Kate felt her heart speed up as she looked into his eyes. "Take me?" she echoed.

She saw his flicker of uncertainty as she pressed for clarification.

"Take you fishing," he said, landing on his feet like a cat. "Wolf watching. Bear tracking. Camping. Touristing. Matter of fact, I thought we might go for a short hike tomorrow, up to Wickersham Dome..."

"Sure," she said, the laughter that had filled her only moments before draining away, leaving her hollow inside. "That sounds nice." She pulled away from him and turned back to the salad she'd been making. "You'd better start cooking your gourmet meal. It's getting late, and I'm sure Hayden's hungry."

THEY ATE DINNER by lamplight while the rain drummed hard on the roof. At 11:00 p.m., Hayden's eyelids were drooping, though he protested leaving the old-fashioned puzzle games he'd found on the bookshelf. The park service CEO must have kids or grandkids. Kate supervised Hayden's nighttime washing up and tucked him into one of the four bedrooms that had two twin beds, and he was asleep before she could bend over and kiss his cheek. Thor sprawled on the floor beside him with a contented sigh and gazed up at Kate without remorse.

"I'm not mad," she told him wryly. "Don't lose any sleep over it. In the end, the wig would've had to go."

Mitch had washed the dishes and tidied the kitchen in her absence, and then shut down the diesel generator in the shed out back, leaving them to the sound of the rain and the wind and the soft glow of gas lamps and firelight. He'd been eyeing her warily all night, as if she might suddenly snap and bite. She sat on the couch near the warmth of the fire and curled her legs beneath her, nursing her glass of wine and wearing her black jogging hat. He retrieved another beer and dropped onto the couch next to her, gazing into the fire for a few moments before shifting those keen eyes and zapping her wide-awake.

"So tell me. If the wig was a farce, what does that make the hat?"

She sat up, cradling her wineglass. "Warm," she replied in self-defense. "It can get kind of drafty up top when you don't have all that much hair."

"You didn't eat much supper."

"Neither did you."

"There's a phone here, in the kitchen."

"I saw it," Kate said.

"I'll call the park supervisor in the morning and thank him for the use of his lodge."

"That would be the polite thing for us to do."

"I could call the governor, too, and thank him for putting together the donor drive."

Kate drew a short breath. "Yes, I suppose you could."

"Then there's the chief of Umiak. He had some good points."

"He certainly did."

"You suppose your big boss would take a phone call from me?"

Kate felt herself clench up. "Maybe."

"Think the world might sit up and take notice if we all got together for a powwow about saving people's lives with a bone marrow drive?"

Mitch held her gaze for a long moment before she tore her eyes away and looked back into the fire. Her heart was pounding painfully and it was hard to breathe. She hated to air her private affairs, and yet once again, Mitch was right. This wasn't just about her. Children were dying. Children as precious to their families as Hayden was to her. If she could help them somehow, some way, wasn't she obligated? And what of the adults diagnosed like she had been? What about Tuttu? Maybe her twin brother was still alive and someone might know where he was. What about all the families and friends who agonized over their loved ones' fate and fought the battle alongside them, hoping for miracles that might or might not happen, hoping for bone marrow donors to step up to the plate and give the gift of life?

Kate felt the prickle of tears. "Maybe."

Mitch finished his beer slowly and wondered what Kate was thinking about as she gazed into the flames. They sat side by side on the couch with no more than two feet separating them, but it felt like much more. He wanted to reach out and touch her because he sensed that touch was what she truly needed but he didn't dare and he silently cursed his cowardice. What if she did die? What if he were to allow himself to fall in love with someone who had only a few months to live? A man would be a fool to open himself up to so much pain.

The smartest thing he could do was to keep his distance.

Two feet was just about right.

Still, he wondered what she was thinking.

"Penny for your thoughts," he said.

She stirred, shifted her eyes briefly to his, then gazed back into the flames. "I was thinking about this eighteen-year-old girl who was in the room next to mine at the hospital. Her name was Gail Anne and she wanted to be a concert pianist. She'd been in there for a long time. None of the treatments were working and no suitable bone marrow donor was found. She'd become so weak she was bedridden, but she was so sure they were going to let her go home this spring. She missed her dog and her friends and couldn't wait to see them again. I used to visit with her a lot. She asked me what song cheered me up the most, and I had to think about it a while but I told her it was the theme song from *Annie*. When I was having a down day she'd play that song for me."

"She sounds like a nice girl," Mitch said.

"Gail loved Hayden. She'd let him sit on her bed and play on her keyboard with her. The day the doctors told her she'd probably be sterile from all the chemotherapy and wouldn't be able to have children, she cried like her heart would break. She told me I was so lucky to have such a beautiful boy.

"On the last Friday in April they moved her upstairs," Kate continued, speaking softly. "All her things, the special music box that belonged to her grandmother, the stuffed dog that looked like her dog Scout, her electronic piano, her favorite photographs, all gone. The very next day one of the nurses who came in to check my IV looked like she'd been crying. When I asked her what was wrong she said that after they'd taken Gail upstairs and settled her into the intensive care unit, the doctors finally told her she wouldn't be going home. So she told her mother she was tired, closed her eyes and died."

Shaken, Mitch pushed off the couch to put another log on the fire, then finished off his beer and carried the bottle into the kitchen. Only after returning to the living room did he dare look at her. He thought she'd be crying, but she was just staring into the flames with that same pensive expression. He sat back down with that safe two feet of distance separating them and tried to think of something to say, but couldn't. He no longer had to wonder what she was thinking about, but mortality was a topic he avoided whenever possible.

"I'm not afraid of dying anymore, Mitch," she murmured.

Time to change the subject. "Look, you're going to beat this, and tomorrow we're going to show Hayden Wickersham Dome and maybe see some more wolves, and we still have to find a grizzly—"

"I used to be," she continued, ignoring him, "but now that I know you'll take care of Hayden, I'm not."

"You're not going to die."

She looked at him with a faint smile. "We're all going to

die someday, and I don't have a problem with that, but I don't want to die in a hospital the way Gail Anne did."

Mitch could feel the fight-or-flight response kicking in, but he didn't have a clue which way to go. "You won't. You're going to get that bone marrow transplant and get better."

"All she wanted was to go home. What's so wrong with letting someone die at home if they're going to die anyway? She wanted to see her friends and hug her dog." This time her voice broke and he saw the shine of tears before she looked away. "Even if a bone marrow donor is found, there's a seventy percent chance that the transplant procedure won't be successful, and if everything goes badly I'll be so sick I won't have the strength to get out of that bed and walk out of the hospital, and it scares me to death to think I might die that way."

Goddamn, he was in way over his head. There wasn't anything he could say and he was too close to her now to ever be able to run away so he did the only thing he could do. He erased the safe, protective distance between them on the couch and put his arm around her. When she turned into him with a muffled sob, he put his other arm around her and held her tight and tried to remember that men weren't supposed to shed tears.

"I don't usually cry," she wept, her voice muffled against his flannel shirt.

"I know."

"I keep thinking about how young she was, about all the dreams she had and all the things she was going to do and the two babies she wanted to have, a boy and girl, and how they told her she couldn't. Why would they tell her that, when they knew she wasn't getting out of there?"

"I don't know."

"And I keep thinking about her dog, waiting for her. Scout

must wonder why she never came back home. They took her upstairs and she never went home."

"That's not going to happen to you." He rubbed her back as if she were a small child and felt her body shake with sobs.

"What if they won't let me leave?"

"If you get so sick you can't move and the doctors tell you that you can't ever go home again, and you want out of there, I'll take you out. I swear to God I will. I'll lift you out of that bed and carry you out of that hospital and take you home."

"They wouldn't let you."

"They couldn't stop me if they tried," Mitch assured her, realizing all at once that it was true. "All you have to do is call me. As long as I'm alive, you don't have to worry about dying in a hospital room. I'll come get you, anytime, anywhere. I promise you that."

CHAPTER THIRTEEN

BY MORNING, THE RAIN had stopped but it was still gloomy and overcast at 6:00 a.m. Mitch was the only one awake. He made a pot of coffee in a French press he found in a kitchen cupboard and built another fire in the fireplace. Kate slept through it all, curled beneath the blanket on the couch. She hadn't even moved when he got up. He walked outside with his mug and stood on the deck and guessed he was staring right at Denali but the entire mountain range was still invisible. Canyon Creek was frothy with white water after the rain, thundering over a series of steep falls below the cabin. A raven glided past on the canyon currents, wary and watchful, looking for its next meal. Mitch finished his first cup of coffee on the deck, and the second he drank while making phone calls, the first to Admiral Ransom Gates, whose secretary put him on hold for ten long minutes before the admiral himself came on the line, transmitting from some top-secret locale.

Mitch introduced himself and came straight to the point. "I'm a friend of Captain Kate Jones's and I need to ask a favor of you. We appreciate your offer to sponsor a bone marrow drive. The thing is, we could test every volunteer in the Navy and in Alaska—and it would be great to get those people on the bone marrow registry—but in my opinion Kate's best chance of finding a donor would be to test people on the

Crow reservation in Montana, and the towns around it and near where she grew up. Does the Navy ever send their medical staff that far inland?"

The admiral didn't pause more than a second. "I think it could be arranged. I'll make some calls. Do you have a number where you can be reached?"

Mitch gave it to him. "There's one other thing, sir. The sooner this donor drive happens, the better, and the speed that they work at in the lab getting the results could make the difference between life and death for Kate."

"I understand. I'll let you know when we can schedule it."

"Thank you, sir."

"Take good care of her. She's the best of the best."

"Yes, sir, I know."

And that was just the first call.

It was Hayden who finally woke Kate by crawling onto the couch beside her and burrowing under the blanket. She'd been having the strangest dreams. Good dreams. So good she didn't want to wake up, but when she did and discovered Hayden nestling into her arms she kissed the top of his head and forgave him his trespass.

"I guess I'm the sleepyhead this morning," she murmured.

"Wake up, Mumma, we have to look for grizzly bears."

She tightened her arms around him. "Grizzly bears. Is that what we're looking for?"

"And wolves."

"Mmm."

"Don't sleep, Mumma. Open your eyes. Mitch said it might rain again."

"It's good to sleep late on a rainy morning."

"But we have to find the bears and wolves before it rains."

"Why?"

"Because Mitch said so."

"Well, Mumma says sleep is good."

"But Mitch said we might see bears and wolves and witches' domes."

"Oh, he did, did he?"

"Wake all the way up, Mumma."

"I can't. Are you sure it isn't already raining?"

She heard Thor's paws and a man's tread on the porch steps, and then Mitch was in the room and there was no hiding from the morning, nor did she particularly want to hide when she opened her eyes and saw him standing there. "What time is it?"

"Ten o'clock," he said.

Kate was shocked. She never slept past six. Never.

"And it just started to rain again," Mitch added.

She propped herself up on her elbows and looked out the big glass windows fronting the canyon. Sure enough, raindrops were streaking the glass. "Good. We can sleep in all day long and listen to it on the roof."

"But I want to find a bear." Hayden slid off the couch, clearly not buying into Kate's sedentary plan. "Mitch said we could."

"Then you'd better get dressed," Kate advised. "You can't go bear hunting in the rain wearing pajamas."

Hayden stampeded for his bedroom with Thor at his heels while Mitch brought her a cup of coffee from the kitchen. Kate took it with a murmured thanks and sat up, swinging her legs over the edge of the couch.

"The weather's supposed to clear tomorrow," Mitch said, dropping down beside her. "We can hide out here today. I've been going through the cookbooks in the kitchen and I've found a recipe I'm going to try."

She cast him a questioning glance. "What?"

"Barbecued bear ribs." His expression was deadpan, but she was catching on.

She crinkled her nose. "Is hunting allowed in the park?"

"Not in the wilderness section, where most of the tourists go, but it is here. Don't worry—not this time of year. Most of the shooting is done in fall and winter."

It felt so natural to lean into him, and his arm draped around her as if it belonged there. "I suppose they use this lodge as a deluxe hunting camp."

"I suppose." Mitch pried off his boots and lifted his feet to the coffee table. "I've flown a lot of hunters into this little town. Probably some of them stayed here as guests, same as us. Anyhow, the cookbooks seem to be all game-oriented, and all we brought along to eat was factory-farmed beef and chicken."

"It's my turn to cook. You pick out a recipe you like and I'll follow it. The beef and chicken will become wild game. They have no choice."

"I made some phone calls while you were sleeping. I got in touch with Dan Wills, the park supervisor. Nice guy. Said he was glad we moved into the lodge before the rain started. It looks like we're on for a meeting with the governor. He thinks for maximum impact it should be held at the Anchorage hospital because there are three leukemia patients being treated there in between their trips to the same hospital you were in. I told him I'd run it by you, but that you're here on vacation and the last place you want to be is in a hospital."

Kate was quiet for a few moments, thinking this over.

"None of us wants to be sick and hospitalized, but sometimes we don't have a choice."

"He has the Blood Bank of Alaska on board for the drive, and the Red Cross, as well. He's working on getting the test kits to the villages of Umiak and Kotzebue and all the other major villages along with a team who can take the blood and fly it back for immediate testing. I volunteered for that. He's going to contact the chief of Umiak personally, and the friend of Tuttu's. I gave him the contact numbers."

"When is this meeting scheduled?"

"Monday. That gives us two whole days, and if he comes here, it could be even longer."

"The governor's right. The meeting should take place at the hospital, right in the patients' rooms. If this is a push to make people aware, they need to see how it really is in a cancer ward, and the press should go to Seattle and interview the patients and their families at the cancer research center. They're the real heroes."

"I don't doubt that, but you're my personal hero and Hayden's, too, and besides, I'd just as soon keep you in Alaska as long as possible."

Kate felt her heart lose its rhythm for a moment. She thought about the strange, vivid dreams she'd had the night before, then raised her hand to her head. The warm ski hat was gone and her head was bare. She leaned forward and looked between the couch and the coffee table. The hat was lying on the floor, right where she'd flung it in her dream. She looked back at Mitch. "Did you say those very same words to me last night?"

"We said a lot of things to each other last night."

Caught off balance, Kate set her cup of coffee down and composed her racing thoughts, or tried to. Some of her strange dreams had been somewhat sexual in nature. Very sexual, in fact, and Mitch had stayed with her on the couch, all night long. She'd woken several times, each time reassured by his strong, solid presence. She remembered that. But as to the dreams, had they really and truly been just dreams?

Or had he…

Had they actually…?

Kate sat up and cleared her throat. "Did we…?"

His frank honesty was disarming. "We did," he nodded gravely. "We talked most of the night. That's why you're so tired. Don't you remember?"

Kate slumped back onto the couch. "Of course I do," she lied. Lord, but she was getting good at telling lies.

"I spoke to Admiral Gates, too," Mitch said.

Kate sat back up. "You *did?*"

"He called back a little while ago. He's in Washington and will be for the next week or so, but he wants you to call him."

"He *does?*"

"He wants you to keep him up to speed with what's going on with you. He wants to know when you get a donor. He wants to be there when you walk out of that hospital for the last time."

Kate slumped back again, stunned. "My God."

Mitch nodded. "He even talks like one. Too bad he won't be there on Monday."

"I don't know about this meeting with the governor." Kate felt a surge of panic. "I mean, I just don't know if I can—"

"Of course you can. Think about Gail Anne, and Tuttu, and all the other people you can help by speaking up on their behalf. Think about all the lives that might be saved, including your own. Think about watching Hayden grow up.

Watching him graduate from high school. From college. Fall in love. Catch a really big fish."

Kate gave him a skeptical glance. "Catch a fish?"

"Sure. Catching a really big fish is a big moment in a guy's life."

"Right up there with falling in love?" She watched him scramble with this one, then drew a deep breath and let it out with a whoosh. "Big Wigs," she said.

"What?"

"If I have to meet with the governor, I'll need to pay a visit to Big Wigs."

Mitch gave her a look she couldn't quite fathom. "You look great just the way you are. You look like the most gorgeous woman in the world who just happens to be fighting leukemia, which is pretty much the situation here." And then he reached out his hand, laid it atop her head and gave her a very gentle, warm caress. "You don't need a wig, Kate Jones. You already have everything you need, and then some. Besides, right now you look the way a Navy shavetail should look." His fingers drifted down to catch her chin and tip it up so she was looking directly into his eyes. "How about some breakfast? I'm cooking."

Kate lost herself in his gaze, wishing he'd just stay put and cuddle with her while the rain came down and the words flowed back and forth between them until the past four and a half years were filled up with all that had been missing. She hadn't realized until now just how empty she'd been. She didn't need food.

She needed Mitch.

"I'm not that hungry. I can wait until lunchtime."

"Maybe," Mitch said, pushing off the couch, "but after an

hour or two of searching for grizzly bears in the rain, you'll be wishing you ate my scrambled eggs and bacon."

HAYDEN WASN'T PUT OFF by the wet conditions. He enjoyed stomping through puddles and getting his feet soaked, and Mitch was glad to see it. He'd hate to think that any son of his would shy away from the outdoors just because the weather wasn't perfect. While Kate had an after-lunch nap, he and Hayden filled the wood box, then took the fishing gear up the canyon trail looking for an opportune place to cast a line, which wasn't that easy because the rain made the ground slippery and the last thing he wanted was for Hayden to fall into the water. After about thirty minutes of searching, he picked a nice level spot and assembled his pack rod.

"See that circle of water below that big rock?" he said, tying on an appropriate fly. "I bet there's a big fish waiting there and he's going to bite this fly the minute I cast it in there."

"Because he's hungry?"

"You bet. These fish are all hungry. We'll catch him and bring him home for your mom."

"But, if he's hungry, what will Mumma feed him?"

"Well…" Mitch stripped off some line in preparation for the cast. He glanced down at Hayden, who was watching him with that serious expression. "Fish food," he said. "They'll eat just about anything. Bread, meat, vegetables, eggs. You name it."

Hayden thought about this while Mitch cast his fly into the eddy. "Would a fish eat a fish?"

"Oh, yeah, that's their favorite food. Big fish eat little fish all the time."

"They eat their own babies?"

"Hmm…" He was treading into unknown territory here.

From what little he knew about early childhood years, other than his own, everything he said and did could have a profound effect on the future development of this kid. This was kind of intimidating stuff. He'd have to remember to modify his behavior around Hayden. "They try to avoid that. They want their own kind to survive, just like the rest of us."

The rain came down harder. He cast into the eddy several times while Hayden watched, but the fly generated no interest. "That big old fish probably already ate his lunch," he said, giving up on that spot and moving downstream toward another likely hole. For an hour they prowled along the bank, getting wetter by the moment in spite of the rain gear. Finally Mitch called it quits. "I better get you back before your mom gets worried. Where'd Thor run off to?" He looked around for the black dog but he was nowhere to be seen. "C'mon, Hayden, my guess is he's either lying beside the fireplace or on top of your bed."

They trudged up the path, the rain and the creek filling the air with sound, deafening them to the barking until they were almost upon the dog, who was standing in the middle of the trail not far from where they'd been fishing. Thor's hackles were raised and the way he was braced on all four paws gave Mitch all the warning he needed. He grabbed Hayden's shoulder and turned the boy around. "New plan, pard. We're going back the way we just came and we'll hang out for a while, until Thor tells us it's safe to use the trail."

Thor never looked back, just kept barking as they retreated down the path. When they'd gone a fair distance, Mitch paused. What now? Hayden was soaking wet, but the way Thor'd been acting, there was a bear close by. While he'd wanted to show Hayden a grizzly, this wasn't how he'd planned to do it. Coming face-to-face with one on the same narrow path wasn't such a good idea.

"Why was Thor mad?" Hayden asked.

"He was telling us there was a bear up ahead."

"A bear?" Hayden perked up.

"Probably. But bears are best viewed at a great distance, so we'll just stay put until Thor comes and gets us." What he didn't add was that bears hated dogs, and if Thor came and got them now, it was possible the bear would be right behind. Mitch thought the smartest thing would be to build a little fire, but after searching unsuccessfully for dry tinder he gave up on that idea. Five minutes passed, then ten. Twenty. Hayden was starting to shiver. The burden of fatherhood grew heavier. Hayden was his responsibility. Gone were the days of only having to take care of himself and worry about no one. His son was cold. It was time to move. "Okay, you keep behind me. Right behind me. We're going to try this again. Ready?"

The boy nodded. Mitch started up the path. They'd have made better time if he carried Hayden, but he knew the walking would warm the boy up. When they came to the place where Thor had made his stand, the trail was empty. Any tracks that might have been left behind had been lost in the downpour. No way to see what had happened or what had been there…and no sign of Thor.

"You stay right behind me," Mitch repeated.

Hayden nodded again through the blur of rain.

For the last quarter mile of steep uphill climb, Mitch carried him on his shoulders. The lodge, when it came into view, was a sweet sight, smoke pluming from the big chimney. They burst inside, dripping wet, welcoming the warmth and the smell of something delicious cooking. Kate was in the kitchen, lamps lit against the dull day, and beyond the wide pass-through, Mitch could see the slow yellow lick of flames around a big log in the fireplace.

"You two catch anything, besides pneumonia?" Kate asked, stripping Hayden out of his rain gear.

"Nope," Mitch said. "And we lost Thor. I was hoping he'd be here."

Kate frowned as she hung the dripping garments on a peg beside the door. "He isn't. I've been right in the kitchen so I would've seen if he'd come onto the porch. How long has he been missing?" She grabbed a clean towel and began drying Hayden's hair.

"An hour or so. I think he might have been trying to ward off a grizzly that was in the vicinity when we were headed back."

Kate's brisk toweling faltered and she glanced up. "You saw a bear?"

"Not exactly, but we might have if Thor hadn't warned us." He lowered his voice and leaned toward Kate. "Thing is, the last time he went one-on-one with a grizzly, he barely survived."

"He wouldn't do that again, would he?"

"I don't know, but I'd better go look for him, just in case."

"You get changed into some dry clothes," Kate told Hayden, and when he'd left the room she fixed Mitch with a serious stare. "If there's a bear out there, I'd rather you stay here. Thor'll be back. Give him some time."

"I won't be that long. The spot's not that far from here."

"Mitch."

He met her stare. "I won't be long," he said. He opened the

door and stepped back into the cold rain before she could say anything more, but the look in her eyes haunted him as he started back down the trail.

WHEN MITCH didn't return for a while, Kate knew something bad had happened. She had walked out onto the porch dozens of times in the past two hours, listening in vain for any noise over the muted thunder of the creek, swollen from the rains. Shivering, she'd return to the kitchen to stand watch at the big glass door. Supper preparations were forgotten and she fed Hayden a bowl of cereal and some toast. He was just as happy with that as he would be with a gourmet meal.

At 7:00 p.m. the rain let up. By eight, the clouds had blown free of the mountain range and sunshine swept across the valley. Still no Mitch. Kate became convinced that both he and the dog had both been mauled to death by the grizzly. Should she call the park supervisor?

She was hunting for the envelope that contained his invitation for them to use his lodge along with a contact number when she heard steps on the porch. She ran to the door and flung it open. Thor plodded in, ears flattened in fatigue, and gave Hayden a brief greeting before flopping down on the rug in front of the fireplace and passing out. Mitch's footsteps were equally weary as he reached the top step and paused there to catch his breath.

"We're back," he said. "I hope you saved some supper."

"You said you wouldn't be long," Kate began, then bit back more heated words and instead drew a shaky breath. "What happened?"

"It wasn't a bear."

"What then? You've been gone nearly three hours!"

Mitch came inside and she closed the door behind him. He

drew off his wet coat and hung it, dripping, from a wall peg. He pried off his waterlogged boots and stripped off his soaking wet socks and threw both out on the porch. "Damn, but I'm tired," he muttered, hanging his ball cap on another peg and finally looking her in the eye with a boyish grin. "It was wolves, Kate. A pack of wolves. They'd killed a caribou, or maybe a bear did the killing, I don't know, but the wolves were on the carcass and that's where Thor was, only when I finally found him, the wolves spotted me and bolted and he ran off with the pack. He went with them, just like he belonged." Mitch gave an incredulous laugh as he opened the refrigerator and grabbed a beer. "So I ran after him."

Kate felt her heart rate accelerate with her anger. "No doubt you thought you could catch up to an animal that runs over twenty-five miles an hour."

He gave her a long stare, then shrugged. "I didn't know what else to do. I figured they'd tear Thor apart when they got over being spooked by me. So I ran and hollered, hollered and ran...and you're really mad at me, aren't you?"

"I thought you'd been killed by that bear."

"Never saw a bear, but Kate, damn! I ran with the wolves."

She turned her back on him and crossed to the stove, switching on the burner under the cast-iron pan.

"I don't know what changed Thor's mind about joining the pack, but all at once he was coming over the hill toward me at full speed, so I turned around and we came back."

She heard the sound of the beer bottle being opened and poured some olive oil into the pan, spreading it over the bottom with a spatula. "I thought I'd make a chicken stir-fry," she said. "The rice is already cooked and everything else is prepped and ready to go. This won't take long."

"I'll just take a quick shower and change into something dry," he said, and she heard him leave the kitchen. She blew out her breath and blinked away the dry sting of tears. He was totally without remorse. It never occurred to him that she'd be worried, or wonder where he was and what was taking him so long. He was irresponsible and immature. Men never grew up, they just turned into older and older boys. When they died they probably spent eternity playing with their Tonka toys in the great sandbox in the sky.

She focused on cooking the stir-fry but she was still seething when he came back into the kitchen after his shower, Hayden at his heels, begging Mitch to tell the wolf story one more time. "Mumma, Mitch ran with wolves!"

"Yes, I know," she said, turning off the burner and sliding the pan to the side.

"Did they howl?"

"No, but they might tonight. We'll listen for them," Mitch said. He leaned over Kate's shoulder to peek at the food and she stiffened. "Anything I can help you with, Captain Jones?"

"Nothing," she snapped, dishing rice onto two plates.

"Care for wine with dinner?"

"No, thanks. I'll stick with water." She added the stir-fry on top of the rice and put the plates on the table. "Hayden's already eaten. He prefers cereal to stir-fry."

"Really?" Mitch fixed Hayden with a stern look. "Cereal isn't going to make you big enough and strong enough to run with wolves, Hayden. You sure you don't want some of the good stuff?"

"Can I have some, Mumma?" Hayden gave her that pitiful begging-dog stare.

Kate felt her blood pressure ratchet a few points higher. She got another plate and fixed it for Hayden. "Did you wash your hands?" she said, putting it down. He turned and ran for the bathroom. She poured him a glass of milk and put it beside his plate, not that he'd drink it.

"Still mad at me, huh?" Mitch said, dropping into a seat.

"I'm not mad."

"Whatever you say. This looks great. Sure you don't want a glass of wine?"

"Positive." She sat down, took a sip from her water glass and placed her paper towel in her lap. She watched as Hayden came back into the room and shimmied into his chair, eyes bright with anticipation. "Mumma, can we go see wolves tomorrow?"

"Maybe."

"Mitch says if they get hungry we might see them."

"Eat your stir-fry. You told me you wanted it," Kate said.

"Why are you so mad, Mumma?"

"I'm not mad. Eat."

Hayden picked up his fork and pushed his food around. He squirmed on his chair and cast Mitch a furtive look from beneath furrowed eyebrows, then stabbed up a manly bite and stuffed it into his mouth. Kate took a small swallow of water. Mitch mixed his rice into the stir-fry in a determined effort to destroy the beauty of the dish and topped it off with a massive overdose of unhealthy soy sauce. Kate deliberately left her rice and stir-fry as separate layers and refused to add soy sauce until she tasted it. Predictably, it was fine the way it was. In fact, it was delicious. The one and only thing she could cook with consistent excellence was a stir-fry.

"Mitch says fish don't eat their own babies," Hayden said, chewing away, "and if we caught a hungry one, you could feed it bread."

"That's good to know," Kate replied. "Don't talk with your mouth full."

"This is great," Mitch mumbled, shoveling more food into his mouth.

"Eat," Kate ordered Hayden, who had set aside his fork.

He shifted on his seat. "I'm not hungry."

"You told me you wanted it."

"But you gave me cereal, so I'm full."

Kate glared. Mitch pushed out of his chair and got himself another beer from the refrigerator. She heard him opening the bottle of wine and pouring a glass, which he set in front of her. "Just in case," he said. Then he dropped back into his seat, caught her eye and held it long enough for her to lose her breath. When he finally redirected his attention to the meal, she lifted her wineglass and took a sip. Just a little one. Her stomach didn't need the aggravation, even if her nerves could use the anesthetic. She glanced into the living room. Thor was, for all intents and purposes, dead to the world, but when the black dog had come through the kitchen door with Mitch, she'd caught the expression in his eyes, that flash of canny wariness, the hint of wildness that simmered deep within.

Thor had run with the wolves.

Why did the fact that Mitch had chased after Thor disturb her so? Was it because she was afraid he had that same wild streak? Was it because she was afraid he might keep on running? Was it because Hayden was so swept up in it all, so suddenly attached to a man he hadn't even known a week ago?

Was she jealous?

No. She'd been worried, that's all. Mitch was back, he was safe, she could let it go now.

But could she?

"What if Thor hadn't come back?" she said.

Mitch glanced up from his near-empty plate. "Huh?"

"What if he'd kept running with the wolves? What would you have done?"

He thought for a moment, fork in midair. "I guess I'd have kept chasing after him. Maybe he'd have been all right, maybe what he wants is to be something wild, but I didn't know that. I still don't. He's pretty used to being fed regularly and he's gotten kind of attached to Hayden. Anyhow, he's family, and you can't give up on family."

Kate lifted her wineglass for another tiny sip. There was no arguing with that logic because, when it came down to it, she wouldn't give up on family, either.

AFTER HE WASHED the supper dishes and put them away, Mitch found Kate out on the porch, leaning against the railing, wrapped in her parka and watching the low clouds scud before the ebbing wind, shredding themselves against the peaks of the Alaska Range. They were lit up with all the colors of the rainbow in the last real light of day. Salmon-pinks and violets and buttercup-yellows and reds. There were pale green and blue and tangerine streaks in the western sky. Mitch came up behind her, put his arms around her, dropped his chin onto her shoulder and pulled her close.

"Pretty impressive," he said.

"Pretty impressive," she agreed.

"I'm sorry I made you so mad."

"I'm not mad."

"Hayden's asleep. He wanted to stay up to hear the wolves howl, but he couldn't keep his eyes open."

"It's way past his bedtime."

"This time of year, Alaskans don't recognize a bedtime. Bedtime comes in winter and it's called hibernation, but during the summer solstice the energy levels are so high most everything stays awake 24/7, making up for lost time."

"So I guess this means you aren't tired?"

"I wouldn't go that far. When I thought there was a bear up ahead of us on the trail, I died a thousand deaths worrying about Hayden. Between Hayden's bear and Thor's wolves, I'm played out." Mitch felt the anger flow from her and the tension dissipate as she softened in his arms.

"Welcome to the world of parenting."

"Thanks for inviting me."

Wrong thing for him to say. He felt her tense up again in self-defense, and damned himself for his stupidity. "Let's sit out here a while," he suggested, hoping for a chance to redeem himself. "If we're lucky, we might hear the wolves howl. You warm enough?"

She nodded.

He pulled her into one of the deck chairs and she sat in his lap just as stiff and cold and unyielding as a rock, the disciplined, unemotional, independent, type A fighter pilot to the end.

The colors in the western sky started to fade as he held her, and he let the fingers of one hand massage the tight muscles in her shoulders and neck and took it as a good sign when she didn't pull away and an even better one when she began to relax.

And then, just before that thick, dusky hour, which was as dark as it ever got in an arctic summer, they heard a wolf howl from across the canyon, close enough to be clearly heard over the sound of the creek. This wasn't just any wolf, and it wasn't just any howl. This howl defined the origins and the destiny of the entire universe and lasted a full ten seconds. It encompassed the deepest of pains and the fiercest of joys and everything in between, and when the last notes had faded into silence, Mitch felt a shiver run through Kate. She turned into him, melted against him and wrapped her arms tightly around his neck and he held her in the same fierce way, because he was just beginning to understand how tragic and how beautiful life could be.

CHAPTER FOURTEEN

THEIR LAST DAY at the park supervisor's cabin passed in a blur. Kate, Hayden and Mitch took a short walk down the Canyon Creek trail to where the caribou had been killed, and together they examined the tracks around the scattered remains of bones and hide. Most of the meat had been eaten. Ravens flew away from the kill site at their approach and kept a jealous eye on their meal while Mitch measured the wolf tracks using a dollar bill. "This must be the alpha track. Look at the size of it. Five inches by seven. Wish we could make a plaster cast. That'd make some kind of souvenir. Bet your Montana wolves aren't that big."

"They eat buffalo for breakfast," Kate said. "They're twice as big."

"Hear that, Thor? Maybe you should head for Montana with Hayden and Kate and try running with the big wolves."

Kate felt a pang and turned away, searching the tundra for the delicate anemones, picking a tiny bouquet of alpine rhododendron and trying not to think about leaving Mitch for the second time. If she hadn't been able to say goodbye after one night, how was she going to say goodbye now? And how would she explain to Hayden that his father, who had just been miraculously raised from the dead to become a part of his life, was going to be living so far away?

They ate lunch sitting on the porch, then tidied up the cabin, filled the wood box and left a thank-you note on the counter next to the small bouquet before loading all their gear back into the truck for the journey back to Pike's Creek. Kate gazed out the truck's window as they started down the park road, recalling that Norman Rockwell illustration of the family going on vacation and then returning home. Their great adventure was over and they were subdued and deflated. Tomorrow they'd be in Anchorage, meeting with the governor and Admiral Gates and other leukemia patients and after that...

She didn't want to think about it. She wanted to remember how special these past few days had been. She wanted to remember hearing that wolf howl, and how Mitch had carried her back into the lodge afterward and the way he leaned in her bedroom door after she'd climbed under the covers and said, "Feel like another bedtime story about the Sky Dragons?" And how, for the third morning in a row, she'd woken from a sleep unplagued by nightmares, with Mitch by her side. She knew he'd only spent the night with her because he knew she didn't want to be alone. She told herself over and over not to read anything into it, to take his generous kindness in the spirit it was offered and expect nothing more, but there was no denying that she wanted something more.

There was also no denying that she had little to offer in return. No man would choose to be saddled with a woman battling leukemia. Mitch was tied to her through Hayden, but that was all. He owed her no allegiance, not after the way she'd shut him out for almost five years. He owed her no friendship, and he certainly didn't owe her his undying love. His push for the drives to help find her a bone marrow donor, while touching, was no doubt spurred by his fear of becoming a single parent and of his whole lifestyle changing to care for a three-year-old boy. She couldn't blame him for that. The responsibilities of raising a child were life-altering. If she died, there would be no more late nights at the pool halls for Mitchell McCray.

Kate gazed out at the magnificent landscape, so vast and humbling that from time to time, while walking with Mitch and Hayden that very morning, she'd had to focus on the delicate alpine wildflowers at her feet to bring the world back into perspective. She felt like that now, about her life. The future ahead of her loomed so frightening that she had to concentrate on the here and now to keep from being overwhelmed.

Suddenly, the truck slowed and Mitch pointed to a green patch of willows alongside a glacial stream a hundred yards to the right of the gravel road.

"Bear!" he said.

Sure enough, a silvery-blond grizzly was pawing the grass and roots along the water's edge, digging up great dark clods of dirt searching for grubs and greens while her two cubs wrestled together at the edge of the willows. Kate caught her breath, awed by the sight, committing the moment to yet another special memory she could draw on to get her through the days and months and, hopefully, the years ahead.

"Little bears, too, Mumma!" Hayden said. "Oh, I hope she doesn't eat them!"

BY THE TIME Mitch dropped Hayden and Kate at the Moosewood and returned to his place on Pike's Creek, it was well after midnight. He wandered through the cabin with a restlessness that was completely incongruous with how he should be feeling after such a long day, but sleep was the furthest thing from his mind. He grabbed a beer out of the refrigerator and walked out onto the porch, where he leaned over the railing, took a long, cold draft and pondered the state of things. He'd been a bachelor since his divorce, and a happy one, too. He'd enjoyed living alone, keeping his own hours and answering to no one. He and Thor had shared this place and called it home for two good years.

This strange loneliness that he was feeling tonight, in a place that had never felt lonely to him before, would pass. As soon as Kate and Hayden left he'd get back to normal, but first they had to resolve the issue about the plane. If she left it behind, he'd never get back to normal because he'd have to see it every day, and everyone would know Kate had bought the plane for him, and everyone would know why.

Mitchell McCray couldn't make it on his own.

That's what people would say.

They'd be right, too. Up until now, making the big bucks hadn't mattered to him. He'd been perfectly content working for Wally and earning just enough to keep him in canned beans and toilet paper, but things were different now. He had a son. Living from hand to mouth was no longer an option. He had big responsibilities to shoulder, but he could do it. He didn't need Kate to prop him up financially. Somehow she had to accept that, the same way he had to accept the fact that she'd turned his world upside down.

And that was the hell of it. Even if the plane issue was resolved, he'd never get back to normal. When he'd left her at the Moosewood last night after unloading her bag and Hayden's, she'd walked back out to the truck with him in the dusky light, head down and arms crossed. He paused by the door of his truck, struggling with the undeniable knowledge that he no longer wanted to keep two feet of space between them. He wanted to pull her into his arms and kiss her.

"I'll pick you up tomorrow morning bright and early," he told her. "We have to be at the hospital by eleven, and the governor invited all of us to lunch after the meeting. I told him we'd be honored. Hope that's okay."

"Hayden, too?"

"He told me the restaurant has a children's menu."

"That sounds fine." She paused, then gave him a small smile. "I had a nice time, Mitch. So did Hayden. Thank you." She stood on tiptoe and kissed him very gently on the mouth, then turned and walked away. No goodbye, which was fine with him. He hadn't wanted one, which was exactly why he was pacing his porch at 1:00 a.m., brooding over what he really did want and wondering if he could ever have it.

MONDAY, THE DAY so dreaded by Kate, passed more quickly than Sunday had. The press conference was held at 11:00 a.m. in the oncology wing of the Alaska Medical Center. Attending, in addition to the governor, were the chief of Umiak; three leukemia patients, including a twelve-year-old girl; and two cancer specialists. It was Kate's first public appearance without wearing a wig or a hat, and she joked, "Easiest hairdo I ever had, but I keep forgetting the sunscreen." Her comment broke the ice, got a laugh and jump-started the press conference. Hayden stood by Kate's side and made shy, monosyllabic responses to the reporters' questions. The Blood Bank of Alaska and the Red Cross both had representatives to talk about the process of becoming a bone marrow donor. There were four very professional and polite members of the press, including John and Mike, who had flown down from Fairbanks.

The discussion lasted a little over an hour and wasn't nearly as bad as Kate had feared, mostly because Mitch was there for her to lean on. Lunch afterward lasted over two hours. The restaurant was near the waterfront, very chic and upscale, but the children's menu, so-called, had nothing whatsoever that Hayden would eat. It was merely scaled-down portions of the regular menu, which included portabello pate, artichoke bisque and duck confit. Kate read the selections aloud to Hayden, who was understandably disgruntled, then glanced at Mitch with a barely suppressed smile. This was going to be an interesting experience.

When the food arrived, Hayden stared sullenly at his plate while Kate tried to carry on a conversation with the governor and the chief of Umiak. Several times she urged him to eat, promising dessert if he ate at least one piece of duck, which she assured him tasted just like chicken. At the end of the meal she was surprised to see that all the duck on his plate had disappeared.

"Good for you, Hayden," she praised him. "I'll ask the waiter for a dessert menu."

Fortunately, the restaurant offered something as mundane as ice cream. Hayden ate a big bowl of French vanilla drizzled with chocolate sauce.

On the way back to Mitch's truck, after all the thank-yous, goodbyes and good lucks had been said, they followed a scenic walking path along Cook Inlet, enjoying the afternoon sunshine. Kate had been vaguely aware that Hayden and Mitch were plotting something, but was taken by surprise when Mitch pulled a fine linen restaurant napkin, bundled into a ball, out of his jacket pocket and handed it to Hayden, who carried it to the edge of the walking path, opened it up and pitched two pieces of duck, one after the other, into the inlet. He turned to look at Kate.

"I feed the fish, Mumma, so they don't eat their babies," he announced.

"I couldn't eat it all," Mitch admitted in response to Kate's questioning glance. "I'm no fan of duck myself, or much of anything else on that restaurant's menu, but I figured Hayden might at least get dessert if I helped him out." He reached out his arm and hooked her around the waist, pulling her up against him while Hayden stared down at Cook Inlet, anxiously waiting for the fish to eat his offering. "You did great today, K. C. Jones, and so did Hayden. I'm proud of you both. Whatdya say we hit a burger joint on our way out of town. We got us a hungry kid to feed."

THEY STOPPED at a fast-food place to satisfy Hayden's appetite, and then Yudy's General Store on the way back to the Moosewood. Kate needed to pick up more yogurt and water; Mitch needed dog food. When they were paying up, Yudy plunked a big poster on the counter, advertising the upcoming donor drive.

"Hot off the press," he announced. "Campy's in charge of distributing them all around town. She started today. The donor drive's been scheduled for next Monday." He nodded at Kate. "I sure hope we find one for you, Captain Jones."

"Thank you," Kate said, a little overwhelmed.

Back in Mitch's truck, she handed Hayden the juice he'd asked for, sat back in her seat and sighed. "Everyone's been so nice."

"Alaska's a great place to live," Mitch said, starting the truck. "People have their differences and sometimes they're extreme, but they look out for each other just the same. Let's swing by Brock's Bar and Grill and have a beer. You deserve one after surviving that press conference."

"What about Hayden?"

"He can have a root beer. You like root beer, Hayden?"

Predictably, Hayden nodded. He'd like anything Mitch suggested. Kate smiled. "Okay. That sounds good."

At 4:00 p.m. on a Monday, Brock's was quiet. The parking lot was nearly empty and the bar was smoke free. Campy was there filling in for someone who'd called in sick, and she served them at a table near the jukebox. "Hey, hon," she said as she set the beer in front of Kate. "How'd it go today?"

"Pretty good, I think," Kate said. "We may have sold the governor on a few proactive programs for helping the native Alaskans get better medical treatment."

"We're having a donor drive right here in Pike's Creek," Campy announced with pride.

"Yudy told us you were in charge of the posters. We saw one outside the bar. Thanks." Kate wanted to say more but suddenly her throat tightened up and she couldn't speak. Campy reached out and gave her arm a gentle squeeze, then she set a foamy, frosted mug of root beer in front of Hayden with a wide smile.

"You see any wolves up in Denali, Hayden?"

"Almost," he said, eyeing the mug with interest before glancing up at Campy. "I saw a moose and a caribou and a sheep. And a bear with babies!"

"Wow. I hope you saw that bear from a distance. I have a healthy respect for Alaskan bears. You hungry? We serve up a mean burger and fries here."

Hayden's eyes widened. "Yes, please."

"You just ate a hamburger not two hours ago," Kate reminded him.

"That was two hours ago," Mitch said. "He's a growing boy. Make that three burgers and fries, Campy. We ate lunch with the governor in Anchorage, and those fancy restaurants serve up mighty stingy portions for the big bucks they charge. Nothing like Brock's."

Hayden took a sip of root beer. The foam left a moustache on his mouth. He liked the taste enough to immediately try another swallow. Meanwhile, Mitch pushed out of his chair, fed some coins into the jukebox and punched some selections. Kate took a sip of her own beer as a country-and-western foot-stomper filled the empty room with sound. Mitch returned, braced his palms on the table in front of Hayden and said, "Mind if I dance with your mother?"

Hayden shook his head, completely involved with the mug of root beer.

Mitch switched focus. "What do you say, Captain? Think you can manage the Texas two-step?"

"If there are only two steps, I'm sure I'll figure it out."

He extended his hand, she took it and rose from her chair. In three minutes she was up to speed on the two-step, and with Mitch's arm around her and his warm, strong hand holding hers, she was feeling a little tipsy even though she'd had only one sip of beer. It felt so good for him to be holding her, for her to be dancing and for them to be together this way. It had been a long day and she was tired, but somehow the dance rejuvenated her and when the song ended she felt young and happy and sorry it was over.

Her regret lasted only until the next song kicked in. This one was slow and didn't require much effort other than leaning into Mitch and swaying with the music. Kate closed her eyes, rested her head against his chest and pretended for a moment that the way she was feeling was a forever thing, that life would be golden and glorious and she would always be safe and protected in Mitch's arms.

Katherine Carolyn McCray.

She smiled at the sweet, childish fantasy, then the song ended and they returned to the table and the monstrous realities of her future loomed before her. "Hayden and I have to leave soon," she told him, the words coming hard. "I promised my parents I'd have Hayden in Montana for his fourth birthday."

"You said his birthday was next month," Mitch said, clearly taken aback by her abrupt announcement.

"July second," Hayden announced. He'd finished off the mug of root beer.

"That's over two weeks from now. You have plenty of time to get back to Montana. There's lots you haven't seen yet. The Yukon River, the Arctic Circle…" Mitch gave her a puzzled look.

Kate lifted her beer and took a small sip, avoiding his eyes. "My mother wants us to come home. I'm sorry, Mitch, but she was so upset when I talked to her last night, I told her we would. I'm glad we came. I've had a good time, and I think Hayden has, too."

"I'll be four," Hayden piped up.

"So then what?" Mitch said to her in a flinty tone of voice. "You wait around in Montana until the phone call comes from your doctors in Seattle?"

"Or until I have to go back for another round of chemo. Yes. That's how it works."

Mitch studied her across the table. "You could wait here just as well as there. Anchorage has a good hospital, and it's a whole lot closer than the one in Seattle."

Kate struggled to find the words to explain, but she knew nothing she said would help. "I promised my parents I'd go home."

He pushed back in his chair and tried to keep his tone even so as not to upset Hayden. "So you're just going to fly out of here with Hayden and I'm supposed to stay here and wait to hear from you?"

Kate glanced at Hayden, who was examining his empty mug with a studious frown, then sighed. There could be no happy ending to this trip, only a long, hard goodbye. "I'll keep in touch. I'll let you know how things go."

Campy's appearance effectively halted any immediate response from Mitch. She slid a huge plate in front of each of them, another beer in front of Mitch and another frosted mug of root beer in front of Hayden. She gave Kate a questioning glance when she saw her untouched beer. "Can I get you something else to drink?"

"Water, Campy, thanks," Kate replied.

When she had gone, Mitch leaned forward on his elbows and held her gaze until Kate felt herself clench up. "I had to know what kind of a man you were. What kind of father you'd make. Don't you see? I had to come and I'm glad I did, but I never intended to stay."

"I don't wanna go," Hayden said.

They both looked at Hayden while Campy set the big glass of ice water in front of Kate. "Can I get you anything else, hon?"

Kate shook her head.

"Mitch, Sanford's here, along with his cronies," Campy said, bending close. "They just arrived from Dutch Harbor and he's itching to shoot a game of pool with you."

"Tell him I can't right now," Mitch said.

"Okay, hon, but he's hot to trot and he brought a wad of money with him. A big wad."

Mitch shook his head. "Sorry. Not tonight. Tomorrow, maybe."

Kate fixed him with a questioning look after Campy had gone. "Who's Sanford?"

"Pool shark. Makes tons of money working in Dutch and loses most of it right here at Brock's."

"Go ahead and have a game if you want. We'll watch."

Mitch glanced over his shoulder to the group of men clustered at the bar, then looked back at Kate. "I don't give a hoot about shooting pool with Sanford, but I do care about you and Hayden. We've shared a lot in the past few days."

Kate lowered her eyes again. "Yes, we have."

"It just seems wrong for you to take him and go."

"Can't we stay, Mumma?" Hayden interjected, chewing his French fries.

"No, we can't, and don't talk with your mouth full." She glanced back up at Mitch. "Try to understand my position."

"Believe me, I am."

They stared at each other while Hayden looked between them, frowning. "Mitch, you're Hayden's father and you'll always be a part of his life. That's why I brought him here, so the two of you could get to know each other."

"And I appreciate that, believe me, I do, but what about you and me, Kate? What part are we playing in this little family scenario? What part do I play?"

Kate drew a steadying breath. "I'm just trying to survive this. That's about all I can do right now."

"Right now you seem to be focused on running away from me."

"I'm sorry you feel that way, Mitch. Believe me, I'd love to stay longer, and I'm grateful for all you've done, but we have to go."

"I don't wanna go, Mumma. I wanna stay here with Mitch," Hayden said.

"Eat your burger, Hayden. You know we have to leave. We had this conversation last night. Gram and Gramp are waiting for us in Montana. There are horses there, remember? You're going to learn to ride."

Mitch pushed away from the table in an abrupt movement. "I told Wally to buy a Cessna 185 with the insurance money. The 185's a good plane, and there's one for sale in Anchorage at the Lake Hood base. It's not the same caliber as the Porter, but it's a good plane."

Kate felt herself stiffen. "The Porter's a great plane, perfect for what you do here."

"No arguments there, but I can't accept it." He stood and stared down at her with those keen clear eyes. "I'm glad you came. I guess I'd have liked it a whole lot better if you'd come four years ago, but I can't change that and since I can't convince you to stay, maybe I will go shoot a game of pool with Sanford. I could use the money."

"I wanna stay with you, Mitch," Hayden said, looking perilously close to tears. "Can I stay? I'll be good. I promise."

Mitch bent over the table and rumpled Hayden's hair. "Don't worry, pard. I'll come visit you a lot. Meanwhile, you learn to ride those mustangs so you can teach me how when I come. Deal?"

Hayden's eyes filled with tears as he looked up at his father. "I wanna stay."

"I wish you could," Mitch said, straightening. His expression was stony. "The two of you finish your burgers and I'll run you back to the Moosewood. This won't take long. Games with Sanford never do."

Kate watched him walk toward the bar and wished she could have said the things she really wanted to say, but she knew how selfish that would be. Mitch didn't need to be dragged any deeper into the nightmares she faced. She would deal with them as best she could on her own, and maybe, just maybe, if things worked out, if a donor was found and if the transplant was successful…maybe one day she and Hayden could come back together.

In the meantime, all she could do was hope…and dream.

MITCH ANNIHILATED Sanford in less than forty minutes. He showed no mercy. There was none in him tonight. Sanford sulked for a few moments, the way he always did, then demanded a rematch. He plunked another wad of bills on the green velvet of the billiard table but Mitch shook his head, pocketing his winnings. "Maybe later," he said, and returned to where Kate and Hayden waited. Kate had barely touched her burger and Hayden's face was red as though he'd been crying.

"It's getting past your bedtime, Hayden," he said, hearing his own father's words again. "Let's get you back."

"I wanna stay here with you," Hayden whined.

"Well, I'm leaving, so c'mon, pard. Let's go."

Kate was predictably quiet on the drive to the Moosewood. He wondered if she had ever, just once, talked for the sake of talking. Talked about the weather, the crowd at the bar, the price of gas. No, there would be no idle chatter. Everything with Kate had to have a reason, a purpose. Every action, every word.

Back at the Moosewood, Mitch carried a groggy Hayden

to Kate's cabin and handed him off to the hovering Rosa, who took him into the bedroom. He stood for a moment, wondering what to do or say. Kate seemed equally at a loss. Rosa came back into the room, saw them standing there and scowled.

"A fine thing, for the two of you to be inside when outside the sky is so beautiful. I'll watch Hayden. You go out and watch God's handiwork."

They went out on the porch and dutifully admired the alpenglow that lit the snow-clad peaks in the distance. They stood side by side, close together but miles apart. Kate's arms were crossed and Mitch could feel the unhappiness radiating from her. "If Hayden's birthday isn't until July, I don't see why you can't stay for at least another week."

"I think it's for the best that we go."

"Best for who? Hayden?"

"The press conference with the governor is scheduled to be aired after the news tomorrow evening. Campy told me she'd tape it and send me a copy," Kate said, dodging his question. "I hope it helps get more native Alaskans on the donor registry and helps Tuttu find her twin brother."

Mitch shoved his hands in his jeans pockets and leaned against a porch post. "Wally wants to go to Anchorage tomorrow to look at that plane. I'll be gone all morning. Maybe we can get together in the afternoon."

"Maybe." She was completely noncommittal, avoiding his eyes by keeping hers fixed on the mountains.

"What does Hayden want for his birthday?"

She smiled faintly. "Ever since meeting Thor, he's been after me to get him a dog of his own, but if a bone marrow donor is found for me and the transplant takes place, I can't be around them for a year."

"Why?"

"Until my immune system reboots, the doctors advise against exposure to pets, people and public places."

"How long will you be in the hospital?"

"For the actual stem cell transplant, in and out about six months total."

Mitch figured it'd take maybe a couple of months and was shocked by her answer. "Why so long?"

"It's a long process."

"So tell me about it."

"There are a couple weeks of tests involved in the workup phase prior to the transplant, then they insert a Hickman central line catheter into the right atrium of my heart. That's where they'll channel all the chemo, antibiotics, antivirals, liquid food, saline and anti-nauseameds and diluted radioactive antibodies."

"They inject that stuff into your heart?"

Kate nodded. "The huge volume of blood pumping through the heart dilutes the chemicals quickly. That's why they put the IV there. I'll be placed in a lead-lined room for six to eight days for this phase because I'll be too radioactive to be around other people. After all my own marrow cells have been destroyed, then comes the transplant from the donor, and then another three months in the isolation ward before I'm allowed into a regular hospital room for monitoring. That's assuming I don't get graft versus host response, which would be bad."

Mitch stared. He couldn't think of a single positive thing to say. She looked at him with a wry smile. "I know. I can't tell you when anything has scared me more than the six months of hell I'll be facing if a donor is found, but for Hayden's sake I have to do this. Getting a bone marrow transplant is my only chance to watch him grow up and catch that first big fish. I'm sorry for taking Hayden away from you so soon, but don't you see, I have to leave now, because if I stay here any longer I may not be able to go."

As far as Kate was concerned, their conversation was over. She dismissed him with a brief kiss, this time on the cheek, but when she spoke, her voice trembled with emotion. "Thanks again for everything, Mitch. I'm glad I came. You're a great guy, and Hayden's got a great dad. Good night." She turned swiftly and the door closed behind her, leaving him standing on the porch, alone and confused.

He drove back toward Pike's Creek, reeling from this abrupt dismissal and still trying to grasp a cancer treatment so horrific the radioactive meds were administered directly into the heart and the patient was confined in a lead-lined room for one week. His thoughts were tangled in confusion. On the one hand, he didn't want her to go. On the other, he was relieved that she was leaving soon, and stricken with guilt for feeling relieved. But he knew she was right. It was better this way. Staying would only make it harder. Harder for her to go back to that hospital and harder for them to say goodbye.

But what about Hayden?

He swung by the airstrip on his way home to check on the Porter, which was right were he'd chocked it before the camping trip. Wally's Harley was parked in front of the warming shack, pristine, gleaming. He paused beside it for a moment, remembering how Kate had admired it, and realized that no matter how hard he tried to convince himself that Kate's leaving would be a good thing, the best thing for both of them, his heart was saying something completely different.

Wally was inside, working on the books and chewing on an unlit cigar. "What're you doing here?" he growled. "Thought you went to Anchorage for the meeting with the governor."

"We did," Mitch said. "We're back. What are *you* doing here on a Monday?"

"Campy had to work, and I'm trying to balance the books and find us another plane. I lit a fire under the insurance company. It won't take long to get the money."

"The longer it takes, the more business we lose."

"Don't I know it." Wally heaved a weary sigh. "You could always fly the Porter. The lease agreement's been signed and its all insured."

"Let me borrow your Harley and I'll think about it."

"No way in hell," Wally said, coming half out of his seat with an expression of alarm.

"An hour, that's all I'm asking. I'll have it back before you're done with your book work. I just want to take Kate on a nice, gentle cruise."

"Like hell you will!" Wally was standing now, his face darkening with indignation. "Your nice gentle cruise will top out at over a hundred miles an hour. I know you jet-jock types. No way, Mitch. Sorry."

"It's for Kate, Wally. She loves your bike. Let me borrow it just this once."

Wally sagged back into his chair, looked intently at Mitch then reached into his jeans pocket and tossed him the key. "One scratch," he warned in an ominous tone.

"Thanks, boss, I knew you'd come through for me."

Mitch walked out of the shack, climbed aboard the black-and-silver anniversary edition Harley and headed back toward the Moosewood. Kate had, after all, saved his life. Mothered his child. Given him one of the best weeks of his life.

He couldn't let her go without one last chance at redemption.

KATE WAS SITTING on the porch, sipping a glass of water and feeling blue when she heard a big motorcycle stop out in the parking area of the main lodge. She didn't think too much about it. There were multiple guest cabins and the restaurant was busy in the evenings. Vehicles came and went constantly. But then she heard footsteps approaching and Mitch came around the corner. He walked up to the foot of the porch steps and paused, hooked his thumbs in his rear pockets and slouched like a biker. The sun had set, but he was still wearing his tough-guy aviator shades.

"Thought you'd want to see my new wheels," he said.

She set the glass down and stood, her lonesome blues banished by his unexpected appearance. "Wally let you borrow his Harley?"

He grinned and nodded. "C'mon. Let's go for a spin. Shake her down and wring her out."

"That sounds dangerous."

"Damn straight. Dangerous is what you need right now. But don't worry, it'll be a safe kind of dangerous. Hayden won't lose his parents."

She didn't need to be asked twice. Sticking her head in the cabin door, she relayed to Rosa that she'd be gone for a little bit, then followed Mitch out to where the bike was parked. She ran her fingertips over the gleaming fender. "He actually trusts you with it?"

Mitch straddled the leather seat. "Of course he does. Climb aboard, pretty woman."

"You sure you know how to drive this thing? It only has two wheels and no wings," Kate couldn't resist teasing as she hopped up behind him and wrapped her arms around his waist.

Kickstand up, engine revving, Mitch left a trail of dust as they exited the parking area and swung onto the Parks Highway heading north. In a matter of seconds the speedometer was nudging sixty. He throttled back and held it there until Kate tightened her arms around him and shouted, "Faster!" He accelerated slowly. Seventy. Eighty. Kate leaned against him and hung on tight, wind whipping past her ears. No wind through her hair, that's for sure, but suddenly that didn't matter a bit, and when Mitch passed a motor home long enough to qualify as an oceanliner in a mere second and a half, Kate laughed her exhilaration into his ear and wished they could hit two hundred and keep on going straight to the moon.

It was a little dangerous, it was a little crazy and it was just the thing she needed to purge the dark thoughts and grim scenarios from her mind, to remember what it was like to fly at Mach 2 with her hair on fire. To be young and invincible and free.

The only thing missing was Bruce Springsteen belting out "Born to Run."

Too soon he was slowing, slowing, then pulling a U-turn, turning back.

Cruising again at a sedate sixty, big bike purring along, Kate leaned into the solid warmth of Mitch's back and relished the feel of the wind and the open space, the soaring mountains and the open road and, above all else, just being with Mitch. She could spend the rest of her life like this and be happy.

Back at the Moosewood, Mitch cut the ignition. They sat for a moment, reluctant for the adventure to end. Just as Kate was about to slide off the bike, Mitch pivoted his upper body, lifted her into his arms and pulled her onto his lap, all in one smooth and remarkably inspired movement.

And then he kissed her.

This was no tender, gentle, pitying kiss. He didn't kiss her as if she was a cancer patient who had lost all her hair. He didn't kiss her as if she might die any day. Mitch kissed her like he wanted more than just a moment, more than a day or a week, a whole lot more, and she twined her arms around his neck and kissed him back with the same fierce, desperate passion.

Things might have gotten completely out of hand as they embraced on the seat of Wally's Harley, but Mitch had forgotten to put the kickstand down. As he shifted his hands, sliding them down Kate's thighs to swing her astride his hips, he lost his balance, and when the heavy bike tipped over, it took them with it.

With any luck, Wally would never notice that tiny scratch on the left front fender.

CHAPTER FIFTEEN

FIRST THING Tuesday morning, early, Kate went for one last walk on the dirt road that led to the abandoned mining town. She was dressed in her jogging clothes, but had given up the effort after her brief warm-up left her weak and breathless. The air was cool and buoyant and filled with bird song, and the beauty of her surroundings inundated her with bittersweet emotions. She wondered if Mitch had spent as sleepless a night as she had. He didn't know she was planning on leaving today. She hadn't been able to tell him last night that she'd booked an afternoon flight out of Anchorage.

Not after that incredible ride on the Harley.

Not after that unforgettable kiss.

She didn't have the courage.

Her mother was overjoyed and relieved that she was finally coming home. Rosa would fly with them to Seattle, then change flights and head back to Southern California while Kate and Hayden continued on to Bozeman. By dark, they'd be at her parents' home in the foothills of the mountains. Tonight she'd sleep in her childhood bed, surrounded by mementos of days gone by.

At the moment, those thoughts did little to comfort her. She didn't want to leave Alaska. She didn't want to leave Mitch.

She couldn't bear the thought of never seeing him again, and she knew she'd never be able to say goodbye.

She tried not to think about the inevitable as she showered and changed, as she had breakfast with Hayden and Rosa, as she packed her bags and loaded them into the car. But of course, that was impossible. Also impossible was the idea of leaving without at least writing him a goodbye note. She could put it on his kitchen counter. She knew he wouldn't be there. He'd be in Anchorage with Wally, looking at a plane.

"Rosa, I'm going over to Mitch's place," she said quietly so Hayden didn't hear. "We'll check out as soon as I get back."

She stopped at Yudy's to buy a card and her eyes stung at the sight of the donor drive poster displayed prominently in the storefront window. Inside, she gave Yudy a hug. "Hayden and I are leaving today. I wanted to stop by and thank you for being so nice to us."

He blushed to the roots of his hair as all the old-timers got up from their seats around the stove to shake her hand and wish her well. She bought a few things, said her final farewells and then headed for the airstrip. Both Wally and Campy were there, which surprised her.

"Mitch told me you were going to Anchorage with him to look at a plane this morning," she said.

"What plane?" Wally frowned.

"The Cessna 185. The one for sale at Lake Hood."

Campy gave Wally a puzzled glance, then looked at Kate. "Hon, that plane sold the day it went on the market, over a month ago."

It was Kate's turn to be confused. "Then where's Mitch?"

Campy shook her head. "If he's not with you, and he's not here, he must be out at his cabin. Give him a call, Wally."

"No, that's all right," Kate said. "I'll drive out there."

"Not in that rental car, you won't. Take my Subaru, hon. The keys are in it."

Kate nodded. "Thanks, Campy. I won't be long."

Mitch's truck wasn't in the yard, and Thor was nowhere to be seen. She was both bitterly disappointed and wildly relieved. Where had he gone? Why had he told her that he was looking at a plane that didn't exist? Was he trying to avoid her? She took the card with her into the cabin, found a pen on the counter and started to write.

Dear Mitch,
The past week has been one of the best of my life. Thank you so much for giving us such a great Alaskan adventure. Our flight leaves this afternoon. I'm sorry you didn't get a chance to see Hayden one last time. Maybe you could call him on his birthday. For his sake, and for mine, fly the Porter. I wish you all the best, forever and ever.
Kate.

She slipped the card into the envelope, wrote his name on the outside and propped it against the salt-and-pepper shakers. Then she went out into his shed, found a shovel and planted the packet of seeds she'd bought at Yudy's in the overgrown garden plot. It took awhile to dig up the big clumps of sod, but eventually she had a nice weed-free patch of dirt and she sprinkled the seeds over it and firmed them into the soil. With a bucket of water from the creek she watered the newly planted seeds and her job was done. She was ready to go, or as ready as she'd ever be. She took one last look around, said a silent goodbye to the rustic homestead and the big mountain, and climbed back into Campy's Subaru. She drove away with her hands clamped tight on the wheel, her entire body rigid with pain, telling herself she would not cry, because tears were pointless.

She would not cry.

Three hours later Kate, Hayden and Rosa were boarding their Alaska Airlines flight to Seattle. At 3:00 p.m. the flight was airborne, and Kate was unable to hold back her emotions. She watched the mountains fade into the distance behind them and wept the bitter tears of a broken heart, keeping her face turned to the window so Hayden wouldn't see.

MITCH SPENT most of the morning driving aimlessly around. He went clear to Fairbanks and asked about planes for sale at the airport there. He looked at a couple with halfhearted interest, then headed south again, driving past the park entrance where he'd spent two of the most meaningful days of his life with the most extraordinary woman he'd ever known. By the time he reached Pike's Creek, he was working on a big lonesome. It was nearly 3:00 p.m. and he drove to the Moosewood to ask Kate and Hayden to supper at his cabin. He'd beg her to stay one more week. He'd do whatever it took to convince her.

Her car wasn't there and no one answered his knock on the cabin door. Maybe she'd left a message for him at the desk. The girl in the office checked the book, looked up at him with an apologetic frown and said, "I'm sorry, but Ms. Jones checked out this morning."

Mitch was stunned. She wouldn't leave without saying goodbye.

Again.

`He repeated that over and over as he sped back down the Pike's Creek Road. There was no rental car with a flat tire pulled over on the side of the road. No Kate standing beside it, waiting for him to rescue her. No rental car was parked at his cabin. The place was empty. Desolate. Depressing. Without bothering to get out of the truck, he turned around and sped back to the airstrip. Wally and Campy were there.

"Where've you been, hon? Kate came by looking for you," Campy said as he jumped out of his truck.

"When?"

"Oh, about three hours ago. For some reason she thought you'd gone to Anchorage with Wally to see that 185 that sold the week it went on the market. I told her you were probably out at your place. She took the Subaru out and when she came back she said you weren't there."

"Did she say where she was going?"

Campy shook her head. "Back to the Moosewood, I guess. Hayden wasn't with her."

Mitch slumped against the hood of his truck. She'd driven out to his cabin looking for him while he'd been off looking for a plane to take the place of her Porter. She was gone. She'd checked out of the Moosewood, and she and Hayden were on their way to Montana. He should have felt relief that the inevitable goodbyes had been avoided, but instead he was sick at heart. "I have to call the airport."

"Help yourself to the phone," Campy said.

The call confirmed what he already knew. Kate was probably halfway to Seattle by now. He returned to his truck, climbed into the cab and sat in numb stupefaction. Campy walked up to his open window. "You all right?"

"Kate's gone."

Campy lit a cigarette and watched him for a moment, then blew out a thin stream of smoke. "I wondered why she hugged me when she left."

"No goodbye," Mitch said. "Just like before."

"I'm sorry, Mitch. I really am." Campy shook her head. "Is there anything I can do?"

He stared at her for a moment, then reached to take the cigarette from her hand, and stabbed it out in the truck's ashtray. "Yeah. You can quit smoking before you get lung cancer." He started the truck. "And you can tell Wally we have to find us a cheap plane to fly, because we're sure as hell not using Kate's."

He drove back to the cabin and the place felt even lonelier than it had the past two evenings. He was beginning to understand why the musher pulled up stakes and left. He climbed the porch steps and was en route to the refrigerator to grab a beer when he spotted the envelope on the counter. He felt a shock run through him as he reached for it, sliding the card out and unfolding it while his heart hammered in his chest. He read the words twice, then set it on the counter and carried a beer out onto the porch. Thor was pacing the way he'd paced ever since he and Hayden had parted at the end of the camping trip. Pacing through the cabin, pacing onto the porch, whining and pacing and missing the boy.

Driving Mitch crazy.

He leaned on the porch rail and gazed out across the clearing toward the mountain. He could find no solace in the wild beauty, only a greater depth to his loneliness. He took a swallow of beer. It tasted terrible. Thor came to a stop at his side, looked up at him and whined.

"Quit that," he said harshly. "Go get the beast that dug up

the garden," he said, gesturing to the plot with the fresh mounds of dirt thrown up in a pile. Then he looked a little closer. It was too neat a job to be the work of a groundhog or a bear. He descended the porch steps and crossed to the fenced plot. The gate was closed. It hadn't been closed before. He opened it and stepped inside, seeing for the first time that the ground had been freshly dug and smoothed in one corner. All the clumps of sod had been piled to one side. In the center a stick had been driven into the soil and the seed packet was slipped over the top. He moved closer to see what she'd planted just hours ago, and felt a stab of pain when he read the packet.

Forget-me-nots.

As if he could ever forget.

CHAPTER SIXTEEN

KATE'S MOTHER was a wonderful cook. Ruth made her own whole grain breads, specializing in a basic crusty sourdough that, when warm from the oven and slathered with sweet butter, could still bring a glow to Kate's heart. How her mother found the time to create such wonderful feasts always seemed magical to Kate. In charge of the running of the ranch, Ruth spent long days in the saddle or in the farm truck or tractor or wielding a posthole digger or growing a huge garden full of food while Kate's father spent his days in the office, successfully growing other people's investments. Retirement for her father consisted of moving his office to the ranch and conducting business via the Internet. This way he was closer to Ruth, which he much preferred.

Kate's father had begun his career as a lawyer. He'd worked as a public defender in Bozeman until the unfairness of the system caused him chronic insomnia and resulting health problems, whereupon he went into the business of managing other people's money. He was calm and quiet and dignified, and he and Kate had always been close.

She'd been home for three days before he folded the evening paper in the middle of his after-supper read, took his pipe out of his mouth and gave her a somber look through his dark-framed glasses. "How did it *really* go in Alaska?" he said.

Hayden had fallen asleep in Kate's lap, something he still did and she still found endearing. She rocked him in her mother's chair, back and forth, and contemplated her father's question. "It went well," she said. "Really. Hayden's father was very nice."

Seemingly satisfied, her father put his pipe back into his mouth, unfolded the paper and continued reading.

"Kate?" Her mother poked her head into the living room. "I'll be out in the garden if you need anything. Just holler if you want me to put Hayden to bed."

Her mother had fussed over her nonstop for the past three days, refusing to let Kate do anything on her own. "No, you let me do this. You just rest and get strong," Ruth would command in that stern, maternal voice. One didn't argue with Mother Jones. Kate had learned that at an early age. Ruth disappeared to spend the next hour or so weeding and watering, a pleasant evening ritual for her in the long days of summer.

"They're holding a big donor drive for you all across the state this weekend," her father said out of the blue.

"Who is?" Kate asked, startled.

"According to the article, the Navy's sponsoring it. They're sending their own teams of medical specialists to oversee the drive. Because you have a healthy dash of native American DNA, they figure your best bet for a donor lies with the people of Montana, especially those with Crow blood."

"The Navy said that?"

"Admiral Gates," her father replied. "According to the admiral, your Mitchell McCray put the bug in his ear and gave him a push in the right direction. Apparently, McCray was instrumental in getting a donor drive going in Alaska and he was behind the Montana drive, too." He handed the paper to her. "Read it yourself. It's front-page news."

Kate scanned the article. Sure enough, Admiral Gates was quoted stating that Mitch was the driving force behind the effort to find a bone marrow donor, that Mitch had called him in the middle of a meeting and wouldn't be put off until he spoke his piece. He urged the admiral to appeal to the Navy and the native people of Montana to help save Captain Jones, and emphasized that time was of the essence. The Navy's medical specialists were pushing forward at top speed, and hoping for a great turnout of volunteers for the drive to help save this extraordinary woman, and others in need of bone marrow transplants.

Then the Blood Bank of Alaska spokeswoman raved warmly about Mitch offering to transport financially challenged people who volunteered to be on the bone marrow registry. *His generosity will help save lives.* There was more, but Kate folded the paper, handed it back to her father and sat with her arms around the sleeping Hayden, rocking back and forth and thinking about the man she'd left behind and the things she hadn't said to him but wished she had, and the plane he wouldn't fly but should. About him sponsoring the transportation for "financially challenged donors" when he was more financially challenged than anyone she knew. And about a donor drive he'd instigated right here in Montana, through Admiral Ransom Gates, without ever telling her about it.

Then again, why would he? She would only have protested his intervention on her behalf. He was trying to help her and she was trying to help him, but because neither was the least bit comfortable with the idea that they needed help in the first place, they shunned each other's assistance.

Stubborn and prideful, the both of them.

"What about Hayden?" her father said, startling her again.

"What about him?"

"How did it go for him in Alaska?"

Kate kissed the top of her son's head, breathing the mingled scents of Montana sunshine and a little boy's youthful innocence. "He saw wolves and a moose and a grizzly with two cubs, he had a dog of his own for a whole week, and he met his real father and liked him a lot." She gave her own father a bittersweet smile. "He was a busy boy, and a very happy one."

THE WEEKEND of the big Montana donor drive came and went and was a great success, with over a thousand people of Crow ancestry joining the registry. Kate settled into a routine of sorts at the ranch, savoring the good food, tolerating her mother's fussing, enjoying her father's company and thinking about Mitch 24/7, which was okay because it kept her from thinking about something called acute myelogenous leukemia, a lead-lined room and dying in a hospital bed. She went for walks every morning in the foothills, took frequent naps, cuddled with Hayden in the sunny window nook and read aloud to him from the same books her mother had read to her as a child. He could already identify the letters of the alphabet and read certain words. "Dog," he said, pointing to the word.

"That's right. Dog."

"I want one."

"As soon as Mumma's better, you'll have your own dog."

"I want Thor."

"Thor belongs with Mitch. He lives in Alaska."

"I want to live in 'Laska with Mitch."

"Don't you like it here, with Gram and Gramp?"

"Can we go back?"

"Yes, we can go back, but not today and not for a while."

"When?"

"As soon as Mumma's better."

"When will you be better?"

"As soon as the doctors find a good tissue match and I get a bone marrow transplant."

Hayden heaved a big sigh, stared down at the storybook and pointed to another word he recognized. "Daddy," he said.

Oh, God, Kate thought. Here we go.

MITCH WAS UNFAMILIAR with things like mortgages and loan officers and the reams of paperwork required to qualify as a good risk for the bank. He spent the better part of a week filling out the forms to mortgage his Pike's Creek homestead so he could get the money to kick in toward purchasing a half ownership in a 1983 Cessna 185. For a while it was touch-and-go. The loan officer frowned on the feast-or-famine income of a bush pilot flying for a start-up company and wouldn't accept his pool hall winnings as legitimate income, but because his homestead was worth so much more than the loan amount and the bank would get the whole shebang if he defaulted, in the end they took a chance and loaned him the one hundred grand he needed to buy his half of the plane. Wally's insurance money for the Stationair covered the other half and paid for a moderately good, used Quonset hut to use as a better office and work space.

Campy thought they were both crazy, but then, she'd been pretty cranky ever since she quit smoking.

"Why would you idiots want to buy another plane when the hottest aircraft in Alaska is sitting right outside our warming hut?"

"Because it's not our plane and we can't afford to buy it from Kate," Mitch said. "Isn't that right, Wally?"

"He's right," Wally growled, "but if you ever want to buy me a plane like that Porter, Campy, you can bet I won't refuse it."

She looked from one to the other, tossed her hair out of her eyes and turned on her heel. "Idiots," she repeated, leaving them to their business dealings while she went to work.

By 4:00 p.m. the next day the Cessna was sitting next to the Porter and Wally was fiddling with something under the cowling while Mitch cleaned up the interior. Campy came out of the warming hut with a scrap of paper in one hand and a small cloth satchel in the other. "I've figured out how much gas it would take to fly the Porter to Montana," she announced, boarding the plane.

Mitch glanced up from cleaning the Cessna's instrument panel. "Huh?"

She settled herself in the copilot's seat and studied the paper. "One thousand gallons of fuel will land you in Bozeman with thirty gallons to spare. I happen to have enough tip money stashed away to front you the cost of the trip. You can leave today. We don't have another booking for three days because the weather forecast is so lousy on the mountain, and Wally can cover for you if we get anything last minute.

"The airline ticket for your return trip is figured into my costs, and please don't tell me you can't accept this money. You can pay me back later and I'll even charge interest if it'll make you feel better." She fixed him with a bitchy look. "If you're not going to use that plane, Mitchell McCray, the least you can do is give it back to her." She handed him the scrap of paper and the satchel. "And for the record, I think you're making a mistake. You're just being stubborn and stupid, which is exactly why you haven't called her since she left. You've been moping around here like a kicked dog."

"If she wants to talk, she knows where I am." Mitch let the heavy satchel full of Campy's tip money drop to the floor with a muffled thump. "But I doubt she's waiting for her phone to ring. She didn't even bother to say goodbye in person."

"Maybe because she couldn't. Maybe because it's hard saying goodbye to someone when you know you might never see them again, especially if you love them."

"Love?" Mitch snorted. "You're way off base, Campy."

"Am I?" She tossed her hair in an impatient gesture. "I think the world of you, Mitch, you know I do, but you're definitely thick when it comes to matters of the heart. Go to Montana. Don't let things end this way between the two of you." She pushed out of the seat and prepared to disembark. "She needs you now, almost as much as you need her." She slammed the door of the plane behind her when she left, making sure she had the last word.

Just like a woman.

IT WAS A SATURDAY NIGHT, and Brock's Bar and Grill was packed. Mitch had been brooding about what Campy had said, and it hadn't helped any to go back to his newly mortgaged homestead on Pike's Creek to see that Kate's little plot of forget-me-nots had already sprouted. Rather than pace his porch and brood, he headed for town with enough money for a few beers, and by 10:00 p.m. he'd raked in over three hundred in winnings at the pool table. By midnight, he'd stashed away another four. He handed Campy her satchel, retrieved from under the truck seat, before he left at the end of the night.

"Thanks for the loan, but with what I just won and what's left in my bank account I think I'm covered," he said. "Tell

Wally I'm delivering the Porter to Montana and I'll be back by Tuesday. Wednesday at the latest. I talked to Raider and he volunteered one of his newbie pilots to fly for us in the meantime, if it gets busy."

Campy shifted the tray of drinks she was carrying and kissed his cheek. "Give Kate our love, hon, and Hayden, too."

By 6:00 a.m. Sunday morning, Mitch was refueling the Porter at the Talkeetna airport. His duffel bag was in the back, along with a big black dog who didn't think much of flying because there weren't many moose at five thousand feet above sea level. With a top cruising speed of 130 knots, it took them two days to make Bozeman with an overnight in Seattle, landing on vapors and sleeping in the plane for four short hours before continuing eastward toward the Rockies. By the time they landed at the Bozeman airport Thor had finally settled into a state of comatose boredom, but the beast was downright ecstatic to jump into the front seat of the cheapest rental Mitch could finagle out of the young woman who finally succumbed to his charms and said she wouldn't tell anyone his passenger was a dog.

"Pets normally aren't allowed in our rentals," she apologized.

"He's not really a pet," Mitch explained. "He's a therapy dog on a mission."

"Oh, that's so sweet!" she said, and handed him a business card with her phone number written on the back.

Mitch had Kate's address in his wallet and a map on the seat. He figured it was a two-hour drive to her place, which would put them there at 5:00 p.m. or thereabouts. He'd spend some time with Hayden, tell Kate her plane was parked at the airport in Bozeman and then book a flight back to Alaska.

Short and sweet. That was the best kind of visit in a situation like this.

ON MONDAY AFTERNOON Kate got a call from the doctor in Seattle. The news was discouraging. In spite of the donor drives in Alaska and Montana, no suitable tissue match had yet been found. "The lab tests take time. Getting the results can take weeks," she was told by the doctor who called. Meanwhile, she was scheduled for a third bout of chemo. That left her just another week, and each day passed more quickly than the last. Time was running out.

Hayden's birthday was only days away and Ruth was planning a celebration along the lines of a coronation, something Kate had always avoided. "You'll spoil him," she warned her mother.

"He's our only grandchild," Ruth countered. "Indulge us."

Kate acquiesced, against her better judgment. She'd seen way too many overindulged kids living on the base, ten-year-olds with cell phones plastered to their ears, sixteen-year-olds with brand-new cars. Hayden wasn't going to be like that. Or was he? If she wasn't around to rein him in, who would? She'd never had this conversation with Mitch. Then again, if Hayden lived with Mitch, he'd be lucky to even be wearing name-brand clothes. He definitely wouldn't have a cell phone or an iPod or the latest and greatest computer game.

"Mom, I'm going riding," she announced after the call from the doctor.

Her mother was making a batch of bread while Hayden built some sort of space-age vehicle out of interlocking plastic cubes. "Where?"

"Up to the fishing hole. I feel like trying to outsmart a trout."

"Take a quiet horse."

"I'll take Bonnie. She's so old she's practically dead."

"She is not!" Ruth dusted the flour off her hands. "I'll saddle her for you."

"Mom, honestly, I can manage. I'll be back in time for supper. Maybe we'll be eating fish tonight."

"Yuck," Hayden said as Kate left the house.

Bonnie was sleeping in the sun, lower lip sagging, eyes closed. "Sorry, old girl," Kate said as she climbed through the corral fence. "Time to wake up. You can have a nap when we get to the meadow."

It had been years since Kate had ridden. Nearly six, to be exact. It felt good to brush Bonnie, to smooth the blanket over her back and settle the leather saddle onto it. She missed being around horses, the sweet grass smell of them, the mingled scents of leather and sweat and wide open spaces. She tucked her pack rod into the saddlebag, led Bonnie out of the corral and, with a few hops, made it into the saddle. All of sudden she was on top of the world and her spirits lifted accordingly.

"C'mon, old girl," she said, gathering the reins and tugging down the wide brim of her hat. "Let's find a peaceful place."

Bonnie's steady walk was fast enough for Kate, who was content to let the sun beat down on her shoulders and listen to the summer insects buzz in the still heat of the day. As they climbed, the air cooled. A breeze came up, blowing tall, billowy clouds over the peaks and bringing the warm, resiny tang of pine down from the high places. By the time they reached the high meadow, Kate felt more like napping than fishing. She slipped off Bonnie's bridle, loosened the cinch and tethered the mare with enough slack to graze in a shady spot. Then she assembled the pack rod and walked down to the swimming hole. It was almost warm enough for a dip, but knowing how cold the water was, she wisely deferred.

The fly she chose worked well and she caught four beautiful trout, one after the other. She released all of them, then set the rod aside and let the lassitude of the afternoon fill her. She lay back in a sun-warmed grassy hollow, relaxed into the curve of the earth and almost instantly fell asleep listening to the murmur of the water and the lonesome whisper of the wind.

MITCH HAD NEVER BEEN to Montana before and by the time he turned off the dirt road that had Kate's family's ranch sign at the end of it, he understood a little better why Kate was such a down-to-earth girl in spite of her lofty career goals. When he stopped in the yard of the place where she'd grown up, he knew why she'd wanted to come back home. It was like a scene out of another century, or at the very least, an episode of *The Waltons*. Laundry flapped on a clothesline, chickens pecked and scratched in the barnyard, flowers bloomed everywhere, and beyond the reach of the corrals and fields, the mountains rose toward the sky.

The house itself was humble and homey, a simple cape-style with a dormered roof and a covered porch facing the yard. A woman stepped onto that porch as he studied the lay of the place, and wiped her hands on an apron she'd tied over a pair of blue jeans and a T-shirt. She wore her gray hair in a long braid over one shoulder and was slender, attractive and friendly looking. Mitch got out of the rental and quickly shut the car door behind him before Thor could shimmy out and chase after the chickens.

"Hello," the woman said with a surprised expression before Mitch could open his mouth to introduce himself. "You must be Mitch. Hayden looks just like you. Kate told me you were tall, but she didn't tell me how handsome you were. Come inside and bring your dog. I expect Hayden would like to see him."

"Mitch!" a young voice called out. Hayden burst through the screen door and flew down the porch steps. He plastered himself against Mitch's legs the same way he had with Kate, and Mitch felt a twist of pride and something else, too, something distinctly paternal, as he lifted Hayden up and gave him a hug.

"Hey there, pard. How are you doing?"

"You staying?"

"I'm visiting. I brought Thor along. Thought you might like to see him."

"Thor!" Hayden squirmed out of Mitch's grasp and opened the car door before Mitch could shout a warning. Thor emerged like a black blur, streaking toward the barnyard with evil intent. Mitch took after him with a roar and there must have been enough thunder in his voice to squelch the instinctive chase of the squawking, flapping hens because Thor came to a reluctant halt and looked back over his shoulder. Then he spotted Hayden and forgot all about the chickens and moments later the two were wrestling happily in the yard.

Mitch blew out his breath. "Sorry about that," he said to the woman who stood watching the show on the top step.

She smiled warmly and extended her hand to him as he climbed the steps. "Come on inside. I'll get you something cold to drink. I'm Ruth, Kate's mother."

The kitchen was warm and smelled of gingersnap cookies and freshly baked bread. Ruth poured iced tea and sliced a lemon, speaking over her shoulder as she did. "Kate's not here. She went fishing up on the mountain. She said she'd be back in time for supper. Her father should be back by then, too. He went to town to pick up some things and visit the office where he used to work. Do you want sugar in your tea?"

"No, ma'am, that's fine just the way it is," Mitch said. "How's Kate doing?"

"As well as can be expected," Ruth said, and he could read the worry lines in her forehead. "She tires easily and the results of her last tests weren't very good. They haven't found a donor yet but the doctor told her it takes time for the lab to test all the blood samples. She's scheduled for another round of chemotherapy right after Hayden's birthday." Ruth handed him a glass and a plate of cookies. "She didn't mention that you were coming."

"She doesn't know. I didn't know myself until a couple of days ago."

"Come sit out on the porch. It's cooler there," Ruth invited, and when they were seated side by side on the bench beside the door, she said, "Kate tells us you fly for an air taxi service."

"That's right. I suppose she told you about the plane, too." Warm, chewy gingersnap cookies and iced tea were a great combination. Mitch ate four cookies, one right after the other, then took a big swallow of cold, lemony tea.

"The crash. Yes, that sounded terrible. You're lucky you weren't killed."

"Not the plane that crashed, the one she bought."

Ruth frowned and shook her head. "I didn't know she'd bought a plane."

"She bought it because she thought the one that crashed wasn't safe to fly."

"I guess she was right."

Mitch took another swallow of cold iced tea and picked up

another cookie. "The thing is, I can't accept the plane. There's no way I'll ever be able to pay her back. It's a beautiful plane but it's too expensive for my bank account so I'm returning it to her. It's here, in Bozeman."

"You flew it all the way from Alaska?"

"She can keep it here and fly it herself, or sell it and put the money toward Hayden's college education. Half a million bucks'll get him a fine degree."

"Lord a'mighty." Ruth's eyebrows shot up. "She spent that much money on a plane?"

"Good planes are expensive, and that Porter's a great plane."

"Well, she must have wanted you to have it. Kate doesn't do anything on impulse. She's like her father that way." Ruth uttered a rueful laugh. "She said she had a good time in Alaska, but other than that she doesn't say much about it. She's been pretty quiet since she arrived. I read the article in the local paper about the Montana donor drive. They called it the Big Sky Drive. It was quite a success. They got over a thousand donors signed up for the registry, most of them of mixed blood, just like her. Thank you for initiating that. And thank you for what you did in Alaska, too."

"It seemed like everything I tried to do for Kate, she took as a personal insult."

Ruth laughed again, this time wryly. "Sounds like the two of you are a lot alike in that respect, but you know something, Mitch? Sometimes the kindest thing you can do for people is to let them help you."

RUTH INVITED HIM to stay to supper and offered him the use of the old bunkhouse for the night. "There hasn't been a cowboy hired on in years, but it makes a great guesthouse," she said, leading him to the board-and-batten building on the far side of the barn. She opened the door on a small, clean room with bunk beds against the far wall, a woodstove for heat and a tiny bathroom. "Leave your duffel bag in here and I'll show you the trail that leads up to Kate's fishing hole. It's a two-mile walk, and mostly uphill, but the view's great up there. Hayden can help me get supper started."

The trail, Ruth had told him, was originally used by the buffalo and the Crow to cut through the mountain pass back when both freely roamed the foothills. Cattle used it now, and horses, and Kate was up there somewhere, fishing. So Mitch leaned into the steep incline and headed up the mountainside and after about half a mile he was struggling to catch his breath. The trail switched back a couple of times, easing the steepness of the ascent; then cut through a dark, deeply timbered pass between two rugged peaks; climbed a little more, and broke through into a high wild meadow where the sun was so bright and unexpected that he stopped for a moment to let his eyes adjust while his lungs played catch-up.

The meadow was large enough for a sizable herd of buffalo, its perimeters sharply defined by timbered mountainsides that climbed into a hot June sky. A bright spangle of wildflowers carpeted the green stretch of grass that rippled in the breeze and a creek bisected the meadow, curving sharply at one point and nearly reversing direction. The weather-bleached remains of an old log cabin stood on this curve, amidst a grove of trees where a saddled horse grazed, but if Kate was nearby, she wasn't fishing. He could see no activity along the banks of the creek. For a few moments he stood at the meadow's edge, admiring the view and soaking up the peace of the place, and then he set out to find the woman he'd fallen in love with in spite of all his efforts not to.

IT WAS THE MARE that woke her, the sharp snort of alarm penetrating through the layers upon layers of fatigue. Bear? Kate struggled onto her elbows with a surge of adrenaline. The sun had shifted, leaving her mostly in shadow now, but there was plenty of light left to show her what had spooked Bonnie. The sight of Mitchell McCray walking toward the horse was so unexpected that for a long moment she could only stare, and by the time she found her voice to hail him, he'd spotted her and changed his direction.

"Your mother told me you were up here," he said in an offhand way as he approached, as if he'd just seen her yesterday. "She offered me a horse to ride. Said it'd be easier than walking. Stupidly, I declined." He lowered himself into the hollow, he eased himself into a comfortable position and sighed a weary sigh. "Damn, that was a tough hike."

"Pretty near vertical," Kate agreed, still staring as if he might vanish at any moment. Was he real, or was she only dreaming? She resisted the urge to reach out and touch him.

"Catch any fish?" he asked, eyes closed now. In a few breaths he'd probably fall asleep the same way she had. She studied his profile. Just the sight of him restored her vitality and kick-started her heart.

"Four. I let them all go."

"Your mother said you would. She said you loved to eat 'em, hated to kill 'em, so you turned 'em loose and fed the family on your fishing stories."

"So, McCray, what brings you to Montana?"

He laced his fingers together across his lean belly. "Thor wanted to visit Hayden," he muttered, eyes still closed. "I thought it'd make a good birthday present for him."

"Well, I'm glad you came. I'll write you a check for your travel expenses."

"All taken care of." He shifted again, settling more deeply into the hollow. "I gotta tell you, Kate, I'm not sure I have the strength to walk back."

"Bonnie can carry us both," Kate said. "She's sturdy, and it's all downhill."

He opened his eyes and gazed up at her. "I flew the Porter here. I'm returning it. Wally and I bought another plane, so we don't need yours."

Kate felt a hot jolt of anger. "If you insist on returning it, I can assume you want me to just store the plane and pay for it's upkeep until Hayden's old enough to fly."

Mitch worked himself onto his elbows. "At the rate he's progressing, that'll be only another five or six years. Surely you can manage that."

"Mitch, I—"

"I know," he interrupted. "You want me to fly it, but I can't. For the same reason you threw my letter off the flight deck, I can't fly that plane. I'm just as stubborn, prideful and independent as you are. That's all there is to it."

"You have no idea why I flung that letter off the flight deck," Kate shot back. "Besides, how I felt then has nothing to do with what I feel now. I was stupid then, and I spent nearly five years of my life paying for that one rash moment. Don't make the same mistake I did, Mitch. You have a chance to make a good life for yourself and for Hayden, too. Don't let your foolish pride hurt Hayden the way mine did."

"I would never hurt Hayden."

"Then prove it! Take that plane and put Arctic Air on the map. Build your son a legacy that the both of us would be proud of. Do this for me, Mitch. Do this for Hayden." Kate was near tears and her voice tightened up until she could barely get the last word out. "Please."

"Kate…"

Digging her fingernails into her palms helped push back the flood. "And while you're at it, build that addition onto your cabin, and put in a bathroom. Set it up like the park supervisor's cabin. You've got a great place, Mitch, a wonderful place. I've changed my will since I got back. You'll have the money to do all those things and more."

"What?" Mitch sat up and riveted her with those damnably keen eyes. "Don't talk like that."

"I have to face the fact that things don't look so good for me," she said. "I have to plan for the worst-case scenario, so that's what I've done. I've set up a trust fund for Hayden. Try to understand that this isn't about you and me. It's about our son's future."

"I get that part, loud and clear, but as far as I'm concerned, you're going to beat this thing. There isn't going to be a worst-case scenario."

"Fine. I'm all for that. Build the addition anyway. Fly the Porter. Make a lot of money. Kids are expensive."

"I know that, but I don't need your financial help to be a good father to Hayden. I'm leaving that plane here with you, and as for Hayden, I hope you'll let him visit me from time to time. I hope you'll let me take him camping again. Show him wolves and bears. Teach him how to fish and how to use his grandfather's compass and let him pal around with Thor.

That's all I'm asking. And, Kate, I'm too tired to fight." He pushed to his feet. "Your mother told me to make sure you got home in time for supper. We better get going."

She ignored his offered hand, still churning with unspoken thoughts, wanting to forge onward with this discussion until they found some common ground. "I'm not ready to leave just yet."

"And I'm not ready to ride a horse, but your mother wants you home for supper and whatever she was cooking sure smelled good."

Kate looked up at him, filled with helpless frustration. Was this it? Was this the deepest conversation they were ever going to have? She heaved a frustrated sigh. "You are so pigheaded for letting your pride stand in the way of your success."

"If I'm so pigheaded, what does that make you?" he shot back.

Kate stood, her heart pounding, a little dizzy from the surge of emotion that overwhelmed her. "That makes me an idiot who's in love with an idiot, and if it matters to you at all, I'd like to go camping again, too."

Her words clearly took him by surprise. "What did you just say?"

"I said, I'd like to go camping again, too."

"No. The part about being in love."

"I said, I'm in love with an idiot!"

"You're in love with me?"

Campy was right. Sometimes a man needed to be hit over the head with a baseball bat to clue him in. "Yes! I want to go camping lots of times, with you!"

He was staring at her with a dumbfounded expression, as

if he couldn't believe she'd ever say something like that. "If you feel that way about me, why didn't you tell me that before you left?"

She took his hand. "Because I couldn't, and I shouldn't be saying it now, but if things work out for me, I'd really like for us to go camping again, if that's all right."

CHAPTER SEVENTEEN

MITCH TRIED TO REMEMBER that he was supposed to keep his distance and stay clear of this dangerous emotional entanglement. That was the logical thing to do. Run far and run fast. He'd brought back the plane. His debt to Kate was discharged. He owed her nothing. He could leave after supper, catch the red-eye out of Bozeman and be back to work first thing Tuesday morning. That was the plan. That had always been the plan.

Until she spoke those words.

Those words about being in love with him.

Damn it, she was throwing a monkey wrench into his plans.

"Let me get this straight. You're in love with me, and you'll come visit me in Alaska if you get the transplant then get better and we'll go camping and have a happy family-style time together, but if things don't work out for you, I'll be hearing from your lawyer."

Kate hesitated. "I'll keep in touch when I'm in the hospital, so you'll know what's going on. Hayden would love it if you called him from time to time, and it would be especially nice if you could stay until his birthday."

Mitch turned away from her and walked down to the edge of the creek. He stared into the dark swirling eddies that laced the pool and wondered if he was going crazy. He wanted to grab hold of her and shake some sense into that stubborn head of hers. He wanted to hold her in his arms every night and keep her nightmares at bay. He wanted to find the courage to allow himself to fall in love with her the way she'd fallen in love with him. He wanted to teach Hayden how to throw a ball. Ride a bike. Drive a car. Fly a plane. He wanted to go camping with Kate and Hayden. Build an addition on his cabin big enough for all three of them. Stand on the porch and watch Kate out in the garden, tending her flowers.

There was still a part of him that knew it would be far easier for him to run far and run fast and never look back, but he knew he couldn't and never would, no matter what, so he turned around and walked back to where she stood. "Let me try to explain something to you. I'll try to keep it simple, since it appears we're both idiots. You don't have to go it alone anymore, Kate. I'm in this, too. What you're going through now and what you're about to go through, like it or not, I'm a part of it."

He saw the shine of tears in her eyes before she glanced away. "I appreciate what you're trying to say, Mitch, I really do, but you can't do anything to help. This is my fight."

"You are so wrong." He reached out and closed his hands on her shoulders. "This is our fight, and by God, Kate, we're going to fight it together, and you're going to let me because I'm Hayden's father and I have a big stake in this, but mostly you're going to let me because I fell pretty hard for you the first time you flew into my life, and I'm not letting you fly out of it again without a battle bigger than this one we're facing. You got that?"

She stared up at him while the tears made silent tracks down her cheeks.

"And," he continued, "I think we should get married right

away, before Hayden's birthday." He shook his head to silence her, though from her expression she was too dazed by his words to speak. "I know what you're going to say. We've only been seeing each other for less than a month. Well, that's long enough for me to know we could make a go of it. Then maybe you're going to argue that marriage is all about compromising, and you aren't ready to compromise your goals and ambitions. I'm right on track with that one, aren't I, Captain Independence? Don't worry. You won't have to compromise anything. You can have your career and I'll back you all the way to Mars, if that's where you really want to go, just so long as you're home in time for supper.

"So now you'll probably throw out the grim statistics about chemotherapy and sterility and no more babies, but you already killed that argument yourself by giving me Hayden. The only argument you could possibly make that I'd take seriously is if you told me you really didn't give a damn about me, but you've already tipped your hand on that one so I'm hoping you'll say yes. And for the record, this isn't all about Hayden. This part here is all about you and me."

She was still for a long moment, then she lifted her chin and said, "Mitch, do you have any idea what you'd face if I said yes?"

Until that very moment, he hadn't known how much he wanted her to say that word. A part of him had believed that his offer of marriage would be enough. She'd refuse, cut him loose, let him leave with dignity, let him live his life without guilt. She wouldn't want marriage, not even for Hayden's sake. She wasn't the type. She was a go-it-alone gal, tough to the core.

But the truth of it was, Campy was right. He needed Kate more than she needed him. His homestead on the banks of Pike's Creek used to be enough. The bush pilot job flying that junker for Wally Gleason used to be enough. Playing pool at Brock's Bar and Grill used to be enough…until Kate came back into his life from out of the blue and turned him inside out and upside down. Now, nothing of his old life was enough.

He wanted more. A lot more. He wanted Kate and he wanted Hayden and he wanted them to be a real family.

Not just any family.

He wanted them to be *his* family.

Because that's what they were. They were his family. He knew what Kate was facing, and he knew that walking that path with her would be the hardest thing the both of them would ever do, but he also knew he wanted to do it, and this shocked him almost as much as his marriage proposal had shocked Kate. The truth was, he no longer wanted to run far and run fast. He no longer wanted to escape Kate's struggle with the most feared and deadly of foes.

Leukemia wasn't just Kate's enemy. It had become his, as well.

This battle had become personal. Cancer was threatening the life of the woman he loved, and he was going to do everything in his power to fight it with her, and defeat it. Together, they would win this war. He believed this to the depths of his soul.

"I know what we're up against," he said. "And I know I don't have all that much to offer, just a wolf-dog that you won't be able to pat for a year and a rustic cabin on a wild creek with some forget-me-nots blooming in a neglected garden, but what do you say, K. C. Jones? You wanna get hitched? And don't quote me the odds. I don't want to hear them. There are no guarantees. I know that. But if all I get is one day, one hour, one minute as your husband, I'll take it, and as your husband, no doctor can keep me out of any hospital room that has you in it and nobody can keep me from making sure they take damn good care of you." He got down on one knee and took both her hands in his. "I'm not asking you out of pity. I'm asking it because I love you, I'm crazy about you and I want you to be my wife. Say yes, Kate, and make us a real family."

She was silent for so long that he began to have serious doubts, then her eyes flooded with tears again, and she said, in a voice that trembled with emotion, "Oh, Mitch, if I were sure about tomorrow, I wouldn't hesitate, but I need to talk to Hayden first. Can you give me a little time?"

KATE WOULD NEVER forget the ride back to the ranch house: that spectacular sunset coloring the western sky with vermilion streaks; Bonnie's slow, careful descent of the mountain trail and the smell of summer's warmth edged with the chill hint of the mountains as the twilight gathered up the cold from the high places and settled with it into the low-lying valleys. The distant, plaintive bawl of a cow and the evensong of the birds as they settled for the night were poignant reminders that all too soon her world would shrink to the size of a hospital room again, but she'd remember every one of these precious moments, and the feel of Mitch's strong, comforting arms around her was burned into her memory for all eternity.

All the way back to the ranch she thought about his proposal. She knew she couldn't accept it, she knew she wouldn't say yes because to accept would be the most selfish thing she ever did, but for a while she liked to think it would all work out. She liked to think he really did love her, that they really could be a family and that the future really did exist for the three of them together.

The trail flattened out and the lights of the ranch house beckoned. A dog barked and the screen door squeaked open then banged shut. Kate could see her father standing beside Ruth on the porch, his pipe in hand, the two of them waiting for her to come home. She was tired, but it was a bittersweet weariness. Mitch helped her down from the mare and she leaned into him for a moment longer, relishing his closeness and the feel of his arms around her, while Hayden came out of the house with the black dog in tow and cried, "Mumma, look, Thor's here!"

And then her mother descended the porch steps and as she approached, Kate saw the shine of tears in her eyes and a look of barely suppressed joy.

"The hospital in Seattle called an hour ago," Ruth said in a voice tight with emotion. "They found a donor match, Kate. They said it's a good one, as good as they get, a young woman from right here in Montana. They want you in Seattle right after Hayden's birthday. Your doctor wants you to call him. The number's by the phone."

As Kate heard the words, a feeling of disbelief washed over her. "Are you sure?"

Ruth nodded, the tears spilling over. "The doctor said something about an extra pair of antigen markers giving you a perfect match. He said on a scale of one to ten, your donor was a twelve. Oh, honey." Ruth broke down and embraced her fiercely.

"I never thought it would happen," Kate said, hugging her back in a daze. "I'd given up hope." She turned to Mitch, brushing tears from her own cheeks, and wrapped her arms around him tightly, clinging to his solid strength. "I owe you one, Mitch. I owe you my life. But something along the lines of a Porter airplane is a start."

Mitch held her close. "Hold it—let's take a step back to you owing me your life. Consider the debt repaid if you'd just spend it with me. That's all I ask."

Kate felt her heart twist with pain. If she said yes, Mitch would be trapped on the same uncertain road she was heading down. If she said yes, he'd be engaged in the same fierce battle. It would take all his time, all his energy, endless hours and days and weeks and months of watching her struggle through the hospitalized hell of the marrow transplant procedure, and in the end, if she didn't make it...?

No. She couldn't do that to him. Wouldn't. The kindest thing she could do would be to let him go. If she died, he'd take Hayden and be a good father to him. A great father. If she lived through the transplant and the cancer went into remission, and if he still wanted to marry her, then they could take up this conversation where they'd left off. Meanwhile, he'd be free to live his own life. She drew a deep breath, pushed out of his arms and was about to tell him no when she felt Hayden's arms clamp around her knees.

"Will you get better now, Mumma?" he said.

"It's very good news," Kate murmured, fearing to say any more. She knelt to hold him close, then rose to her feet at her father's approach. "Dad, this is Mitchell McCray."

The two men shook hands. "Good to meet you, sir," Mitch said, "and I know this is a little abrupt, but with your permission, I'd like to marry your daughter. That is, if she'd get beyond that stubborn, independent mind-set of hers and consent."

If Mitch's announcement surprised her father, he didn't show it. He puffed on his pipe calmly for a few moments, studying Mitch, then he glanced at Kate, and finally at Ruth. "What do you think, Mother Jones?"

Ruth just smiled. "That's up to Kate, isn't it? Come on, let's go put supper on the table."

After her parents had returned to the house, Kate gave her full attention to Mitch. "Are you sure? Really sure?"

"I wouldn't have asked you if I wasn't."

"I have to go back to Seattle right after Hayden's birthday."

"As I recall, weddings don't take all that long. A few minutes of official mumbo jumbo and a few signatures. We can have the big celebration afterward, after you're out of the hospital and we're back in Alaska. It'll give your parents a chance to see Montana magnified."

"What about your job? You can't just abandon Wally and Campy."

"They can hold the fort for as long as this takes. They're survivors, just like you and me."

Kate felt an electrical tingle shiver through her as he reached out and took her hands in his. "But it could take a while," she said. "I don't think you understand how long or how hard—"

"I like Seattle," Mitch interrupted. "I could pick up a flying job there. As a matter of fact, I was offered one just yesterday when I refueled at the airport there. I could get us an apartment right near the hospital where Hayden could come visit, and your parents, too, and we could all stay there when you weren't confined to a hospital room. C'mon, Kate," he urged. "Say yes. Hayden, tell your mother to say yes."

"Say yes, Mumma," Hayden said.

Kate's vision blurred. "You're ganging up on me."

"Damn straight."

"You may regret this a thousand times over," she said, "but yes, Mitchell McCray. I'll marry you."

AFTER THE CELEBRATORY SUPPER, and after the phone calls to the justice of the peace to arrange a small wedding at the ranch and to the Seattle hospital to confirm her bone marrow transplant countdown, Kate was exhausted. She put Hayden to bed, pulled the covers up over him, kissed his cheek, gave the ever-watchful Thor a grateful pat and went back downstairs to where Mitch waited for her.

Quietly.

Patiently.

The way she sensed he'd always be waiting for her, no matter what.

"I'm staying out in the bunkhouse," he said when she rejoined him in the quiet of the living room, Hayden already asleep and her parents gone to bed, as well.

"What a coincidence. So am I," she said.

Kate didn't know if there would be a tomorrow for her, or a day after, let alone a year. She didn't know if she'd be around to see Hayden graduate high school and college, find a sweetheart, get married, or catch his first real big fish. But she did know that no matter what, from this moment on, she wouldn't be alone to face her greatest fears. Mitch had chased her nightmares up into the hills and banished them forever and tonight they'd start building a sturdy corral together and fill it with their dreams.

Good dreams.

Great dreams.

That night, Kate's future looked as bright as the stars spangling the black velvet sky. As Mitch's warm, strong hand clasped around hers, as they walked side by side down the path, she wondered what had taken her so long to realize that needing someone wasn't a sign of weakness, and that loving someone was the greatest strength of all.

EPILOGUE

Pike's Creek Chronicle
Lofty Arrival

Mitchell and Katherine McCray are pleased to announce the birth of their daughter, Gail Anne McCray, on December 19 at 11:00 p.m. in the middle of the first real snowstorm of the season. Gail was due to arrive on January 20 but was born, a healthy six pounds, nine ounces, while en route to the Fairbanks hospital in a plane piloted by her father. Camilla Clarke and Wally Gleason helped her into the world and are equally proud to be named as godparents. Mitchell, Katherine and Wally are partners in one of Alaska's most successful new charters, Arctic Air. Gail Anne joins her eight-year-old brother, Hayden, as the newest member of the McCray family and a treasured addition to Pike's Creek. We wish them all the best and would just like to add, good job, Kate. We're proud of you, and we love you.

* * * * *

Happily ever after is just the beginning...

Turn the page for a sneak preview of
DANCING ON SUNDAY AFTERNOONS
by
Linda Cardillo

Harlequin Everlasting—Every great love
has a story to tell. ™
A brand-new line from Harlequin Books
launching this February!

PROLOGUE

Giulia D'Orazio
1983

I had two husbands—Paolo and Salvatore.

Salvatore and I were married for thirty-two years. I still live in the house he bought for us; I still sleep in our bed. All around me are the signs of our life together. My bedroom window looks out over the garden he planted. In the middle of the city, he coaxed tomatoes, peppers, zucchini—even grapes for his wine—out of the ground. On weekends, he used to drive up to his cousin's farm in Waterbury and bring back manure. In the winter, he wrapped the peach tree and the fig tree with rags and black rubber hoses against the cold, his massive, coarse hands gentling those trees as if they were his fragile-skinned babies. My neighbor, Dominic Grazza, does that for me now. My boys have no time for the garden.

In the front of the house, Salvatore planted roses. The roses I take care of myself. They are giant, cream-colored, fragrant. In the afternoons, I like to sit out on the porch with my coffee, protected from the eyes of the neighborhood by that curtain of flowers.

Salvatore died in this house thirty-five years ago. In the last months, he lay on the sofa in the parlor so he could be in the middle of everything. Except for the two oldest boys, all the children were still at home and we ate together every evening. Salvatore could see the dining room table from the sofa, and he could hear everything that was said. "I'm not dead, yet," he told me. "I want to know what's going on."

When my first grandchild, Cara, was born, we brought her to him, and he held her on his chest, stroking her tiny head. Sometimes they fell asleep together.

Over on the radiator cover in the corner of the parlor is the portrait Salvatore and I had taken on our twenty-fifth anniversary. This brooch I'm wearing today, with the diamonds—I'm wearing it in the photograph also—Salvatore gave it to me that day. Upstairs on my dresser is a jewelry box filled with necklaces and bracelets and earrings. All from Salvatore.

I am surrounded by the things Salvatore gave me, or did for me. But, God forgive me, as I lie alone now in my bed, it is Paolo I remember.

Paolo left me nothing. Nothing, that is, that my family, especially my sisters, thought had any value. No house. No diamonds. Not even a photograph.

But after he was gone, and I could catch my breath from the pain, I knew that I still had something. In the middle of the night, I sat alone and held them in my hands, reading the words over and over until I heard his voice in my head. I had Paolo's letters.

* * * * *

Be sure to look for
DANCING ON SUNDAY AFTERNOONS
available January 30, 2007.
And look, too, for our other Everlasting title available,
FALL FROM GRACE by Kristi Gold.

FALL FROM GRACE is a deeply emotional story
of what a long-term love really means.
As Jack and Anne Morgan discover,
marriage vows can be broken—but they
can be mended, too.
And the memories of their marriage
have an unexpected power
to bring back a love that never really left....

This February…

Catch NASCAR Superstar **Carl Edwards** *in*
SPEED DATING!

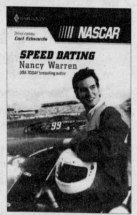

Kendall assesses risk for a living—
so she's the last person you'd
expect to see on the arm of a
race-car driver who thrives on the
unpredictable. But when a bizarre
turn of events—and NASCAR
hotshot Dylan Hargreave—inspire
her to trade in her ever-so-structured
existence for "life in the fast lane"
she starts to feel she might be
on to something!

Collect all 4 debut novels in the Harlequin NASCAR series.

SPEED DATING
by *USA TODAY* bestselling author
Nancy Warren

THUNDERSTRUCK
by Roxanne St. Claire

HEARTS UNDER CAUTION
by Gina Wilkins

DANGER ZONE
by Debra Webb

**On sale
February
2007**

Silhouette®
ROMANTIC SUSPENSE

Excitement, danger and passion guaranteed!

Same great authors and riveting editorial you've come to know and love.

Look for our new name next month as Silhouette Intimate Moments® becomes Silhouette® Romantic Suspense.

REQUEST YOUR FREE BOOKS!
2 FREE NOVELS PLUS 2 FREE GIFTS!

HARLEQUIN®

Super Romance®

Exciting, emotional, unexpected!

YES! Please send me 2 FREE Harlequin Superromance® novels and my 2 FREE gifts. After receiving them, if I don't wish to receive any more books, I can return the shipping statement marked "cancel." If I don't cancel, I will receive 6 brand-new novels every month and be billed just $4.69 per book in the U.S., or $5.24 per book in Canada, plus 25¢ shipping and handling per book and applicable taxes, if any*. That's a savings of close to 15% off the cover price! I understand that accepting the 2 free books and gifts places me under no obligation to buy anything. I can always return a shipment and cancel at any time. Even if I never buy another book from Harlequin, the two free books and gifts are mine to keep forever.

135 HDN EEX7   336 HDN EEYK

Name	(PLEASE PRINT)	
Address		Apt.
City	State/Prov.	Zip/Postal Code

Signature (if under 18, a parent or guardian must sign)

Mail to the **Harlequin Reader Service®**:
IN U.S.A.: P.O. Box 1867, Buffalo, NY 14240-1867
IN CANADA: P.O. Box 609, Fort Erie, Ontario L2A 5X3

Not valid to current Harlequin Superromance subscribers.

Want to try two free books from another line?
Call 1-800-873-8635 or visit www.morefreebooks.com.

* Terms and prices subject to change without notice. NY residents add applicable sales tax. Canadian residents will be charged applicable provincial taxes and GST. This offer is limited to one order per household. All orders subject to approval. Credit or debit balances in a customer's account(s) may be offset by any other outstanding balance owed by or to the customer. Please allow 4 to 6 weeks for delivery.

Your Privacy: Harlequin is committed to protecting your privacy. Our Privacy Policy is available online at www.eHarlequin.com or upon request from the Reader Service. From time to time we make our lists of customers available to reputable firms who may have a product or service of interest to you. If you would prefer we not share your name and address, please check here. ☐

HSR07

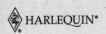

Every great love has a story to tell™

Save $1.⁰⁰ off

the purchase of any Harlequin Everlasting Love novel

Coupon valid from January 1, 2007 until April 30, 2007.

Valid at retail outlets in the U.S. only. Limit one coupon per customer.

5 65373 00076 2   (8100) 0 11302

HEUSCPN0407

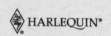

EVERLASTING LOVE™

Every great love has a story to tell™

Fall from Grace

Kristi Gold

Save $1.⁰⁰ off

the purchase of any Harlequin Everlasting Love novel

Coupon valid from January 1, 2007 until April 30, 2007.

Valid at retail outlets in Canada only.
Limit one coupon per customer.

52607370

HECDNCPN0407

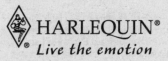

COMING NEXT MONTH

#1398 LOVE AND THE SINGLE MOM • C.J. Carmichael
Singles...with Kids
When Margo almost loses her bistro...and custody of her children...she realizes a real family is about more than owning a pretty house and being a perfect mother. And then there's Robert... But like the other single parents in her support group, she has to make sure he wants the whole package. Is it really possible to find true love the second time around when you're single...with kids?
The first in a wonderful new series!

#1399 THE PERFECT DAUGHTER • Anna DeStefano
Count on a Cop
Detective Matt Lebrettie can't be the man for Maggie Rivers. She just can't watch him face danger every day. But will keeping her heart safe rob her of her chance for happiness?

#1400 THE RANCHER NEEDS A WIFE • Terry McLaughlin
Bright Lights, Big Sky
After his divorce, Wayne Hammond resisted making anyone the second Mrs. Hammond. Topping the list of the women he wouldn't pick is Maggie Harrison Sinclair, who's taken refuge at her family's ranch until she can figure out which big city is for her. He's not about to make the mistake of picking a city woman again. Or is he?

#1401 BECAUSE OF OUR CHILD • Margot Early
A Little Secret
More than a decade ago, Jen Delazzeri and Max Rickman had a brief, intense love affair—and then disappeared from each other's lives. Now Jen's work as a TV reporter brings her into Max's world again, the world of smoke jumpers and Hotshots, of men and women who risk their lives to fight wildfires. Should she use this opportunity to tell him the secret she's kept for twelve years—a secret named Elena?

#1402 THE BOY NEXT DOOR • Amy Knupp
Going Back
In Lone Oak, Kansas, Rundles and Salingers don't mix. Not since the tragic accident involving Zach Rundle's brother and Lindsey Salinger's mother. But when the well-being of a young boy is at stake, Zach and Lindsey are unwillingly dragged together again. Fighting the same attraction they'd felt twelve years ago.

#1403 TREASURE • Helen Brenna
Jake Rawlings is a treasure hunter and Annie Miller is going to lead him to the mother lode. But what he finds with beautiful Annie is much more than he bargained for.

HSRCNM0107